The
*Genesis
Code*

The
Genesis
Code

Christopher
FORREST

A TOM DOHERTY ASSOCIATES BOOK
NEW YORK

This is a work of fiction. All of the characters, organizations, and events portrayed in this novel are either products of the author's imagination or are used fictitiously.

THE GENESIS CODE

A Forge Book
Published by Tom Doherty Associates, LLC
175 Fifth Avenue
New York, NY 10010

www.tor-forge.com

Forge® is a registered trademark of Tom Doherty Associates, LLC.

ISBN-13: 978-0-7653-5514-0
ISBN-10: 0-7653-5514-0

First Edition: August 2007
First Mass Market Edition: December 2008

Printed in the United States of America

0 9 8 7 6 5 4 3 2 1

For Amy,
my angel,

and for my parents,
Betty and Jim

Acknowledgments

A veritable army of generous people gave their support to make *The Genesis Code* a reality. I would like to thank my agent, Susan Crawford, and my editor, Natalia Aponte, for taking a chance on a new author and believing in *The Genesis Code* when it was little more than a fledgling attempt at a first novel. My deep appreciation to Tom Doherty, for allowing me to join the ranks of Tor/Forge authors. Thanks also to Paul Stevens, for his guidance and assistance, and to all the good folks at Tor/Forge for their support.

Special thanks to author James Rollins, for his support and encouragement. If you haven't read James Rollins's novels, you simply must go out and buy them today. For the inspiration for this story, I gratefully credit the works of Graham Hancock and Robert Bauval.

Appreciation and love to my family: my parents, Betty and Jim, to whom I owe everything; my brother, Brett, for his unwavering support; my aunt, Bev Marshall, a truly gifted author who inspired me to write, and my uncle, Butch, who always believed in me; my grandfather, Ernest, the great storyteller; Steve Carle; Don Gouger; my stepson, Kyle; and my adopted parents, Ronda and David Raymond. Thanks also to my colleagues at the firm for their support and encouragement: Dave Bowman, Eugene George, Jim Toale, David Bowman, Jr., and Robert Scheb.

But first and foremost, I would like to thank my wife, my friend, and my soul mate—my angel, Amy—for sharing her life with me.

Since I entered politics, I have chiefly had men's views confided to me privately. Some of the biggest men in the U.S., in the field of commerce and manufacturing, are afraid of somebody, are afraid of something. They know that there is a power somewhere so organized, so subtle, so watchful, so interlocked, so complete, so pervasive, that they had better not speak above their breath when they speak in condemnation of it.

—Woodrow Wilson

The important thing is not to stop questioning. One cannot help but be in awe when he contemplates the mysteries of eternity, of life, of the marvelous structure of reality.

—Albert Einstein

Prologue

Sometimes stealing is the best way to make a living. After all, reasoned eleven-year-old Pakal, the dead no longer had any need for their earthly possessions. So he didn't really feel guilty.

The average annual income of Mayan Indian families in Central America is about six hundred dollars. In the tropical jungles of western Belize, Pakal's family was slightly below average. Poverty provided a strong incentive to overlook any moral ambiguities inherent in grave robbing.

Pakal's mother and grandparents definitely would not agree. But he was young, and therefore secure in the knowledge that he knew better than they did. So at the age of eleven, Pakal Q'eqchi began looting the tombs and temples of his ancestors. Many unexplored Mayan ruins lay hidden deep within the jungles of Belize. For the enterprising grave robber, discovering a Mayan ruin is like finding an unlocked bank vault. Local antiquities dealers in Belize will pay as much as $1,000 for a single polychrome plate, for which a gallery in New York or Brussels will offer $20,000 to $30,000.

After several months of exploration in the foothills of the Maya Mountains, Pakal discovered a crumbling Mayan pyramid built over a network of caverns. The ruin yielded only broken pottery and shattered human remains. But in the caverns beneath, Pakal unearthed three polychrome plates, an ornate bowl decorated with a bas-relief jaguar, a handful of obsidian figurines, and a human skull. The skull's teeth were inlaid with jade.

Fortified by his success, Pakal recruited an assistant, his seventeen-year-old sister Aluna. With tropical green eyes and long black hair, Aluna possessed a surprisingly languid beauty. She resisted at first, but warmed to the idea after Pakal displayed a stack of Belizean twenties he received in exchange for the Mayan relics from the cave. The antiquities dealer had refused to buy the skull and cautioned Pakal against disturbing human remains.

"Bad business," he said. "Leave the dead lie where they lay."

Pakal didn't tell Aluna about the tarantulas. Dozens of tarantulas inhabited the cave Pakal had looted, prompting him to name it Labertinto de las Tarantulas. Maybe they were avoiding the sweltering summer heat, or perhaps they were feasting on the hundreds of assassin beetles lurking about. Pakal shivered as he remembered the assassin beetles hunting in the cool caverns, impaling their insect victims with stout beaks and injecting a toxin that liquefied their prey.

Pakal and Aluna rose at dawn and hiked all morning, stopping only once to dine on heart-of-palm soup and rest on the *maguey* reed mats they carried slung from their backs. The tropical jungle was filled with colorful birds perched in towering trees covered with orchids and bromeliads. The broad, irregular crowns of the trees formed a tight, continuous canopy sixty feet above the ground. The foliage above was wet and dripped constantly like a continuous light rain.

On the jungle floor, Pakal and Aluna walked amid a bright green carpet of broad ferns on a thin layer of fallen leaves, seeds, and branches. Very little sunlight filtered through the dense canopy. The howls of monkeys and screeches of macaws echoed through the dense humid air.

Aluna's *huipil,* the traditional Mayan blouse, was wet with perspiration. The fabric of the poncholike garment, covered with colorful embroidered geometric patterns, clung to her skin. She tied back her long hair in a loose ponytail and fanned her face with a woven reed fan.

By early afternoon, Aluna and Pakal reached the ruin in the foothills of the Maya Mountains.

"Look, there it is," whispered Pakal as he pointed.

In the distance, Aluna saw the moss-covered rocks of a large stone wall, barely visible under dense jungle foliage. Behind it, the entrance to a cave yawned like a black hole in the jungle.

Far beyond the wall, a terraced stone pyramid covered with lianas and strangler vines was shrouded in mist. Small plants and vines covered a broad stone plaza, infiltrating through cracks between large stone slabs. Lichens and moss covered almost every surface. Several mahogany trees grew straight up through the middle of the plaza, standing like sentries guarding the temple.

"Let's start with the cave. It will be cool inside," said Pakal.

A pause. "Okay, but you go first."

As they descended into the winding network of subterranean passages, a mysterious world took shape. Stalactites of blood-red limestone seemed to ooze from the dripping ceiling. Above strange pools of green iridescent water, hundreds of sinewy tree roots penetrated the ceiling and dropped fifty feet into the water below. A piercing beam of sunlight streamed in through a small fissure in the ceiling, illuminating the eerie underground forest. The air was damp and stale.

Pakal withdrew a butane lighter from his pocket and lit two torches. He handed one to Aluna.

The narrow passageway descended for several yards before it broadened into an expansive subterranean chamber. Glistening stalactites hung from the ceiling. The terrain was rocky and potsherds littered the ground. Their torches threw ominous shadows against the cavern walls.

Pakal and Aluna walked carefully across the underground chamber through a forest of stalagmites. Towering rock formations formed slender fingers that dipped into the cool waters of an underground stream.

"Pakal, I see something," said Aluna.

She pointed off to the left where a small ledge jutted out from the cavern wall at shoulder height. They cautiously approached. Peering over the edge, Pakal and Aluna could see the skeletal remains of a small child lying face down in a dry limestone pool. Aluna stifled a gasp.

"Don't touch it," warned Pakal. "And don't worry, it's been here a really long time."

Aluna averted her eyes.

Near the child was a stone hearth that contained the charred remains of ears of corn and other botanical detritus. Carbonized husks, stems, and leaves covered several pieces of pottery. Aluna plucked a small vessel from the hearth and examined it.

"Look, it's painted. Here's a man with the head of a jaguar. And there's some writing around the top."

The ceramic cup was decorated with hieroglyphic writing around the circumference of its top edge. Slip paint, a mixture of finely ground pigment, clay, and water, decorated the vessel with a rendering of the Jaguar God who inhabited the underworld, home of the dead.

"Mr. Q'axaca told me about him," said Pakal. "The ancients believed that each morning, the Jaguar God became the Sun God, traveling across the sky to the west, where he fell back into the underworld. To make sure that the Jaguar God rose each day, Mayan kings performed rituals to appease the gods."

"Now there are no kings left to perform the rituals," said Aluna.

Pakal laughed. "Maybe the Jaguar God is still stuck in the underworld!"

Pakal spotted a bowl off to one side of the hearth. It was a wide, flared bowl decorated with intricate carvings and pigments.

"Look at this one. Two intertwined snakes that wrap around the bowl and slither under this band of writing."

"I hate snakes," said Aluna. "Why couldn't they paint butterflies and birds?"

Aluna spied a peculiar-looking formation in the recessed shadows ahead. Three cave formations called draperies flowed from a ledge twenty feet overhead and cascaded down onto the cavern floor. The solid rock looked as if it had been poured down the cavern wall. In the center drapery, the Maya had carved a doorway-sized hole and fitted it with a stout wooden door.

Around the door were handprints stamped onto the rock in bright pigments. Mayan petroglyphs conveyed a message, but neither Pakal nor Aluna could read it.

"I've never heard of anything like this," said Pakal.

Aluna pursed her lips.

"I don't know. Maybe we should just leave it alone. There must be lots of things we can find without opening that door."

"But think of what could be on the other side. Enough treasures to move us away from here. We could move into Belize City, buy a house and maybe a car," said Pakal.

He hesitated for a moment.

"I'm going to open it," he said.

"Please be careful."

Pakal grasped the ornate copper handle and pulled. The door was stuck fast, its edges swelled by moisture against the stone frame. Pakal tried again, planting his foot against the cavern wall for leverage. He strained and cursed. Finally, the door came free with a loud splintering noise.

The half-open doorway exhaled a breath of dry, foul-smelling air. Pakal and Aluna's torches were snuffed out. There was a loud thump and a grunt of pain. In the blackness, Aluna reached out blindly, fighting the terror rising from the pit of her stomach.

"Pakal!" she screamed. "Pakal, where are you?"

A quick scratching sound. A whiff of sulfur.

In the dancing light of a small match, Aluna saw the strained face of her brother as he relit his torch. Blood streamed from a large gash on his forehead.

"Calm down. I'm okay. I just stumbled."

He reached up and felt his forehead. There was blood on his fingertips. "I must have hit my head."

"Hold out your torch." Pakal relit his sister's torch. It sputtered and crackled in the rank air.

"Come on. It's okay. Don't worry."

He took Aluna's hand and led her through the open doorway. The darkness inside was pitch-black and stifling. The light from their struggling torches seemed to smother out after only a few feet. Slowly, they crept forward into the chamber.

In the dim illumination, Aluna could barely discern the outline of an ancient sarcophagus. Its massive stone lid rested on the cavern floor.

"Pakal, I think this is a tomb. I don't like being in here."

"Don't worry," Pakal replied. "We'll just look around and then go."

The chamber was at least fifty feet long and twenty feet wide. At the opposite end, a dark opening led farther into the caverns. The floor was covered with dead leaves, cohune nuts, and heart-of-palm seeds.

Pakal dropped to one knee and began clearing away the organic sediment, revealing a pile of human bones and polychrome ceramic vessels.

"Look. Lots of pottery. And it's in good condition."

Aluna paused and listened intently.

"Pakal, do you hear that?"

There was a soft, wet wheezing noise.

Aluna looked frightened. "What is that?"

"It's probably nothing. Just wind coming through a crack in the ceiling or something." But he didn't sound very confident.

The wet wheezing noise grew louder, echoing off the stone walls.

"Pakal, I don't like this. Let's go. Please."

"Okay, but put a few of those pieces of pottery into your bag. And the jade jewelry too. Then we'll go."

Pakal turned and hurriedly began to collect artifacts

that would command a decent price from the dealer in Punta Gorda. As he reached for a small piece of sculpted jade, Pakal accidentally knocked over one of the female skulls. A large tarantula scurried from the recesses of the skull and disappeared into the pile of bones.

Aluna was already heading for the door. Her torchlight cast long shadows on the stone drapery. "Come on, let's get out of here!"

"Okay, I'm coming."

Pakal stood and turned toward the door.

Aluna had reached the doorway and looked over her shoulder toward her brother. His torch cast a small circle of light in the black void around him. The air in the tomb was warm and smelled foul.

The wheezing sound grew louder.

Then, behind Pakal, barely discernible against the black void of the tomb, Aluna saw the faint outline of something large.

Something alive.

Something menacing.

She screamed.

As Pakal turned in fright to see what had terrified his sister, his torch suddenly went out, casting the tomb back into darkness. Aluna's torch, still lit, was too weak to shed enough light to illuminate her brother.

Pakal cried out, a high-pitched wailing scream. The muffled whispering noise grew frantic.

There was a ripping, tearing sound. Aluna was splattered with something warm and wet. She looked down at her *huipil* in the flickering torchlight. A fine mist of dark red blood and bits of pale flesh covered her clothing and bare arms. Unreasoning terror took hold.

Aluna turned and ran, screaming.

A wet wheezing sound pursued her into the blackness.

Part I

Heaven from all creatures
Hides the book of fate,
All but the pages prescribed,
Their present state.

—Alexander Pope, *An Essay on Man*

Heaven above, Heaven Below
Stars above, Stars Below,
All that is over, under shall show.
Happy thou who the riddle readest.

—Tabula Smaragdina

One

The clock on the bedside table read 4:32 A.M.

And still no sleep.

Again.

Dr. Christian Madison, Ph.D. in genetics from Stanford and nonlinear mathematics from Columbia, hated taking pills.

Especially sleeping pills.

They left him with a sleep hangover in the morning, feeling groggy and dulled. So he tossed and turned, hour after hour, longing for a few hours of unconsciousness.

Time heals all wounds.

How many well-meaning friends and colleagues had trotted out that sad refrain? Madison had lost count.

Time had brought no healing. His memories of Justin were as sharp and penetrating as ever. Most nights, after the world became still, he would just lie in the darkness and remember.

Madison would remember the crushing sense of help-lessness that tortured his soul as his six-year-old son's withered body consumed itself.

Madison hated cancer.

He *HATED* cancer, with terrible raging anger buried in unexamined quarters of his mind.

The sheets were damp from night sweats. Madison kicked off the down comforter. He flipped his pillow, ex-posing the cool side beneath.

Madison closed his eyes and prayed for dreamless sleep.

Across town on the thirty-fourth floor of the Millennium Tower in lower Manhattan, Dr. Joshua Ambergris peered at a flat-panel plasma screen with weary eyes. He punched at his computer keyboard with two index fingers.

An antique mahogany desk clock ticked away the minutes toward four-thirty A.M. The silence of the early morning hours was deafening.

How long have I been awake? Forty-eight hours? Fifty-six?

Ambergris wiped a trail of perspiration from his forehead and pushed his fingers through a mop of dark hair, longish and peppered with invading streaks of gray marching outward from his temples. At forty-three, Ambergris was an undeniable giant in his profession. A Nobel Prize–winning geneticist and a founding partner of the global biotech titan Triad Genomics, he was both rich and revered.

A faint noise broke the silence.

Ambergris froze, his eyes darting toward the open door of his office. His heart thumped in his chest.

Seconds passed.

The noise did not repeat.

Dr. Ambergris glanced nervously around the room. His spacious office was a study in contrasts. A sleek, state-of-the-art computer workstation adorned a seventeenth century French desk. Leather-bound volumes rested on metal bookshelves next to stacks of technical journals. On the desktop, piles of books on Hebrew mysticism, the great Pyramid of Giza, and ancient mythology held down the corners of computer printouts detailing lengthy sequences of genetic code: ACT GCT GAG TCT AGC TGT CAG AGC TGT GAA GTC GAG CTA GTC ACT GCT GAG TCT AGC TGT CAG AGC TGT GAA GTC GAG CTA GTC ACT GCT GAG TCT AGC TGT CAG AGC TGT GAA GTC GAG CTA GTC. The margins of the printouts were filled with Ambergris' handwritten notations.

For a moment, Dr. Ambergris' eyes lingered on a framed photograph on the wall opposite his desk. The image captured his father, Maximillian Ambergris, a prominent historian, shaking hands with President Lyndon B. Johnson at a reception at Yale University's Peabody Museum of Natural History.

Hanging next to the photo was a reproduction of images from the Dresden Codex, a pre-Columbian Mayan text. Rows of Mayan hieroglyphs were arranged in a grid above a rendering of two intertwined serpents. On the credenza below, a diagram of the Mayan calendar rested atop an astronomical chart detailing the precession of the equinoxes.

Dr. Ambergris turned his attention back to the computer screen.

Almost finished.

With several rapid strokes, Ambergris finished typing. His finger hovered over the enter key.

Perhaps the most astounding discovery in the history of mankind.

Humanity's oldest secret.

A shadow fell across the plasma screen. From the corner of his eye, Ambergris was startled to see a figure standing in the doorway. He quickly pressed the enter key.

The man in the doorway cleared his throat.

Ambergris pivoted in his chair.

A wiry Asian man dressed all in white leaned casually against the door frame. His hands were covered by latex surgical gloves. The intruder's silky black hair fell across his muscular shoulders in long braids. Inscribed in red on the snowy white fabric of his left pant leg was a single character from the Japanese alphabet.

Ambergris felt a cold chill dance across his clammy skin.

It's over. My time has come.

The intruder held up a long syringe, tapping it several times with the nail of his forefinger. A thin stream of liquid spurted from the long needle as he cleared air bubbles from the murky fluid.

"Good evening, Dr. Ambergris. I'm pleased to make your acquaintance," said the man with the needle.

He smiled pleasantly. "You may call me Mr. Arakai. In fact, I insist that you do."

Ambergris clutched the arms of his chair with white-knuckled hands.

"If you're going to kill me, just get it over with," said Ambergris.

Arakai smiled. His amber eyes glinted with malice.

"Have patience, Dr. Ambergris. Let's have a little chat first. The killing will begin soon enough."

Arakai removed a long, thin knife from within the folds of his jacket. His fluid movements revealed a tattoo on the inside of his left wrist.

A tattoo of two intertwined serpents.

Two

APARTMENT OF CHRISTIAN MADISON
MANHATTAN, NEW YORK

It always began with the screaming. Before the horrific visions of billowing smoke, orange flames, and hulking ruins of concrete and steel assaulted his mind, before the acrid smell of burning wood, paper, and plastic affronted his beleaguered senses, Madison always heard the screaming.

In the haze of early morning, replayed in vivid detail in his recurring dream, he watched helplessly as a tremendous explosion rocketed through a mammoth skyscraper, blasting a maelstrom of dark smoke, glass, and concrete into the dawn sky. Above the deafening roar of the blast, the screams of men, women, and children echoed in his mind.

One screaming voice always rose above the din.

Justin, his son, calling out his name, pleading for rescue, begging for redemption.

Justin, who had died only a year ago, his small body hollow and broken from the leukemia that consumed him.

And as always, Madison could only watch, helpless, as the towering skyscraper imploded, falling inward on itself, collapsing into a massive pile of twisted steel and debris.

A shrill ringing filled the air.

Madison fumbled for the phone, the sounds and screams of his recurring nightmare still echoing in the hollows of his head. Beads of cold sweat dripped from his hairline into the dampness of his pillow.

He rubbed his eyes and pressed the phone to his ear.

"Hello."

"Good morning, Christian. It's your mother. Are you up? It's after seven . . ."

Madison took a deep breath and tried to ignore his heart pounding in his chest. He wrestled with the dingy white cotton sheets twisted around his torso.

"Hi, Mom."

He wiped a sweaty palm across his face.

"I'm up," Madison lied. "Been up since six. Just finishing the paper and a cup of coffee."

A pause on the line.

"I just wanted to check in. Make sure you were okay," she said.

"I'm fine, Mom. Don't worry. And tell Dad not to worry. I'll be fine."

She sighed softly. "Are you sure you won't come up to the house for a day or two? Stay in the guest room. Let me feed you some home-cooked meals. You shouldn't be by yourself today."

Madison squinted at the digital alarm clock on his nightstand with one eye.

7:04 A.M.

June 11.

Justin's birthday.

Next to the Sharper Image alarm clock was a framed photograph of a small boy in a gray Scooby-Doo sweatshirt, at least one size too big, grinning at the camera from astride an old trail horse at the base of the Grand Canyon. Madison's gaze lingered on his crooked smile and bright blue eyes.

"Christian, are you there?"

For a moment he considered, and then rejected, the offer.

"Thanks anyway, but I'll be okay. Besides, I've got the Biogenetics Conference just around the corner. I really can't afford to be away."

Another uncomfortable pause.

"Did you get the card I sent?"

"I did. Sorry. I meant to call and tell you thanks for the card. And for the money."

Mrs. Madison always sent a crisp ten dollar bill in each greeting card to her son, delivered well in advance of holidays and other noteworthy occasions by U.S. mail.

"And I promise to buy something that will cheer me up." That was the perennial condition of Mrs. Madison's maternal cash gifts, folded between the front and back covers of Hallmark greeting cards. She required that the cash be used to purchase an item solely for the purpose of self-gratification.

"You better," she replied.

Madison could hear the smile in her voice.

After another beat of silence, she asked the dreaded question.

"Have you spoken to Kate?"

Madison's stomach knotted instantly. He flopped back sideways on the bed, hanging his head upside down over the edge of the mattress.

"No. Not for quite a while."

"Maybe you should call her again."

"I don't think so, Mom."

Christian and Kate had separated shortly after Justin breathed his final breath. The loss of their only child had ripped apart the marriage in a way that Madison now knew could never be mended.

For once, his mother let the issue drop.

"Christian, I'm going to light a candle for Justin at mass. You should start going to church again. Attending services would be good for you. Father Donovan always asks how you're doing."

Madison hadn't been to church for years. Raised Catholic, he had stopped going to mass after graduating from high school and going away to college. The only time he had set foot in a church in at least the past decade had been the day of Justin's funeral service.

"Maybe you're right," he said.

"Okay. Well, I won't keep you. But call me tonight. Just to let me know you're okay," she said.

Madison shifted the phone to his other ear.

"Okay, Mom. Deal. I'll speak with you soon."

"Have a good day, Christian."

Madison placed the phone back in the receiver and sat on the edge of his bed, rubbing his eyes. Memories of his son's final days surged into his thoughts.

Justin was a ghost of a child, lying thin and frail under the starched white sheets of a hospital bed. A tangle of tubes and wires crisscrossed his chest, connecting his dying body with IV bags, monitors, and machines.

"No," said Madison. He pushed the memories from his conscious mind. Madison looked around the bedroom of his small apartment.

It was an absolute mess.

A pile of dirty laundry dominated one corner of the room. Boxes of books were piled against the wall opposite his queen-sized bed, partially obscuring the large window overlooking a tiny park three stories below.

On a large mahogany desk, surrounding a laptop computer in the center of the desktop, haphazard mountains of paper and research materials marked with a riot of yellow Post-it notes threatened to spill off their precarious perch and onto the floor.

Stretching his arms above his head to free the kinks from his neck and shoulders, Madison forced himself out of bed and onto the polished wood floor. He caught sight of his reflection in the antique mirror above his mahogany dresser. The reflection, staring back at him with vague curiosity, looked tired.

His pale blue eyes, framed within red-rimmed eyelids, were slightly puffy from too many nights of fitful sleep. His strong jawline bore the stubble of a day's growth of beard, and his dark hair stuck up in several different directions above a handsome but weary face.

This, he could tell already, *is not going to be a pleasant day.*

Three

DESERTED PARKING GARAGE
HARLEM, NEW YORK

A man in a dark Italian suit sat behind the wheel of a 700 series BMW parked in a row of empty spaces in the derelict parking garage. He kept the windows rolled up to keep out the stench of stale urine. The car idled softly, its engine running to keep the AC cool. The man checked his watch and sighed impatiently.

Within moments, the passenger door opened and Takeyo Arakai sat down on the black leather passenger seat. The interior of the BMW smelled faintly of expensive cigars.

Arakai paused a moment before speaking.

"It's done," he said, cracking the knuckles on his left hand.

"You're certain?"

Arakai turned and flashed a cold smile. "Quite."

"And the rest?"

"The stage is set," Arakai replied.

"Excellent. The Council will be pleased."

The man reached into the inside breast pocket of his suit jacket and removed an envelope. He handed it to Arakai.

Arakai took the envelope without comment and deposited it into a pocket in the folds of his jacket.

"What about Ambergris' notes and papers?" the man asked.

"Not to worry. I've destroyed his papers. Removed his hard drive. Unfortunately . . ."

The man raised an eyebrow. "Yes?"

"I was unable to access the Triad Genomics mainframe. We have no way of knowing if Dr. Ambergris stored any of his notes on the main server."

The man removed his eyeglasses and rubbed the bridge of his nose with a thumb and forefinger.

"I understand," he said.

"There is also one loose end left to tie up," said Arakai, holding up an electronic key card he had removed from Dr. Ambergris' office.

"Very well. But remain accessible. We may require your services again shortly. I will contact you within the next twelve hours."

Four

MILLENNIUM TOWER, STREET LEVEL
MANHATTAN, NEW YORK

Flavia Veloso was going to make it big. Fresh out of journalism school at NYU, she had recently landed a much-coveted job as a field reporter for the morning news on WXNY, Channel 10. With her exotic Brazilian good looks and driving ambition, Flavia was determined to climb to the top of her profession.

And yesterday, her producer had dispensed her biggest assignment yet, a series of reports on the much-anticipated International Biogenetics Conference at New York's premier convention facilities in the Millennium Tower.

Flavia was tired from a night of only four hours of sleep, but her late-night Internet research session had paid dividends, providing useful background information that she could include in her on-the-scene reports. She reviewed the facts catalogued in her mind.

Built in tribute to its own stunning global success, and the resulting dizzying heights of its stock price, biotech conglomerate Triad Genomics' seventy-five-story Millennium Tower dominated lower Manhattan. The elegant high-tech tower, designed by the most prestigious architectural and engineering firms from a dozen countries, was the latest jewel in the New York skyline.

Constructed from high-strength concrete, a material twice as effective as steel in reducing the wind sway that plagues modern skyscrapers, the Millennium Tower's immense weight was supported by an inner ring of thick concrete cores and an outer ring of widely spaced "super columns"—a sophisticated structural system that accommodated its slender profile.

The Millennium Tower boasted a full forty floors of palatial office suites, fifteen floors of luxury hotel rooms, twenty floors of multimillion-dollar apartments, and was the chosen address for the headquarters of a dozen Fortune 500 companies.

But perhaps the most acclaimed feature of the massive postmodern structure was the colossal, six-story atrium in the base of the tower, featuring five-star restaurants, high-end retail, and a perfectly manicured mini–rain forest, complete with misting falls and hooting tropical birds. Prominently displayed in the first-floor colonnade of the cavernous lobby, a large, slowly spinning hologram of the Triad Genomics' logo incorporated a colorful representation of the intertwined double helix of human DNA.

The Millennium Tower had become the preferred convention spot for business and scientific conferences, hosted in internationally renowned convention facilities overlooking the financial district and downtown Manhattan. On this particular day, Flavia noted a marquis in the lobby that heralded the upcoming arrival of the week-long Ninth Annual International Biogenetics Conference. Hundreds of the world's top geneticists would gather to present their latest research and discuss new discoveries that promised to usher in a new era of human history.

Standing on the sidewalk across the street from the Millennium Tower's magnificent main entrance, Flavia smoothed the front of her cherry-red suit as she surveyed the scene, looking for the best location to film the lead-in to her report. Randy, her cameraman, lounged patiently on a bench sipping a café mocha as Flavia deliberated.

As she considered several different alternatives, Flavia's attention was drawn to a small crowd that was gathering across the street near the enormous glass doors leading into the Millennium Tower's atrium. Several posterboard signs on wooden sticks poked up above the motley-looking group.

Now, this might be interesting, Flavia thought as she interrupted Randy's morning coffee, dragging him across the street with his camera in tow.

Five

34TH FLOOR, MILLENNIUM TOWER
MANHATTAN, NEW YORK

Madison was late for work. Again. It was three minutes after eight when he finally drove into the ground-floor entrance to the parking garage in his black Jeep Cherokee.

He took it as a bad omen.

Despite having worked in the Millennium Tower since it opened, Christian Madison rarely visited any of the shops or restaurants in the atrium. He arrived in the building's underground parking garage each morning and rocketed up to the thirty-fourth-floor offices of Triad Genomics by express elevator. Madison often worked until late into the evening, declining polite dinner invitations from colleagues in favor of taking dinner at his desk in Styrofoam containers filled with sushi delivered by androgynous Japanese teens from the Pacific Rim Restaurant on the third floor.

By the time Madison stepped off the elevator onto the thirty-fourth floor, it was almost eight-fifteen.

Occupying eight floors of the Millennium Tower, the headquarters of Triad Genomics housed a world-class genetics research lab, high-tech offices for its geneticists and support staff, administrative facilities, boardrooms, and plush guest suites for visiting scientists and investors. Security was of the highest caliber, and Madison waited impatiently for the high-tech security system to detect the RFID chip implanted in his security badge.

With an audible click, the thick Plexiglas door unlocked and swung open.

"Dr. Madison, how are you this morning?" asked Michael Zoovas, seated behind the reception desk in the foyer. A former NYPD police officer, Zoovas had taken a job as a security officer with Triad Genomics following a short, unsuccessful attempt at retirement.

After Zoovas left the NYPD, he grew out his beard, put on twenty pounds, and bought a bass boat. He was bored out of his skull within six months. Drove his wife crazy. Zoovas was fond of saying that in order to save his marriage, he had to go back to work.

"Sandy was just asking about you the other day," said Zoovas. "Wondered how you were doing."

Madison had met Zoovas's wife, Sandy, last year at Justin's funeral. She was a Rubenesque blonde with creative tendencies and a short attention span.

"And how is Mrs. Zoovas these days? Still painting watercolor landscapes?" asked Madison.

Zoovas chuckled.

"Nope. That lasted about two weeks. Now she's taking pottery classes."

"As in shaping-clay-on-a-wheel pottery classes?"

"Exactly right. Need any bowls or cups? I've got pottery coming out my wazoo. All different colors too."

"No, I think I'm good. But thanks for asking."

"How about charcoal renderings? Japanese calligraphy? African tribal art? My house looks like a gallery for the artistically challenged."

"No, thanks, chief. I'm all set on artwork."

Zoovas chuckled. "Dr. Madison, have you met David Occam?" he said, gesturing at a burly uniformed security officer seated to his left.

"No, I haven't," said Madison, extending his hand in greeting to the young man.

"Good to meet you."

"Good to meet you, sir," said Occam. "I just started last week." His speech was flavored with traces of a British accent.

"Are you assigned to our floor?"

Occam's handshake squeezed Madison's fingers like a vise.

"No, sir. I'm going through your orientation and training program. They rotate me around through different departments. This week, Mr. Zoovas is putting me through the paces."

"Well, then you're in good hands," said Madison, extricating himself from the painful handshake. He noted Occam's rigid posture and crew cut, and the punctuation of his responses to Madison's questions with a crisp "sir."

"Former military?" Madison asked.

"Yes, sir. Ten years in Her Majesty's Armed Forces. Eight of those ten in the Twenty-second SAS Regiment. Special air service."

"Special air service—is that part of the Royal Air Force?"

"No, sir. British army, actually. A common misperception."

"Did you and Omar serve together?" asked Madison. "I believe he was British army as well."

"Omar?"

"Omar Crowe," offered Zoovas, referring to the head of security at Triad Genomics. "Some of the higher-ups here call Mr. Crowe by his first name. But unless he asks you to call him Omar, I wouldn't recommend it."

"Ah, yes. I believe I'll continue to address him as Mr. Crowe. And to answer your question, Dr. Madison, no, I didn't know Mr. Crowe in the service."

He smiled. "But I'm sure that my time in Her Majesty's Armed Forces didn't exactly hurt my prospects for employment here."

"I'm sure it didn't," said Madison. He glanced at the Tag Heuer watch on his wrist.

"I'm running late. I'll see you both later. And Mr. Occam, welcome to Triad Genomics."

"Thank you, sir," replied Occam.

"Take it easy, Dr. Madison," said Zoovas.

Madison strolled off down the hallway, forcing himself to toss a friendly wave and good-morning smile to his colleagues as he made his way to his office.

Once Madison was out of earshot, Zoovas turned to Occam.

"Nice guy. Very sad story," he said.

"How do you mean?"

Zoovas glanced around and self-consciously lowered his voice.

"Dr. Madison is a real whiz kid. A little odd, but a true genius. I swear he's got one of those photographic memories. Doesn't forget a thing. And he was quite the rising star here at Triad Genomics. He was Dr. Ambergris' protégé. They worked together on the human genome project. Triad Genomics was the first biotech firm to completely sequence human DNA."

Occam leaned back in his chair. "But?"

Zoovas sighed. "Madison had a kid. A little boy named Justin. It was a terrible thing. About a year and a half ago, his kid was diagnosed with leukemia. Died six months later."

Occam let out a low whistle. "That's awful."

"Yeah. Madison's wife just lost it. Couldn't cope. She left him not long after the funeral. Since then, he just hasn't been the same. Madison used to work seventy, eighty hours a week. He'd be in here before six A.M. Sometimes he wouldn't leave until after midnight. Not anymore. Sometimes I don't see him for days. Actually, I'm surprised he still has a job here at all."

"Maybe Dr. Ambergris protects him?" ventured Occam.

"Maybe. But I don't know. After Justin died, things went south between them too. They had some kind of falling-out. I'm not sure they even work together anymore."

"A falling-out? About what?"

"I'm not sure. Madison requested reassignment. Now he works on the Ark Project, decoding and cataloguing DNA from all kinds of different animals. Moved to a new office on the other side of the building."

"And Ambergris?"

"Around the same time, Ambergris lost his father, a big-shot professor at Yale. It did something to him. Dr. Ambergris was always eccentric—you know, in that charming, absentminded professor kind of way? But since last year, he's been different. People don't smile anymore when they say he's eccentric."

"But he's still one of the big shots around here, though."

"No question about it. He's got some big new research project going on. And he took on a new protégé—a young woman by the name of Grace Nguyen. Dr. Madison's no longer the heir apparent, that's for sure. She even moved into his old office."

"That's too bad. He seemed like a nice guy."

"Yeah. But you know what they say about nice guys," said Zoovas. "They always finish last."

Six

As she walked the six blocks from her apartment building to her office at Triad Genomics, Grace Nguyen was greeted with the sights and smells of a typical weekday morning in Manhattan. A cacophony of car horns, cell phones, and voices emanated from the herds of commuters migrating in the morning rush hour. The aroma of freshly baked breads and pastries wafted from a corner bakery, displaced only a moment later by the sharp odor of exhaust from a red double-decker transit bus.

Nguyen recalled the days when New York seemed vibrant and alive—a living, breathing metropolis, brimming with opportunity and possibility. Over the past year, the teeming city had lost its luster in her eyes, and felt crowded, dark, and dirty.

Grace navigated through the morning crowds with long, fluid strides, purposeful but unhurried. Dressed in a simple white linen shirt and tan skirt, with long, dark hair and Asian features, Grace had grown accustomed to the unwelcome stares from male passersby on the street.

As she neared the front entrance to the Millennium Tower, she realized that a group of roughly twenty people were congregated on the sidewalk outside. Several of them held homemade signs emblazoned with protest slogans.

An overweight middle-aged woman clutched a sign in a meaty hand that read: *STEM CELL RESEARCH IS IMMORAL!*

A young man with longish hair and a colorful tattoo of Jesus on his forearm held a placard that declared: *EMBRYOS ARE PEOPLE TOO!*

Down the block at the corner, a large black man was

filming the scene with a television camera perched atop his shoulder. An attractive young woman, presumably a reporter, hovered nearby, gesturing instructions to the cameraman.

Grace's cheeks flushed with annoyance.

You have got to be kidding me.

Grace was just beginning to consider skirting back around the block to the side entrance when a young woman in the group spotted the Triad Genomics identification badge hanging from a cord around Grace's neck. Perhaps emboldened by the presence of a television crew, she placed herself squarely in Grace's path.

"Stop stem cell research now!" she yelled, locking eyes with the approaching geneticist.

Grace's annoyance swelled into anger.

"You're blocking my way," she said in a stern voice. Other members of the group took notice of the exchange and watched with anticipation.

The young woman held her ground. And although there was ample room for Grace to walk around the female protester, she refused to alter her course, walking directly toward her verbal assailant.

"We're here to protect the unborn, those who can't protect themselves!" shouted the woman.

"How nice for you. Now step out of my way," she said, continuing on a collision course with the protester.

The confrontation had begun to draw the attention of people passing on the sidewalk, some of whom stopped to watch the encounter. One of the protesters, an older man in a white oxford shirt and blue jeans, handed his sign to a teen standing nearby and attempted to intervene.

"Jennifer, this is a peaceful demonstration," he said.

The young woman was undeterred. Emboldened by the gathering crowd, she held her sign high above her head and stuck her chin out defiantly.

"People like you have no respect for the value of human life!" she cried.

Grace stopped dead in her tracks. The two women were

separated by only a few feet. Grace's eyes narrowed and her hands clenched into small fists.

When she finally spoke, her voice was low and razor-sharp.

"People like me? Listen to me, you ignorant girl," she said, anger blazing in her eyes. "I lost a child to a genetic disease. She died before she was born. Have you ever lost a child?"

The moral indignation drained from Jennifer's face. She slowly shook her head.

"I thought not. Stem cell research may find a cure for the disease that took my daughter," said Grace. "Not that you have any idea what stem cell research really means. And I don't even do that type of work. Not that you have any comprehension of what geneticists actually do."

Jennifer opened her mouth.

"Don't you dare say another word to me," said Grace.

The woman visibly wilted under Grace's onslaught. The crowd of protesters and onlookers were silent.

"Now step out of my way before I knock you to the ground."

Jennifer lowered her sign and moved to the side.

Without uttering another word, Grace walked defiantly through the small crowd of protesters toward the entrance to the Millennium Tower.

Down the block, Flavia Veloso turned to the cameraman standing beside her.

"Please tell me you got that . . ."

Seven

Madison's office at Triad Genomics was one hundred and ninety-four paces from the security station in the thirty-fourth-floor lobby. He unconsciously counted them off in his head as he walked through the tangle of sterile hallways and plain doors toward his assigned environs.

As he neared his office, the Triad Genomics security system detected the RFID tag embedded in the ID card clipped to Madison's shirt pocket, confirmed his identity, and courteously unlocked the office door. The computer system also increased the ambient lighting and temperature in Madison's office to suit his personal preferences, and began piping in soft classical music through hidden speakers.

Madison tossed his battered leather shoulder bag onto the credenza. As he sat down at his desk, Triad Genomics' computer system unlocked his workstation and opened a secure socket to the central server. Then, as if on cue, his phone rang.

"Christian Madison," he answered.

"Hi, Christian, it's Kate."

Madison felt like he had been kicked in the stomach.

"Kate," he said, trying to keep the emotion out of his voice. "It's been a while."

"Christian, I just wanted to see if you were okay. I mean, today has been really hard for me, and I know it must be hard on you too."

"Did my mother call you?"

Silence.

"Umm, yeah. She did. Don't be upset with her. She's just worried about you."

"So this phone call wasn't your idea."

"Christian, don't be like that."

"Don't be like that? Give me a break. We haven't talked in weeks. And now you decide to call me and see how I'm feeling?"

A diminutive twenty-something in wire-rimmed glasses strolled into Madison's office, slurping from a can of Diet Coke. He looked like the young CEO of a dot-com start-up from the nineties. He wore pleated khaki pants and a black T-shirt. His dark brown hair was longish and stylishly unkempt.

"Bad time?" asked Stefan "Quiz" Goertz, Triad Genomics' systems engineer and resident computer guru.

"No, I'm finished," said Madison. He turned his attention back to the phone.

"So, as I was saying, thanks for calling. Don't be a stranger."

"Christian, wait—"

Madison hung up the phone.

"You're late again," said Quiz, deliberately ignoring the tension in the room.

"Your point being?"

Quiz smiled. "Big conference got you off your game?"

"Piece of cake," said Madison. "Dr. Ambergris is giving the big speech for Triad Genomics. I've just got the breakout session, a discussion group on the Ark Project."

"How many species are you up to?" asked Quiz.

"Just over eleven thousand. Noah may have assembled two of every animal in the days before the Great Flood, but he had divine assistance."

Madison sighed and leaned back in his chair.

Quiz pointed to a framed *Time* magazine cover on the wall. The cover story featured Triad Genomics, the first biotech company to sequence the entire human genome. Beneath a photo of Madison and his mentor, Dr. Joshua Ambergris, the title read, "The DNA Codebreakers."

"You and Dr. Ambergris. Always playing God."

"Beg your pardon?"

"Mapping the human genome wasn't enough," said Quiz. "Now you want to play Darwin and reinvent the origin of species."

"We can't all be genius computer gods like you," replied Madison. "Besides, Ambergris hasn't been involved in the Ark Project for at least six months. He's keeping his current research all to himself."

"Yes, but—"

"Look," interrupted Madison. "I have no idea what he's working on."

"You two used to be thick as thieves."

"Not anymore. Grace Nguyen is his new pet. She works with him on his new projects."

"And the Biogenetics Conference?"

"He's giving the keynote speech. The rumor mill has it that he plans to announce some new groundbreaking discovery."

"Ambergris is an odd bird," said Quiz. "Great taste in assistants, though," he said, reflecting for a moment on the attractive geneticist with whom Dr. Ambergris currently shared his secrets.

"But enough about the enterprising, young Dr. Grace Nguyen," said Madison, casting a disapproving look at Quiz as he turned toward his computer.

Madison's workstation loaded the documents and data he had been working on the previous day. On his computer monitor, a three-dimensional double helix revolved slowly in cyberspace.

A synthesized chime alerted Madison to the presence of new e-mail messages. He clicked on the mail icon. The first entry on the list of unread e-mail was dated June 11, 4:40 A.M. The sender of the e-mail was identified as Dr. Joshua Ambergris.

An e-mail from Dr. Ambergris.

At 4:40 A.M.?

Madison clicked open the e-mail. A puzzled look

dashed across his face. Curious, Quiz leaned over the desk to view Madison's computer monitor.

<<<
Priority: Urgent
[This message is not flagged]

Date: Tue., 14 June 04:39:57 -0400(EDT)
To: Dr. Christian Madison
    (CMadison@TriadGenomics.com)
From: Dr. Joshua Ambergris
    (JAmbergris@TriadGenomics.com)
Subject: [none]

52	61	4	13	20	29	36	45
14	3	62	51	46	35	30	19
53	60	5	12	21	28	37	44
11	6	59	54	43	38	27	22
55	58	7	10	23	26	39	42
9	8	57	56	41	40	25	24
50	63	2	15	18	31	34	47
16	1	64	49	48	33	32	17

Beneath the grid was a single line of text: *This is the beginning of the ancient word.*

"What's that?" asked Quiz.

"I have no idea."

Eight

Grace Nguyen stepped off the elevator into the thirty-fourth-floor lobby of Triad Genomics. She was still seething from her confrontation with the protesters on the street, and her eyes glinted with anger. Security officer Michael Zoovas looked up as she approached.

"Mornin', Dr. Nguyen."

"Good morning. Mr. Zoovas, would you kindly phone the NYPD and inform them that a group of protesters has assembled on the street in front of the building? They have apparently chosen the Biogenetics Conference as a venue to air their opposition to stem cell research. And probably to science and progress in general."

Zoovas tried not to smile.

"I was harassed by one of them when I entered the building."

"Yes, ma'am. I'll inform the police. I'll alert Mr. Crowe as well."

"Thank you," she said, rapping her knuckles on the countertop as she passed.

Zoovas picked up the phone at his desk and dialed a number he knew by heart from his years on the force. "John? Michael Zoovas here . . . I'm doing well, and yourself? Listen, we have a bit of a problem over here at the Millennium Tower . . ."

Four minutes later, after alerting the NYPD to the presence of the protesters downstairs and dispatching a brief e-mail report to Omar Crowe, Zoovas turned his attention back to the security monitors arrayed behind the security desk.

Several black and white displays showed images from

security cameras located throughout the thirty-fourth floor. Zoovas also kept an eye on the small color television set he had placed unobtrusively beneath the security monitors. On the TV screen, a BBC reporter was doing the lead-in for an interview with a distinguished-looking woman in a crisp white lab coat.

". . . Dr. Bancroft has found a way to use the information-carrying capacity of DNA to transmit and receive secret messages. Espionage has embraced biotechnology with Dr. Bancroft's creation of the microdot, which conceals secret messages in the immense complexity of human DNA."

Zoovas turned the volume on the TV set up a notch.

"In a recent experiment, Dr. Bancroft's team of researchers proved that the DNA microdot technique works. An account of this remarkable experiment was published this month in the highly respected scientific journal *Nature*. With us today is Dr. Catherine Bancroft, of the Mount Sinai School of Medicine in New York. Dr. Bancroft, can you explain to us what you've achieved in this experiment?"

"Hey, Occam, check this out," said Zoovas.

Occam stepped over and peered at the small TV over Zoovas's shoulder. On the screen, Dr. Bancroft folded her hands and gathered her thoughts.

"What we've done is encode a short, four-word secret message using the natural properties of human DNA. We've created a way to transmit a coded message in DNA that is completely undetectable," she replied.

The reporter leaned forward.

"And how was this accomplished, in layman's terms, Dr. Bancroft?"

"Well, the first step of the technique is to use a simple code to convert the letters of the alphabet into combinations of the chemical bases which make up DNA."

The reporter looked puzzled.

"And how is the coded message inserted into a strand of DNA?"

"Once the message is encoded, a piece of DNA spelling

out the message is synthetically created. It contains the secret message in the middle, plus short marker sequences at each end. This is slipped into a normal piece of human DNA."

"Remarkable," said the reporter. "And how would the message be decoded by the person who receives it?"

"The key to unraveling the message is knowing what the markers at each end of the DNA message are. The markers allow the message recipient to use a standard biotechnology technique, the polymerase chain reaction, or PCR, to multiply only the DNA that contains the message."

"I'm afraid that's way above my head, Dr. Bancroft."

"Let me put it this way. If the recipient of the message knows where to look for the message in the strand of DNA, that portion of the DNA can then be sequenced and the coded message can be read."

"And have you been approached by the government about your experiment?" asked the reporter.

"No, there haven't been any inquiries yet. But I did wonder if I would get the security clearance to publish the paper in the first place. This is very cutting-edge science," said Dr. Bancroft.

Zoovas scratched his head and chuckled.

"Amazing," he said, turning to Occam. "What will they think of next?"

Nine

DR. CHRISTIAN MADISON'S OFFICE
34TH FLOOR, MILLENNIUM TOWER
MANHATTAN, NEW YORK

Madison glared at the strange e-mail.

"I really don't have time for this," he said, irritation flaring in his voice. He reached for the phone, intending to dial Dr. Ambergris' extension. He halted midreach when Grace Nguyen appeared in his doorway.

"Good morning, Christian. Quiz."

Her usual poise was rough at the edges. Madison noted the furrows that stress etched between Grace's eyebrows when she was upset.

"Good morning," said Madison.

"Hello, Dr. Nguyen," said Quiz, tipping an imaginary hat.

She smiled at Quiz. "Enough already. My name is Grace. Stop calling me Dr. Nguyen."

"My mother always told me it was impolite to address my elders by their first name." He suppressed a mischievous grin.

She raised one eyebrow.

"Do I look 'elder' to you?"

He looked her up and down. "Elder than me."

"Don't make me come over there and give you a spanking, Stefan."

Quiz groaned. As Grace was well aware, he hated his given name. He held up his hands in mock surrender.

Madison leaned back in his chair. "What brings you to the wrong side of the tracks?" His words had a sharp edge.

Grace raised her deep blue eyes to meet Madison's. Her azure irises were a genetic gift from her British father, a striking splash of color on a canvas of Asian features.

Grace stifled a retort. Unvoiced, it was bitter on her tongue.

"Christian, I need to talk to you," she said.

"Everything okay?" asked Christian.

A pause.

"No," she said.

Another pause.

Madison took his cue to inquire. "What is it?"

Grace shifted her weight back and forth from one foot to the other. "I think I made a mistake."

"How so?"

"When I came to work this morning, there was a group

of protesters outside the building. Maybe twenty or so. One of them really got under my skin. She baited me and I fell for it. I think I really overreacted."

"Overreacted how?" asked Madison.

"Wait a minute," said Quiz. "Protesters?"

"They're demonstrating against stem cell research," said Grace.

"Do we even do that?" asked Quiz.

"No," said Madison. "We don't."

"But the Biogenetics Conference is going to get a lot of press," said Grace. "They're probably looking for media exposure."

"Overreacted how?" repeated Madison.

"I said some things I shouldn't have." She briefly related the encounter.

"Well, that doesn't sound so bad," said Quiz.

"Ordinarily, I might agree, but I think we were filmed. There was a reporter and cameraman down the street."

Madison shook his head slowly. The corporate suits that steered the financial course of Triad Genomics were very sensitive to bad publicity. A negative news report could have adverse effects on the stock price. Triad Genomics paid millions of dollars each year to Madison Avenue wizards to wage a public relations war against its critics and to paint a positive image of the company in the public mind.

"If that gets aired, the board of directors will want your head. On a platter," said Madison.

"That's what I'm afraid of," she said. "What do you think I should do?"

"Why don't you ask Dr. Ambergris?"

"I'm asking you."

"You want to know what I think? I think you opened your mouth again without thinking."

"Christian, of all people, I thought you would understand."

"Look, I don't know why you—"

Quiz interjected. "Hey, guys?"

"Quiz, she always does this," said Madison. "She never stops to consider—"

When he saw the alarmed expression on Quiz's face, Madison stopped abruptly, midsentence.

Ten

DR. CHRISTIAN MADISON'S OFFICE
34TH FLOOR, MILLENNIUM TOWER
MANHATTAN, NEW YORK

"No. Stop it. Stop it." Quiz frantically rubbed the palm of his right hand with the thumb of his left. His fingers curled inward in a contorted muscle spasm.

"What is it?" asked Grace.

Beads of sweat popped out on Quiz's forehead. The color drained from his face.

"Your pills," Madison prompted.

Quiz dug in his pocket for the plastic prescription vial. He struggled to remove the cap, finally wrenching it free and spilling dozens of tiny blue pills to the floor. With a trembling finger, he fished out one caplet and popped it in his mouth, swallowing hard.

Grace's eyes grew wide. "What's happening?"

"He's having another seizure," said Madison.

"They always start like this," said Quiz, grimacing in pain. "My hand twists up. God, that hurts . . ."

"You need to sit down," said Madison, rising from his chair. "Grace, can you—"

Grace took Quiz by the arm, leading him to one of two chairs parked in front of Madison's desk.

The memory of Quiz's first seizure six weeks ago flashed in Madison's mind. Madison had stopped by Quiz's office one morning with a sack of onion bagels and cream cheese and found him lying on the floor in the throes of a full grand mal attack. Madison would never forget the look of sheer terror in Quiz's eyes as he lay helpless on the concrete floor, his limbs jerking and twitching uncontrollably.

Quiz closed his eyes. Cold sweat trickled down his face. His breath came in short gasps.

"Breathe, Stefan," urged Grace.

"Do you want me to call an ambulance?" asked Madison.

Quiz shook his head. "No . . . I think it's easing up."

Slowly his breathing returned to normal and the muscles in his fingers and hand began to relax.

"Thank God for Depakote," he said.

"I didn't know you had epilepsy," said Grace.

"I didn't either. At least until last month. If Madison hadn't been there to call 911 . . ."

"What did the doctors say?"

"Adult-onset epilepsy. Unknown cause. These pills really seem to help," he said, shaking the prescription vial. "No driving for at least six months. That's state law. Other than that, take my meds and try to avoid stress," said Quiz.

"Not much chance of that around here," said Madison, smiling.

"No," said Quiz. "No, I suppose not." He sighed.

"Grace, I'd rather that people didn't know about this," said Quiz. "I don't feel comfortable with—"

There was a loud knock at the door.

Before Madison could respond, his office door swung open. An enormous black man, with a shaved head and barrel chest, filled the doorway. His eyes scanned the room.

Eleven

"Pardon the interruption, Dr. Madison," said Omar Crowe, Triad Genomics' chief of security. He spoke the Queen's English with a proper British accent.

As he scanned the room, his eyes lingered on Quiz.

"Is everything okay here?" he asked.

Crowe towered over the office's occupants. The top of his shaved head barely cleared the door frame. Powerful shoulders and thick musculature strained the seams of his navy-blue blazer, adorned with the Triad Genomics logo on its breast pocket.

Quiz nodded.

"Yes," said Madison. "Everything's fine. Why?"

Crowe ignored the question.

"Dr. Madison, will you come with me, please?"

An alarm sounded from the intercom speakers mounted in the ceiling of Madison's office. The three shrill electronic warbles were followed by a voice.

"Attention, please. May I have your attention. Triad Genomics is now operating under a level-one security lockdown. External communications are now prohibited. Please return to your stations and await further instructions."

The computer on Madison's desk chirped and text began scrolling up the screen.

<< PRIORITY ALERT >>
<< From: TRIAD GENOMICS SECURITY
<< Priority: ALPHA
<< To: ALL
<< Level-one security lockdown in effect. >>

<< External communications suspended. >>
<< All stations directed to implement security protocols. >>

"Another security drill? We just had one last week," said Quiz.

"Quiz, Dr. Nguyen, please return to your offices."

"I'm not going anywhere until you tell us what this is about," said Grace.

Crowe retrieved what appeared to be a small cell phone from the inside pocket of his blazer. He punched three buttons and spoke into the receiver.

"Mr. Occam, please report to Dr. Madison's office to escort Dr. Grace Nguyen to her workstation."

Ignoring Grace's protests, Crowe turned to Quiz.

"Will you require an escort as well?"

Quiz shook his head. "No, that won't be necessary."

Crowe placed the phone back in his pocket.

"Dr. Madison, will you come with me, please."

It was not a request.

Twelve

DR. CHRISTIAN MADISON'S OFFICE
34TH FLOOR, MILLENNIUM TOWER
MANHATTAN, NEW YORK

"We're not going to the executive suite?" Madison asked his burly escort.

"No," Crowe replied. "Mr. Giovanni is waiting for you at Dr. Ambergris' office."

Dante Giovanni and Joshua Ambergris were the original founding partners of Triad Genomics. Ambergris directed the genetic research that led to the successful completion of the Human Genome Project, but it was Giovanni who brought the financial acumen and business connections to the company, shepherding it from its humble beginnings as a fledgling start-up to a multibillion-dollar IPO. Dante Giovanni was Triad Genomics' CEO and chairman of the board.

They rounded a corner in the maze of hallways on the thirty-fourth floor and Madison spotted Giovanni standing in the hallway outside of Dr. Ambergris' corner office. He spoke in clipped sentences to a young female security officer. She dashed off down the hall to carry out her instructions.

Dante Giovanni was, as always, an impressive sight. He was perfectly coiffed and manicured, as if he had just come from a press conference. With a full head of graying hair and two rows of pearly white teeth, Giovanni embodied the stereotypical image of the corporate CEO.

He gripped Madison's hand in a firm handshake and clasped Madison's elbow with his other hand in the familiar politician's gesture.

"Dr. Madison. Thank you for coming. I'm afraid I have some grave news."

Madison waited expectantly.

"Dr. Ambergris is dead. He was found in his office, at his desk, this morning."

Madison stared in stunned silence.

"What? That can't be. He was in good health. You must be mistaken."

"No. There's no mistake," said Giovanni. "Dr. Madison, Joshua Ambergris was murdered."

Madison's brain refused to process the information.

"What?"

Giovanni placed a hand against Ambergris' office door and pushed it open. The room was in complete disarray. Papers and books were scattered everywhere. On the floor beside the massive desk, a white sheet covered Ambergris' still form.

"My god," said Madison. His heart pounded in his ears.

Crowe displayed no emotional reaction. His expression

remained stoic, poker-faced and unrevealing. But Madison noticed that his left hand was tightly clenched in a fist.

"How did this happen?" asked Madison. "Who did this?"

"I don't know," said Giovanni, placing a hand on Madison's shoulder. "But we're going to find out."

Thirteen

63RD FLOOR, PETRONAS TOWERS
KUALA LUMPUR, MALAYSIA

Until 1996, the world's tallest skyscraper had always been in the United States. But the completion of Kuala Lumpur's twin eighty-eight-story buildings, the Petronas Towers, ended America's claim to that title. On April 15, 1996, the Petronas Towers became the tallest skyscrapers in the world. Surpassing Chicago's Sears Tower by thirty-six feet, the Petronas Towers were a tribute to Malaysia's emerging economic might, and to Kuala Lumpur's prominence as a commercial and cultural capital.

The uniquely Malaysian architecture of the dual skyscrapers, with their elegant proportions and design, captured the attention of the world. Each tower's floor plan forms an eight-pointed star created by two intersecting squares, a design that evokes Islamic arabesques and repetitive geometric figures characteristic of Muslim architecture. Curved and pointed bays create a scalloped facade that suggests the form of ancient temple towers.

The two towers, joined by a skybridge on the forty-second floor, have been described as two cosmic pillars spiraling endlessly toward the heavens. For Malaysian industrialist and billionaire Kai Tanaka, the Petronas Towers were a fitting location to showcase the headquarters of his growing business empire.

One entire wall of Tanaka's opulently furnished executive office suite on the sixty-third floor was covered from floor to ceiling with a massive LCD screen divided into a grid of boxes, each displaying the real-time digital image of a participant in the videoconference that was under way.

Arrayed around the room, museum-quality pieces from ancient human civilizations were illuminated in eerie blue light from xenon spotlights in climate-controlled glass display cases.

A Sumerian tablet.

A Mayan stela.

An Egyptian ankh.

An Assyrian sculpture of two intertwined serpents.

Tanaka paced the length of his plush office, speaking in a commanding voice to the group.

"Gentlemen," he began. "The threat has been eliminated. Our agent was successful in his assignment."

He paused to allow for the slight delay in transmission created by the use of sophisticated encryption software. Relief at Tanaka's announcement was evident on many of the faces displayed on the videoconference screen.

"Unfortunately, our agent was unable to access the Triad Genomics' mainframe. We cannot be certain that evidence of the discovery does not remain on the company's computer system."

Tanaka paused.

"The good doctor was remarkably uncooperative when questioned before his untimely demise. He displayed an unforeseen resistance to our man's . . . novel techniques of persuasion."

An older man with a leathery face addressed the group.

"So we have accomplished little and created much additional risk. This is precisely why I was opposed to such an action."

Tanaka fixed his gaze firmly on the reticent man.

"This was the will of the Order. You were all aware of the potential risks. The Order has killed many times before to prevent the discovery of our secrets. Those who came before us eliminated many scholars and students of history who stumbled upon fragments of the truth. It is necessary."

Tanaka spread out his hands in front of him.

"Our first attempt to suppress the truth in this instance was simply incomplete. We only have to finish the job. In a more . . . shall we say . . . thorough manner."

"Meaning?"

"First, the Triad Genomics computer server must be neutralized."

"What do you propose? A computer virus? A fire?"

"No. That will not be sufficient," said Tanaka.

He sat down on a steel and leather chair and folded his hands in his lap.

"Our agent was unable to extract from Dr. Ambergris whether or not he communicated his discoveries to any of his colleagues. We cannot afford the possibility that our secrets have been revealed to others within the Triad Genomics group."

Tanaka's thin lips parted in a malevolent smile.

"We must employ more extreme measures."

Fourteen

ROOM 714, UNITED NATIONS PLAZA HOTEL
MANHATTAN, NEW YORK

Arakai sipped from a small teacup. The faint aroma of green tea reminded him of home. He stared out the long window in his room at the UN Plaza Hotel. Across the street, the sprawling United Nations complex overlooked the East River.

We the Peoples of the United Nations, United for a Better World . . .

The towering UN Secretariat Building dominated the United Nations campus in New York. Its narrow end walls rose like sheer white cliffs. The long sides of the structure were clad in green-tinted glass curtains.

We the Peoples of the United Nations, determined to save succeeding generations from the scourge of war . . .

The light blue UN flag flapped in the wind.

. . . to maintain international peace and security, and to that end, to take effective collective measures for the prevention and removal of threats to the peace . . .

Arakai reflected on the flag's design: a map of the world, inscribed in white and gold within a wreath, an equidistant projection of the earth centered on the North Pole on a field of light blue.

Turning away from the window, Arakai sat cross-legged on the floor of his hotel room. From his pocket, he retrieved a silver coin. Flexing his fingers with great dexterity, Arakai coaxed the coin into performing numismatic acrobatics, dancing across his knuckles.

Two additional silver coins joined the first in the palm of his left hand.

Arakai closed his eyes and prepared to begin divination of the Taoist oracle, the *I Ching*. He wrote out a single question on a tablet of white paper.

Images from Arakai's childhood passed through his mind. His grandfather had taught him the secrets of the *I Ching* when Arakai was a child. He remembered his grandfather's words:

The I Ching, *the* Book of Changes, *is the oldest of the classic texts. It is the ancient system of cosmology and philosophy at the heart of our beliefs.*

Arakai cast the coins in the air.

Each moment of his past and the myriad possibilities of the future all came together in one single moment of time, joining in a complex web of synchronicity to divine a precise insight from the *I Ching*. The coins fell silently on the thickly carpeted floor. Arakai wrote down the orientation of the coins on his tablet.

Nine more tosses of the coins completed a six-line hexagram.

The voice of Arakai's grandfather echoed in his head.

With six such lines stacked from bottom to top in each hexagram, there are sixty-four possible combinations that can result from each divination.

Sixty-four possible combinations.

As Arakai had recently been taught, there are extraordinary similarities that link the ancient knowledge of the *I Ching* to contemporary knowledge of the structure of human DNA. All human DNA is constructed from four genetic letters, each representing an amino acid. These genetic letters are grouped together in sets of three called codons. In human DNA, there are sixty-four different codons.

Sixty-four.

Sixty-four possible combinations in the I Ching.

Sixty-four possible combinations in human DNA.

Arakai immediately recognized the configuration of the hexagram.

Sung. Conflict.

He consulted a thin, worn book—the *Book of Changes*—and read the appropriate passage.

THE JUDGMENT

> *Conflict. You are sincere*
> *and are being obstructed.*
> *A cautious halt halfway brings good fortune.*
> *Going through to the end brings misfortune.*
> *It furthers one to see the great man.*
> *It does not further one to cross the great water.*

THE IMAGE

> *Heaven and water go their opposite ways:*
> *The image of Conflict.*
> *Thus in all his transactions the superior man*
> *Carefully considers the beginning.*

Arakai's consciousness filled with serenity. The oracle was clear. He knew what he must do.

Fifteen

Madison's eyes were locked on the still form of Joshua Ambergris, lying on his office floor, covered by a thin white sheet. His mind reeled from news of Dr. Ambergris' murder. Despite the fine sheen of sweat that had appeared on his forehead, Madison felt a cold chill sweep through his arms and legs.

"No . . . not again . . ."

Painful memories welled in his mind.

Justin was a ghost of a child, lying thin and frail under the starched white sheets of a hospital bed. A tangle of tubes and wires crisscrossed his chest, connecting his dying body with IV bags, monitors, and machines.

The monotonous beep of a heart monitor ticked off the passage of seconds. Christian Madison sat at his bedside, gently holding Justin's hand.

Madison realized that Giovanni was speaking.

"It's my understanding that Dr. Ambergris had made significant discoveries that he planned to announce at the Biogenetics Conference. Can you tell me what Dr. Ambergris was working on?" asked Giovanni.

"I feel sick," said Madison. His face was pale and his knees felt weak.

Giovanni grasped Madison's shoulder. Tightly.

"Dr. Madison, focus for a minute. This is very important."

Cold beads of sweat ran down the back of Madison's shirt. His hands were damp and clammy.

"I have to know what Joshua was working on," said Giovanni.

"I wasn't involved in Dr. Ambergris' current research project. I have no idea what he planned to present at the conference. Why? Do you think his research has something to do with his murder?"

"I don't know," said Giovanni, "but it's a possibility. Triad Genomics has been the target of corporate espionage before. Theft. Blackmail. But never this. Never murder."

Madison looked around. "Where are the police?"

"We'll alert the authorities in due course," said Giovanni. "But first I need to get a handle on what we're dealing with."

Madison was stunned. "You haven't called the police?"

"Listen to me," said Giovanni. "The death of our senior geneticist could send our stock price plunging. Rumors of corporate espionage and murder could be disastrous if not handled carefully."

"I don't believe this," said Madison. "Dr. Ambergris was murdered, in his office, and your first priority is the company's stock price?"

Giovanni grabbed his shoulder.

"I need to obtain as much control over this situation as possible before I allow it to become public knowledge. With all due respect to the NYPD, I need some answers before I invite a bull into the china shop."

Crowe folded his arms across his massive chest, straining the fabric of his blazer.

"Dr. Madison, when was the last time you spoke with Dr. Ambergris?" asked Crowe.

Madison stared at Crowe for a moment, then turned to Giovanni.

"What is this, an interrogation?"

"No, of course not," said Giovanni. He buttoned the middle button of his suit jacket and straightened his cuffs. "But we do need your help. I'd like for you to assist Crowe in his investigation."

"With all due respect, I don't want to get involved," said Madison. "If you want to delay informing the police, that's your choice. But I want nothing to do with it."

"Dr. Madison, this is important. Ambergris was your mentor. He recruited you, brought you to Triad Genomics. For God's sake, working with Dr. Ambergris got you on the cover of *Time* magazine. Don't you think you owe it to him to help investigate his murder?"

Madison's face flushed with emotion.

"Owe it to him?"

His voice rose.

"All Ambergris ever did for me was lead me down the primrose path. Genetic research with absolutely no practical application. Did those years of research accomplish anything worthwhile? I wasted years of my life in the lab with Dr. Ambergris. Nights. Weekends. Time I should have spent with my family . . ."

His voice cracked.

". . . time I should have spent with my son."

Madison locked eyes with Dante Giovanni.

"Did our research save any lives? Did we stop even one child from dying of cancer? Of leukemia?"

Giovanni held up a hand.

"That's enough, Dr. Madison. I know you're upset. But this is helping no one. Take a few minutes. Go back to your office. Cool off. Think things through. Rationally. Then we'll talk."

Madison took a deep breath, then slowly exhaled.

"Look, all I know is that Ambergris was working with introns. Anyone who has read the agenda for the Biogenetics Conference knows that much. If you want the details on his research, you should speak with Grace Nguyen."

Sixteen

Introns.

With a few discreet inquiries, Flavia Veloso easily identified the woman who had clashed with the protesters outside the Millennium Tower—Dr. Grace Nguyen. Digging for background information on the hotheaded young scientist had been just as easy. A quick review of the press packet for the International Biogenetics Conference revealed that Dr. Nguyen, a geneticist with Triad Genomics, was slated to give a joint presentation with Dr. Joshua Ambergris on introns.

Introns?

Flavia's cameraman, Randy, was holed up in WXNY's production studio, editing the film of Dr. Nguyen's hostile exchange with the protesters and adding Flavia's voice-over to the footage. With a little luck, and creative editing, they just might snag the lead story on the ten o'clock local news.

While Randy worked his magic with the footage, Flavia was determined to learn as much as she could about Dr. Grace Nguyen. Her first step was to hunt down WXNY's science and technology correspondent. After adjusting her push-up bra for maximum effect, she cornered Donald Ebersole in his cubicle on the third floor. He was busy at work on a ham and egg breakfast sandwich.

"Hi, Donald," said Flavia, giving him her best smile. "Do you have time for a favor?"

Ebersole set his breakfast sandwich down on the sports section of yesterday's *New York Times*. He hiked up the bifocals on his nose with a greasy index finger. His narrow head was crowded between two large ears.

"You are asking for my help? My pleasure. What can I do for you?"

Ebersole took a quick slug from a mug of lukewarm coffee and a surreptitious leer at Flavia's cleavage.

"I need to tap into that encyclopedic storehouse of knowledge in that brain of yours. Some background info for an assignment I'm working on," she said.

Flavia retrieved a chair from the next cubicle and sat, crossing one slim thigh over the other.

Ebersole grinned. "Flattery, my dear, will get you everywhere."

Flavia flipped to a blank page in her pad, armed with a ballpoint pen. "Donald, what can you tell me about introns?"

"Introns," repeated Ebersole. He searched his mind for information. He wanted to make a good impression on the attractive young reporter.

"Well, introns are also called junk DNA. They're long sequences of DNA in the human genome. Scientists don't really know what introns do. They don't appear to serve any useful purpose."

Flavia was puzzled.

"Back up. More basic. Science wasn't really my thing in school. What exactly is DNA? I mean, I know the basics, but what is it really?"

Ebersole leaned forward and cracked his knuckles.

"Okay. Let me give you a brief overview to get you oriented. Two minutes on genetics. It's like this. High school textbooks refer to DNA as the blueprint of life. It exists in every single organism, from the smallest virus to the largest mammal. DNA, or deoxyribonucleic acid, is the chemical inside our cells that carries the genetic instructions for making living organisms. It's passed along from generation to generation."

"Right," said Flavia. "Genes. Heredity. I remember that much."

"The interesting question is this: What is it about DNA that makes it the key to heredity?"

"The double helix?" Flavia ventured.

"Exactly. See, you know more than you realize. Two intertwined spirals form what looks like a long, thin, twisted ladder. This is called the double helix. This structure enables DNA to reproduce itself."

"Reproduce itself?"

"Yes. Interesting, is it not? DNA can make a copy of itself, a twin, if you will, to pass along to new cells or to a new generation."

Ebersole took another sip of coffee, patted Flavia on the knee, then continued.

"DNA is like a master pattern from which living things can be replicated again and again. Inside each human cell are two complete copies of the human genome. Each set contains around seventy thousand genes on twenty-three sets of chromosomes."

Ebersole's hand remained on Flavia's knee. Her skin crawled at his touch, but she didn't flinch, encouraging Ebersole with a smile to continue his lecture. Ebersole removed his hand and pulled a book from a shelf above his desk. He opened it at random to a page near the middle and set it on Flavia's lap.

"How shall we visualize it? Like this. You can think of the human genome like a book," he said, pointing to the open page in the book. "It has twenty-three chapters called *chromosomes*. Each chapter contains thousands of paragraphs called *genes*. Each paragraph is made up of sentences called *exons*. Each sentence is composed of words called *codons*. And each word is written in letters called *bases*."

"Okay, I'm with you."

"But instead of being written on pages of paper, like this book, the human genome is written on long chains of sugar and phosphate called DNA molecules."

"And how long is this book?" asked Flavia, warming to the analogy.

"There are over a billion words in the human genomic book. It's as long as eight hundred King James Bibles.

Incredible, no? If you were to read the human genome aloud at a rate of one second per word for eight hours a day, seven days a week, it would take over a hundred years to read it all."

"Wow."

It seemed to Flavia that Ebersole was dredging up every bit of information on DNA from his memory.

"You can think of human DNA as a message written in a code of chemicals, one chemical for each letter. The language of DNA is an alphabet with only four letters—A, C, G, and T—adenine, cytosine, guanine, and thymine. The DNA message carries the chemical instructions for assembling a new person."

"A recipe for making humans?"

"In a manner of speaking, yes. DNA is the code for life, and that code has been replicated in every person who has ever lived. Some might call it the secret language of God."

Seventeen

63RD FLOOR, PETRONAS TOWERS
KUALA LUMPUR, MALAYSIA

"Here is what I propose," said Tanaka to the group. "Decisive action."

Tanaka's demeanor radiated confidence and power. He looked into the eyes of each member of the Council in turn.

"The day after tomorrow begins the Ninth Annual International Biogenetics Conference at the Millennium Tower, only ten floors below the offices of Triad Genomics. Assembled at that conference will be most of the world's leading geneticists. We have the opportunity, with one decisive action, to eliminate both the unascertained threat at Triad Genomics and to impede the progress of biogenetics research for decades. Research that threatens to uncover the secrets of the Genesis Code."

"You propose that we destroy the Millennium Tower during the middle of the Biogenetics Conference?" asked a senior member of the Order. "That this Council should sanction the murder of hundreds of scientists? And the killing of thousands of innocent men and women who work in the Millennium Tower?"

Tanaka picked up a Japanese sword from its display stand and slid the blade from its scabbard.

"Some must be sacrificed for a higher purpose. It has always been so."

Surveying the faces of the Council members, Tanaka knew that his will would prevail. There would be dissenters. But ultimately, he would strike them all down.

Tanaka swung the katana in an overhead arc, executing an offensive attack from the aikido school of martial arts.

"How long to set this course of action in motion?" asked a member of the Council.

"We can begin moving assets into place immediately. Zero-hour will be nine-fifteen A.M. on the first day of the Biogenetics Conference."

Eighteen

DANTE GIOVANNI'S OFFICE
EXECUTIVE SUITE, TRIAD GENOMICS
MANHATTAN, NEW YORK

Dante Giovanni's expansive corner office offered a breathtaking panoramic view of Central Park and the Manhattan skyline. On a typical day, Giovanni began his morning by reading *The New York Times* and *The Wall Street Journal,* sipping Columbian coffee, and enjoying the view.

Today, however, was not a typical day.

Today he was seated with his chief of security at a round mahogany conference table, calmly discussing the murder of Dr. Joshua Ambergris—his business partner, his oldest friend, and Triad Genomics' top geneticist.

"Barring some personal vendetta against Dr. Ambergris, which I find highly unlikely, the motive for his murder must be related in some way to his work," said Crowe.

Giovanni folded his arms and sat back in his chair. Along each wall of the ornate office, at ceiling level, small unobtrusive speakers emitted "pink noise." At frequencies indiscernible to the human ear, the emissions from the speakers blocked any attempts at eavesdropping by electronic devices either smuggled into the room or directed at the office from outside.

"That may be," said Giovanni.

"Dr. Ambergris had a limited circle of friends and acquaintances," said Crowe. "He was a widower. No children. No gambling habits or unusual sexual preferences. If he was concealing something in his personal life that would provide a motive for murder, it is not evident to me."

There was a tentative knock at the door.

Giovanni pressed a button hidden beneath the tabletop. The office door unlocked and swung open. One of Giovanni's young female assistants hastily deposited a carafe of coffee, two ceramic mugs, and a tray of breakfast pastries on the conference table. At a nod from Giovanni, she scurried out the door.

"Let's look at this from another angle," said Crowe, turning back to the conversation. "Ambergris' killer was able to compromise our security. Unless we're dealing with an extremely sophisticated operation—sponsored by a foreign government, perhaps—it is inconceivable that our security system could be breached unless the intruder had intimate knowledge of our facility. Inside information. That leaves only two possibilities."

He drummed his fingers on the mahogany table.

"Either the killer already had security clearance, or

Dr. Ambergris' murderer had help from the inside," said Crowe.

"Yes. I suppose that's the logical conclusion."

Crowe served himself a cup of steaming black coffee.

"Either way, we're dealing with a traitor within our ranks."

Nineteen

DONALD EBERSOLE'S CUBICLE
WXNY, CHANNEL 10
QUEENS, NEW YORK

Ebersole continued his impromptu lecture while Flavia scribbled notes on her pad.

"Every second, roughly fifty million of the cells in your body die. Amazing, is it not? From the recipe contained in your DNA, new cells are created to take their place. Your genetic code, written in every cell in your body, recreates your body as you age."

"Okay, I think I've got it. So where do introns fit in?"

"Good question," said Ebersole. "So what about introns? Big chunks of our DNA appear to be nothing more than a jumble of repetitive, random sequences that are rarely, if ever, used. Geneticists call these junk sequences introns."

Flavia frowned.

"How can we visualize introns? Try this. If DNA is like a television show, then introns are like enormous commercial breaks that interrupt the real program. Except in our DNA, the commercials are longer than the actual show."

"I think I understand," said Flavia.

Ebersole continued. "Do we really understand them? No. We still have no idea why introns are present in our DNA or what they actually do, if anything. And what is being done? Nothing. No significant research on introns has been done in years."

Flavia flipped to a fresh page in her notebook and continued writing.

Ebersole took another bite from his breakfast sandwich. When he spoke, crumbs fell from his mouth onto his wrinkled shirt.

"Interesting, is it not? A few years back, there was one paper published by a pair of geneticists from Japan. As I recall, it wasn't well regarded by the mainstream scientific community. These Japanese scientists claimed that their measurements clearly revealed the Fibonacci sequence and the Golden Ratio in the structure of human DNA."

"You've lost me again. The Fibonacci sequence? The Golden Ratio?"

"Not given to mathematics, are we? These are mathematical concepts. There's an easy way to explain the Fibonacci sequence. Start making a list of numbers. The first two numbers on your list are zero and one."

"Okay," said Flavia, jotting numbers on her pad.

"Now add a third number to your list by adding the first and second numbers together."

"Okay. Zero plus one equals one."

"Now make a fourth number by adding the second and third numbers in your list. Keep doing this, over and over."

Flavia stopped writing.

"The series that you get is zero, one, one, two, three, five, eight, thirteen, and so on. Mathematicians call this the Fibonacci sequence. And if you divide any number in the Fibonacci sequence by the one before it, the answer is always close to 1.61803."

"What's so special about that?"

"The relationship between successive numbers in the Fibonacci sequence, 1.61803, is called the Golden Ratio. It's also called phi. You can find the Golden Ratio in nature, art, and music."

"I don't get it. How?"

"It's a puzzle, is it not? The Golden Ratio shows up in nature in the arrangements of leaves on plants, patterns in the growth of crystals, graphs of animal populations, critical values of spinning black holes, and the shapes of pine trees and chicken eggs."

Ebersole logged on to the Internet. He typed as he talked.

"Where else do we see it? Many places. Claude Debussy used phi in his music, and Le Corbusier employed it in his architecture. Leonardo da Vinci used the Golden Ratio when he painted the *Mona Lisa,* and the Greeks used it when they built the Parthenon."

Flavia consulted her notes. "And these Japanese geneticists found the Fibonacci sequence and the Golden Ratio in DNA?"

"Here it is," he said, reading from the computer screen. "What did they find? According to their calculations, human DNA measures thirty-four angstroms long by twenty-one angstroms wide for each full cycle of the double helix spiral. Thirty-four and twenty-one are numbers in the Fibonacci sequence, and their ratio is 1.618, the Golden Ratio."

Ebersole smiled. "Remarkable, yes?

"But like I said, no one seemed to take much notice. And that was years ago. For at least the last five years, no one has made any progress on introns."

Flavia thought for a moment. "What if I told you that one of the keynote speeches at this year's International Biogenetics Conference was going to be about introns?"

"Who's the speaker?"

"There are two copresenters listed on the agenda. Dr. Grace Nguyen and Dr. Joshua Ambergris, both from Triad Genomics."

"I don't know Nguyen," said Ebersole. "But what do I know about Ambergris? He's a heavy hitter. He won a Nobel Prize for his work on the Human Genome Project."

Ebersole smoothed the wispy goatee on his chin.

"The International Biogenetics Conference is like the

Super Bowl for geneticists. If Dr. Ambergris is giving a big presentation on introns, I'd wager that he plans to announce a major discovery. What do I think? I think you may have a big story here."

Twenty

DR. CHRISTIAN MADISON'S OFFICE
34TH FLOOR, MILLENNIUM TOWER
MANHATTAN, NEW YORK

When Madison returned to his office, Grace was waiting inside.

"Grace?"

She turned to face him. Her eyes were red from crying.

"I thought security escorted you to your office. How did you get back in here?" asked Madison.

"Quiz. I called him and asked. He worked some magic to override the security lock on your door."

Her lower lip quivered.

"Is it true?" she asked. "People are starting to talk. Is he really dead?"

Madison nodded grimly. "I'm afraid so."

Fresh tears welled in Grace's eyes. She reached out to Madison. He held her tightly as she cried.

"I can't believe this is happening."

Grace stepped back from Madison's embrace and smoothed the wrinkles in her white linen shirt. She wiped at her eyes with the flat of her hand.

"They want to talk to you," said Madison.

"Who does?"

"Giovanni. And Crowe. They want to know what Dr. Ambergris was working on. I told them as much as I knew. Which wasn't much," said Madison.

Grace bit her lower lip. "He didn't want anyone to know. At least not until tomorrow."

"Giovanni thinks someone may have been after his research."

Madison related the substance of his conversations with Giovanni and Crowe. Grace's hands trembled.

"I suppose it's possible," she said. "Dr. Ambergris made a big breakthrough," she said. "He was going to announce it at the Biogenetics Conference."

"Tell me," said Madison.

Twenty-one

DR. CHRISTIAN MADISON'S OFFICE
34TH FLOOR, MILLENNIUM TOWER
MANHATTAN, NEW YORK

She took a deep breath, then slowly exhaled.

"I don't know everything," she said. "Dr. Ambergris kept a lot of his work to himself."

Madison rolled his eyes.

"You may think I was Ambergris' new golden child, but that's just not true. Sure, I worked with him a lot, but Ambergris kept me at arm's length. He was very secretive. Almost obsessively so."

Madison was silent.

"Why don't you believe me?"

"Okay," he said. "For the sake of argument, let's say I believe you."

Grace sat on the edge of Madison's desk. For a moment she seemed lost in thought.

"I don't suppose it matters anymore," she said finally. "This is what I know. Dr. Ambergris planned to announce his discovery during our presentation at the Biogenetics

Conference. His research clearly shows that certain introns in human DNA follow Zipf's law."

"Zipf's law?"

"Yes. It's a statistical pattern common to all human languages. All languages follow what linguists call Zipf's law."

"I've never heard of Zipf's law," said Madison.

"I hadn't either. It's an odd concept, but it's not that hard to understand. If you take any book, written in any language, you can see Zipf's law at work. Count the number of times each word appears in the book. You might find that the most frequently recurring word is 'the,' followed by the second most recurring word, 'of.' The least common word might be xylophone, which appears only once in our imaginary book."

Grace picked up a yellow notepad and pen from Madison's desk. Flipping to a blank page, she drew a graph with a straight line running from the upper left corner to the lower right corner of the graph.

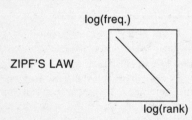

"If you plot this data on a graph, with the frequency of recurrence on one axis and the ranking of the word according to its frequency on the other axis, you get a perfectly straight line."

Grace pushed several strands of fine black hair behind her ear, then continued.

"This straight line will appear for every human language, whether it's English, Chinese, Greek, or Swahili. If you try and perform the same analysis on a bunch of randomly generated characters, you just get a chaotic-looking graph—no order at all. The Zipf's law pattern shows up only for human languages."

"But if that's true . . . if Zipf's law only applies to human languages . . ."

"Yes," said Grace. "The logical conclusion is inescapable. It's the revelation of a lifetime. Of a hundred lifetimes. Think about this for a moment. If genetic sequences in human DNA follow Zipf's law, then the human genome, or at least part of it, hides some form of language."

"That can't be . . ." said Madison.

"I know it seems impossible to believe," said Grace, "but Dr. Ambergris was absolutely convinced that human DNA hides a coded message. An enciphered text. Hidden in the building blocks of the genome."

"What kind of message?"

"An intelligent communication. A message we should be able to decode and read. Dr. Ambergris called it the 'Genesis Code.' He worked countless hours trying to decipher it."

"Did he have any success?"

"He thought he was very close. But he wouldn't even let me help him with the decryption. He worked mostly at night, alone here at the lab, keeping notes on his computer."

Madison grimaced. "Whoever killed Dr. Ambergris also stole his optical drive. His notes are gone."

"Maybe not," said Grace. "He never saved files or data to the mainframe or his hard drive. But I know he was in the habit of hiding his research journal on the Triad security server. To him, that was like hiding a valuable diamond inside the dial of a safe. It was a place no one would think to look."

Madison thought for a moment.

"We have to find that journal," he said.

Madison picked up the phone and dialed Quiz's extension. Quiz answered the phone on the first ring.

"This is Quiz."

"It's Christian. I need a favor. It's important."

Twenty-two

Crowe picked up Giovanni's phone and dialed a three digit extension. "This is Crowe. I—"

The voice on the other end of the line interrupted.

"I don't care who's been complaining," Crowe barked into the receiver. "The lockdown will remain in effect until I tell you otherwise. Are we clear?"

Crowe waited for an affirmation.

"Good. Now, I want you to scan the security logs. The system logs everyone in and everyone out each day. Find out for me who was on the thirty-fourth floor between ten-thirty last night and six A.M. this morning."

Crowe switched the phone to his other hand and leaned on the edge of Giovanni's desk.

"No," he said. "I'll wait for the results."

Giovanni, still seated at the conference table, crossed one leg over the other and plucked a small piece of lint from his trousers.

"Put it on speaker," he instructed.

Crowe punched a button on the base of the telephone and replaced the receiver into its cradle. For almost a minute, only silence emanated from the speakerphone.

Then, a voice.

"Sir, after you left at ten thirty-two P.M., only three people remained on the thirty-fourth floor—Dr. Amber-gris, Dr. D'Amico, and Marilyn Sams."

Crowe addressed the speakerphone.

"Dr. D'Amico works in the animal labs. I am familiar with her. Who is Marilyn Sams?"

"Technician, sir. In our IT department."

"And does Ms. Sams generally keep such unorthodox hours?" asked Crowe.

"One minute, sir."

There was a short, staccato burst of typing.

"I'm showing an IT service ticket for Marilyn Sams for the thirty-fourth floor router," said the voice. "Service log notes report servicing completed at nine fifty-five P.M."

Another burst of typing.

"Sams left the floor at ten-oh-three. Security log shows Dr. D'Amico left the floor at eleven-oh-three. Not unusual for her. D'Amico is a night owl."

Crowe leaned forward. "So Dr. Ambergris was alone on the floor after about eleven P.M. Did anyone arrive on the floor between eleven P.M. and six A.M.?"

"One minute."

More typing.

"Yes," said the voice. "Just one person entered the floor during that time frame. Dr. Grace Nguyen passed through the security door adjacent to the elevator banks at four-eleven A.M."

Twenty-three

PRODUCTION STUDIO
WXNY, CHANNEL 10
QUEENS, NEW YORK

"How's it going?" asked Flavia as she plopped down on the battered sofa in WXNY's production studio. Randy was seated at a computer workstation, digitally cutting and splicing the footage he had filmed at the Millennium Tower. A half-eaten glazed donut lounged on a paper plate in his lap.

"Not bad."

After she had pumped Ebersole for everything useful

that he knew about introns and DNA, Flavia had dismissed the socially awkward science correspondent with the vague promise of joining him for a cocktail at some uncertain date in the future. She gave him a quick kiss on the cheek to keep him on the hook.

You never know when you might need a favor.

Flavia wasn't above granting sexual favors to co-workers to get ahead, but Ebersole was not going to be one of them. The mental image of a naked Ebersole lying on top of her, flailing about, made Flavia shudder with revulsion.

"I think you'll be pleased with the footage," said Randy, bringing her back to the present. "Maximum bang for the buck."

Flavia crossed her legs and leaned back, throwing one arm along the back of the couch. Her short skirt was tight against her tan thighs. She inspected the French manicure on her nails.

"How do I look?"

"Fabulous," he said. "As always."

Randy leaned forward until his face was only three inches from the monitor. He squinted at the slow-motion video, and then made some minor adjustments to the digital images with three clicks of his optical mouse.

"You're going to ruin your eyes if you keep doing that," said Flavia.

Randy turned and made an outlandish face at her.

"And will my face freeze like this if I don't stop making faces?"

Flavia rolled her eyes. Randy turned back to the screen and continued editing the footage.

"When do you want me to do the voice-overs?" asked Flavia.

"Give me another hour. I'll be ready for you then."

Maximum bang for the buck.

Flavia stood up and walked across the room. She stood behind Randy's chair, pressing her breasts against his back, and massaged his shoulders.

"Do a good job for me, Randy," she purred.

Twenty-four

Arakai surveyed Dr. Joshua Ambergris' three-story brownstone, located on a quiet side street in uptown Manhattan. Stately and imposing, the brownstone had been in Ambergris' family for three generations. A tarnished bronze plaque mounted on the dark red brick to the right of the front door read, simply: *Ambergris.*

Seeing no one on the street, Arakai moved closer to the front of the building. Ducking behind a row of manicured shrubs, he peered into a window.

The living room was empty.

Arakai circled around to the back of the brownstone through a small alley. Through a rear window, he could see a female figure in a faded apron moving about the kitchen. She was wiping the kitchen counter with a pink sponge.

Ambergris' housekeeper.

In quick succession, Arakai examined each of the three rear windows on the bottom floor. They were latched, but Arakai could see no evidence of an electronic security system.

Careless, Dr. Ambergris.

Arakai retrieved his knife from its hidden scabbard and slipped the blade between the upper and lower window frames. With a quick flick of his wrist, he disengaged the window's single, ineffectual lock.

Placing the blade between his teeth, Arakai quietly raised the window and hoisted himself inside.

Quiz cradled the phone against his ear with his shoulder. "What do you need?" he asked, taking a slug from his third Diet Coke of the day.

"There's a lot going on right now, Quiz. I'll explain everything later. But right now I need for you to search the Triad security server for a hidden file. Grace and I need to access Dr. Ambergris' research journal. She tells me that he had it hidden by saving the file on the security server under an innocuous-sounding file name. I need you to find it for me."

"Shouldn't be too hard to find," said Quiz. "But why don't you just ask Dr. Ambergris where it's located?"

"I can't do that, Quiz. I'll fill you in on everything soon, but things are happening fast. Can you do this for me?"

"Sure. What do you want me to do when I find the journal?"

"Don't do anything with it. And don't tell anyone what I've asked you to do. I'll get back to you as soon as I can."

"Okay, Christian."

Madison placed the phone back in its cradle. He felt decidedly uneasy.

"Ambergris sent me an e-mail last night. At four-thirty A.M. I didn't think much about it, but now . . ."

Madison clicked open the e-mail and spooled it to the laser printer on his desk.

"What did it say?" asked Grace.

Madison retrieved a single sheet of white paper from his printer tray and handed it to Grace.

"That's just it. No explanations. Just this."

52	61	4	13	20	29	36	45
14	3	62	51	46	35	30	19
53	60	5	12	21	28	37	44
11	6	59	54	43	38	27	22
55	58	7	10	23	26	39	42
9	8	57	56	41	40	25	24
50	63	2	15	18	31	34	47
16	1	64	49	48	33	32	17

Beneath the text was a single cryptic sentence: *This is the beginning of the ancient word.*

"I know what this is," said Grace, running a finger across the rows of digits. "It's called a Magic Square."

"A what?"

"Magic Square. Dr. Ambergris used to talk about these. He called them Chinese number mysteries. They've been around for thousands of years."

Grace thought for a moment. "Christian, I think Ambergris was trying to send you a message."

Crowe marched down a corridor on the thirty-fourth floor, his jaw set in grim determination. As he rushed down the hallway, Crowe spoke into a handheld radio transmitter.

"Override the security lock on the door to office number 2427," he instructed a subordinate in the security control room.

Crowe came to a sudden stop in front of a plain office door. Plastic numbers denoted the office as number 2427. Crowe thought he could hear voices inside.

"Yes, sir. Done."

Crowe heard a small click as the locking mechanism for the door disengaged.

Quietly turning the doorknob, he drew his 9mm from a leather shoulder holster concealed beneath his navy blazer.

Twenty-five

63RD FLOOR, PETRONAS TOWERS
KUALA LUMPUR, MALAYSIA

"Extreme measures?" asked a man in a three-piece suit, echoing Tanaka's pronouncement. "I must object. Any use of extreme measures would draw a great deal of attention and scrutiny. A tremendous amount of risk."

Tanaka appeared to thoughtfully consider the prime minister's remarks.

"But also great opportunity," he finally responded.

Tanaka steepled his fingers and spoke forcefully.

"Gentlemen, scientists in two dozen countries are relentlessly pursuing genomic research. Granted, many have been coopted by the Order, or have been sufficiently manipulated to direct the focus of their scientific inquiries away from areas of concern. But how many years will it be before some brilliant young geneticist stumbles upon the same discovery as the dearly departed Dr. Ambergris?"

Tanaka placed his palms on his knees and leaned forward.

"Our scientists are making progress in unlocking the secrets of the Genesis Code, but we must have more time."

Tanaka's eyes narrowed.

"Gentlemen, the potential rewards are too great. And the potential risks of inaction are too severe. Who among you would stand idly by while the secrets of God Himself are within our reach? We can only speculate about what rest of the Genesis Code will reveal to us. The ability to dramatically extend the human life-span. The possibility of eliminating all disease. Genetic manipulation taken to its highest and best uses."

Tanaka slowly shook his head.

"No. We cannot fail to act. We stand at the precipice. We are approaching a paradigm shift that will change the very nature of human existence. It would be foolish . . . unconscionable . . . no, *immoral,* to allow a sin of omission to destroy what we, and those before us, have labored to protect."

Murmurs of assent rippled through the assembled members of the Council.

"Here is what I propose," said Tanaka.

Crowe took a deep breath, raised his 9mm, and threw open the office door.

Grace's office was empty.

Goddammit.

Crowe holstered his weapon and yelled into his hand-held radio.

"Listen up. I want you to run the face recognition proto-col on all feeds from every security camera in the building for the past hour. All floors. Your target is Dr. Grace Nguyen. I need to know which camera spotted her last, and how long ago."

"That will take a while," said the voice crackling over the radio.

"You have three minutes. Call me back when you're fin-ished. Do not be late."

Crowe surveyed the interior of Grace's office. Her purse was sitting on the credenza. A picture of an elderly Asian couple sat in a metal frame on her desk.

Parents? Grandparents?

Grace's computer was on, but she had not yet logged in to the network. Triad Genomics' logo, two intertwined strands of DNA forming a double helix, rotated on the screen.

Grace's desk was covered with piles of photocopied ar-ticles and handwritten notes. One small colorful slip of paper caught his eye. It was a color copy of a Mayan ren-dering of two intertwined serpents.

A burst of static spewed from Crowe's radio transmitter, startling him.

"I've got her," said the disembodied voice. "The last camera to spot Dr. Grace Nguyen was on the thirty-fourth floor, in Corridor H. She was heading south."

Corridor H. Dr. Madison's office is on Corridor H.

Crowe keyed the transmit button on the radio. "Lock down all of the doors on the thirty-fourth floor. Security access level alpha only. Exits, offices, conference rooms, stairwells . . . everything."

"Yes, sir."

Crowe rubbed a hand across his bald head, thinking.

"And dispatch two security teams to the thirty-fourth floor. Where is Mr. Occam?"

There was a pause as the security officer consulted his computer.

"In the atrium."

"Tell Mr. Occam to join me in Dr. Madison's office. Immediately."

Twenty-six

QUIZ'S OFFICE
SUBBASEMENT, MILLENNIUM TOWER
MANHATTAN, NEW YORK

The maintenance levels of the Millennium Tower possessed none of the restrained elegance on display in the public areas of the Triad Genomics headquarters.

That suited Quiz just fine.

His office overlooked the server farm in the subbasement of the Millennium Tower. Through a large window, Quiz could see the long rows of slender computer servers and squat genetic sequencers that made the work of Traid Genomics' geneticists possible. Quiz's job was to ensure that it all functioned. And that it all functioned correctly.

Quiz was a genius with computers, and the management at Triad Genomics gave him wide latitude and significant autonomy, provided that everything ran smoothly.

It usually did.

Finding Ambergris' hidden journal will be a piece of cake.

One of the first lessons Quiz had learned in the profesional world was to never promise too much. It was a lesson he taught to his favorite techs on the IT staff.

"Figure out how long it will take you to complete a task," he advised, "and then tell them it will take twenty-five percent longer than your estimate. If you get it done in the time you estimated, you're a hero. And if you run into problems and it takes you longer, then you've covered your arse."

Ghostly blue light from five flat-screen monitors provided the only illumination in the otherwise darkened office. The plasma screens were arrayed on a metal frame, mounted at various heights in a 180-degree arc around a seated figure.

"Barkley, hold my calls," he announced to a small chihuahua sleeping on a dog bed under the desk. Barkley cocked his head and snorted.

"He may only weigh four pounds," Quiz would say to anyone who would listen, "but he thinks he's a big dog."

He cracked open a fresh Diet Coke.

"And we're off," said Quiz, as he began writing a short program to ferret out Ambergris' hidden data.

Four custom-built CPUs were vertically tiered in a metal rack against the wall. Cooling fans droned in the background. A riot of wires and cables snaked across the U-shaped computer workstation and spilled onto the floor. Scanners, digital cameras, stylus pads, and an assortment of digital accessories covered the surface of the workstation. At the other end of the room was a battered leather sofa adorned with a beat-up pillow and dingy blue comforter. Quiz often spent several days at a time in his office, taking catnaps when needed and showering in the gym at the hotel.

Quiz didn't sleep much. He wasn't very good at it. Instead, he often stayed up most of the night, prowling the Triad Genomics network, writing code, or challenging online players in the latest computer games.

An antique trunk served as a coffee table, piled high with copies of technical journals and computer magazines. Several empty pizza boxes were stacked by the door. A blue recycling bin next to the computer workstation was filled with empty Diet Coke cans. An *X-Files* poster hung on one wall. Across the bottom, it read: *I Want to Believe.*

In ten minutes, Quiz compiled the sixty lines of code

needed to search the security server and identify the hidden files. A pretty nifty little algorithm, actually, thought Quiz, patting himself on the back.

He executed the command to start the program. Lines of text began scrolling down the screen as the algorithm evaluated possible targets. The computer chirped each time it found a possible hit.

Soon it began chirping every ten or fifteen seconds.

"Houston, we have a problem," said Quiz.

The small chihuahua barked in agreement.

Twenty-seven

DR. CHRISTIAN MADISON'S OFFICE
34TH FLOOR, MILLENNIUM TOWER
MANHATTAN, NEW YORK

"You think this grid of numbers is a message from Dr. Ambergris?" asked Madison. "Why wouldn't he just write it out?"

"He must have been afraid that someone else might try to read it," said Grace. "So he sent it in code."

Madison was skeptical. "A code that only you would recognize?"

Grace examined the printout. "Look, Dr. Ambergris must have anticipated that if something happened to him, I would come to you. The only way this message could be read would be if you and I tried to figure it out together—an additional safeguard to keep his message hidden from others."

"That doesn't make any sense," said Madison. "Only Triad Genomics personnel would have access to the e-mail server or my computer."

Grace chewed on her lower lip. "It makes sense if he was concerned about a traitor inside the company. Someone who works for Triad Genomics."

Grace directed Madison's attention to the eight-by-eight grid of digits, crisply printed in black ink on white paper.

"Let me show you how this works," said Grace. "Add up the numbers across the top row."

Madison took a moment to make the mental calculation.

"They total two hundred sixty."

"Right. Now pick any other row or column and add the digits."

Madison placed a finger on the third row and mentally tabulated the sum.

52	61	4	13	20	29	36	45
14	3	62	51	46	35	30	19
53	60	5	12	21	28	37	44
11	6	59	54	43	38	27	22
55	58	7	10	23	26	39	42
9	8	57	56	41	40	25	24
50	63	2	15	18	31	34	47
16	1	64	49	48	33	32	17

"Two hundred sixty," he said. In quick succession, he added the digits in each of the columns.

"They all add up to two hundred sixty," said Madison.

"That's a Magic Square. The numbers are arranged so that every row and column adds up to the same number," said Grace.

"What's the significance of two-sixty?"

She pointed to a small statue resting on Madison's credenza. The stone figure brandished a feathered staff adorned with two intertwined serpents coiled along its length.

"A gift from Dr. Ambergris?" she asked.

"Yes. It's Mayan—a representation of Chac, the Sky Serpent and Rain God."

"Ambergris' father was a tenured professor at Yale, a respected archaeologist and historian."

"I know this," said Madison.

"But did you know that the ancient Maya were one of his father's passions? He spent a lifetime studying the Maya. And he shared this passion with his son. I know that Dr. Ambergris sometimes went with his father on archaeological digs in the Yucatán Peninsula when he was a boy. He even considered a career in archeology, following in his father's footsteps, before he discovered his passion for science and genetics. But clearly, Dr. Ambergris' interest in the Maya and other ancient cultures survived as more than just a curious son's peek into his father's world."

"Why do you say that?" asked Madison.

"Dr. Ambergris was an only child. When his father died, he was the sole recipient of his father's inheritance, including his brownstone uptown, the Ambergris family trust, and his father's extensive library—a collection of books and manuscripts he spent a lifetime assembling."

"But—"

"Give me a second," said Grace, raising a finger. "After his father died, Dr. Ambergris renewed his interest in his father's work. Maybe it was his way of staying connected to his father, even in death. Who knows? But the point is that Dr. Ambergris began studying his father's research. He spent hours, days, weeks studying his father's notes and the books in his library."

Madison drummed his fingers impatiently.

"Sometimes he talked about it. That's how I recognized the significance of these numbers," she said, pointing to the eight-by-eight grid. "The root number of this Magic Square, two hundred sixty, is the number of days in one year of the Mayan calendar."

Madison was exasperated. "But what does any of this have to do with his genetics research?"

Grace shook her head. "I have no idea."

"And this line of text. This is the beginning of the ancient word?"

Grace shrugged. "Again, no idea."

Madison studied the cryptic Magic Square.

"Grace, this grid has sixty-four digits," he said, in a flash of inspiration.

Grace's eyes grew wide.

"DNA has sixty-four codons. That can't be a coincidence."

Twenty-eight

DR. JOSHUA AMBERGRIS' RESIDENCE
UPTOWN MANHATTAN, NEW YORK

Arakai quietly slipped through the window and lowered himself to the floor in the dining room, listening intently for any sign that Ambergris' housekeeper had detected his illicit entry. From the direction of the kitchen, Arakai could hear the housekeeper humming a game-show tune as she cleaned.

The interior of the brownstone was dark and uninviting, but well kept. Brick walls, heavy curtains, and wood floors seemed to absorb most of the ambient light, creating a dreary effect. Arakai gingerly closed the open window and crouched behind Ambergris' dining room table. He removed the knife from between his teeth and wiped the flat of the silver blade once across his black trousers.

A grandfather clock in the living room chimed the quarter hour. The sound brought a flash of childhood memories to Arakai's mind. Many nights, Arakai had listened to an antique clock chime away the dark hours as he lay awake in his bed, alone, waiting for his mother to return home from work, stinking of gin and cigarettes. He had never known his father. The clock had belonged to Arakai's grandparents, a family heirloom passed to Arakai's mother after their death in 1945.

Arakai's grandparents had lived in Japan, on the outskirts

of Nagasaki, for decades. On the day that America unleashed hell on the city of Nagasaki, Arakai's grandparents had been entertaining neighbors for dinner at their home. Spared the horrific death that consumed tens of thousands in the epicenter of the thermonuclear blast, Arakai's grandparents instead lingered in agony for weeks, suffering from terrible radiation sickness, before finally crossing the void in a makeshift hospital hastily erected by the defeated Imperial Army on the outskirts of the ruins of Nagasaki.

There was a faint sound from Dr. Ambergris' kitchen. Arakai forced his thoughts to return to the present. He slowed his breathing, relaxed his grip on the handle of his knife, and crept across the dining room toward the kitchen.

Twenty=nine

DR. CHRISTIAN MADISON'S OFFICE
34TH FLOOR, MILLENNIUM TOWER
MANHATTAN, NEW YORK

The phone on Madison's desk chirped. A blinking red light indicated an incoming call.

"How are you getting a call? What about the security lockdown?"

"I don't know," said Madison.

The phone chirped again. Reluctantly, he answered it, placing the telephone receiver against his ear.

"This is Dr. Madison."

"I want you to listen very carefully." The voice on the phone was slightly garbled and had a flat, synthetic sound. *Digitally disguised,* thought Madison. "Who is this?"

"You are in danger. Your life and the lives of thousands of others are in jeopardy."

Grace pointed to the speakerphone button. Nodding,

Madison pushed it and gently set the handset back into its cradle.

"Tell me who this is," said Madison, "or I'm hanging up the phone."

"Dr. Madison, by now you must be aware of the murder of Dr. Joshua Ambergris."

"Yes."

"The same individuals who plotted Dr. Ambergris' murder have set in motion a plan to detonate a bomb in the Millennium Tower on the first day of the Biogenetics Conference."

Grace's jaw dropped.

"What? Are you insane?" said Madison.

"Dr. Madison, I assure you that I am perfectly sane. I have risked my life to convey this warning to you. I will not call again. The detonation will occur at nine-thirty A.M. on the first day of the conference."

Madison's face went white.

"Who is doing this? Who killed Dr. Ambergris?" he asked.

Grace screamed as the door to Madison's office swung open and slammed into the wall, punching a hole in the plasterboard with a loud bang.

Crowe's immense form filled the doorway.

"Good luck," said the voice. Then the line went dead.

Thirty

QUIZ'S OFFICE
SUBBASEMENT, MILLENNIUM TOWER
MANHATTAN, NEW YORK

Quiz finished off his Diet Coke and leaned back in a black leather executive chair. On a flat-panel display to his left, a music video featured waiflike blondes with thick blue eye shadow and Lycra bodysuits undulating to the rhythms of trance music in a postindustrial urban wasteland. Hi-fi speakers hidden around the room pulsed with futuristic electronica.

Quiz had located the error in his programming and quickly corrected the flaw in the code.

"No need to tell anyone about that one, eh, Barkley?" he said to the diminutive canine. Barkley opened one eye, then closed it again.

Another flat-panel display silently played a pirated copy of *Raiders of the Lost Ark*. On the screen, Harrison Ford used his coiled whip to brush a herd of tarantulas from the back of his unsuspecting companion. Torchlight cast flickering shadows against the walls of a cavern passageway enshrouded with spider webs.

On a third screen, a three-dimensional chessboard slowly rotated against a black background. The chess pieces were fashioned from the characters of *Alice in Wonderland*. Quiz glanced up to see a black bishop float across the board and descend on a square next to his queen.

"The French suck at chess," he muttered. With two keystrokes, his queen swept in to capture his opponent's only remaining rook. "That's five moves to checkmate."

A fourth screen displayed an ongoing conversation in an Internet chat room with RIGHTSEDFRED and SCULLY2000.

RIGHTSEDFRED: No way the Egyptians built the Sphinx.
SCULLY2000: LOL. Dude, it was built during the Fourth Dynasty.
RIGHTSEDFRED: No. The Sphinx is much older than that. Prof. Schoch of BU has shown that the erosion of the Sphinx was caused by thousands of years of rainfall, ages before the Old Kingdom ever existed.
SCULLY2000: ROTFL. Most Egyptologists think Schoch is wrong. But just for the sake of argument, who do you think built the Sphinx?

Shaking his head to clear the cobwebs from his brain, Quiz turned his attention back to the errant program he had just fixed.

"Forgot to take my Ritalin this morning, Barkley," he said.

That's what two nights of no sleep will do to you, he thought. *Things get a little blurry around the edges.*

The edited program quickly located four suspicious files. Quiz examined each one in turn.

You've been busy, Dr. Ambergris, he thought.

He began reading.

An alarm sounded on Quiz's computer. Punching at the keys on his keyboard, he opened a secure socket to the Triad Genomics security server. He reviewed the latest entries on the security logs.

```
00.854745
<< Run face recognition protocol C; all feeds. >>
<< Target: employee file #0028473. >>
<< Match found: 98% confidence level. >>
<< Camera location: Cam 24-H3 >>
00.954326
<< Security restriction—access level D only >>
<< Sectors 2400-2479. >>
<< Authorization OC. >>
```

That's a restriction on the entire floor. Authorized by OC. Omar Crowe. What's going on?

Shaking his head in dismay, Quiz keyed off the alarm and refocused his attention on the computer screen displaying Dr. Ambergris' research journal. After the fourth paragraph, his mind was spinning.

Thirty-one

DR. CHRISTIAN MADISON'S OFFICE
34TH FLOOR, MILLENNIUM TOWER
MANHATTAN, NEW YORK

"Crowe, what the hell do you think you're doing?" yelled Madison.

"Dr. Nguyen," Crowe said. "Would you care to tell me why you were in the building last night between four-eleven and four forty-six A.M.?"

"What? I was nowhere near the office last night," said Grace. "I was home sleeping, like normal people."

Crowe's eyes narrowed as he spoke. "The security logs place you on the thirty-fourth floor at four-eleven A.M. You were the only one on the floor around the time Dr. Ambergris was murdered."

"Bullshit," yelled Grace. "Did you review the tape from the security cameras?"

Crowe shook his head and smirked. "As I'm sure you already know, that data has conveniently been erased from the server. For all of the cameras on that floor, from four A.M. to five A.M. Quite convenient, wouldn't you say?"

Madison tried to interject. "Crowe, wait a minute—"

"Stay out of it, Dr. Madison," Crowe snapped.

"You know me," said Grace. "I had nothing to do with this."

"No," said Crowe. "It's quite apparent that I don't know you at all."

"Crowe," said Madison, raising his voice in anger. "Just stop for a minute. Listen to me! I just got a telephone call warning me that the same people who killed Dr. Ambergris are planning to detonate a bomb in the Millennium Tower on the first day of the Biogenetics Conference. Grace has nothing to do with this!"

"I warned you to stay out of it, Madison," yelled Crowe. "And I'd like to know why Grace is here in your office. What's your interest in defending her? Perhaps you're involved in this as well?"

Grace started to back away from Crowe.

"You aren't going anywhere," he said, grabbing her roughly by the arm.

Grace cried out in pain and twisted her body away from Crowe, trying to free her arm from his painful grip.

"I said stop!" yelled Crowe, pulling hard on Grace's arm. She stumbled and fell, banging her head against the wall.

Madison, outmatched by at least eighty pounds, grabbed Crowe's wrist and tried to release Grace from his grasp. Crowe backhanded him across the face with a loud smack, sending Madison crashing to the floor.

Grace twisted her upper body, bringing her teeth within range of Crowe's arm. She bit down hard on the meaty muscle of his inner forearm.

"Goddamn you," roared Crowe, turning toward Grace and grabbing a fistful of her hair.

Rising to his feet, Madison took advantage of Grace's momentary distraction and launched himself at Crowe's back.

He wrapped one arm around Crowe's neck, pulling hard on it with the other, trying to fasten a chokehold around his throat.

"Let her go," he yelled, jamming his knees into Crowe's kidneys.

Crowe brought both hands to his neck and fastened his fingers around Madison's arm with a viselike grip. Struggling for breath, he began to spin around the room, smashing Madison's body into the walls and furniture in a desperate attempt to dislodge him.

Grace, suddenly free, grabbed a brass reading lamp from Madison's desk. Crowe spun around, slamming Madison's legs into the desk.

Grace raised the heavy lamp above her head and jumped at Crowe, smashing the lamp down on the back of his head.

Crowe dropped like a rag doll. Madison fell to the ground beside him.

"Christian!" yelled Grace. "Are you okay?"

Madison, his chest heaving with exertion, pulled himself up onto his knees. He took a quick inventory of his pains and injuries.

"I don't think I broke anything," he said, pressing on his ribs.

Madison crawled over and checked the back of Crowe's head for a skull fracture. He felt a knot the size of a golf ball. His hand came away red with Crowe's blood.

Thirty-two

QUIZ'S OFFICE
SUBBASEMENT, MILLENNIUM TOWER
MANHATTAN, NEW YORK

Quiz scrolled through page after page of Dr. Ambergris' research journal. The lines of text were periodically punctuated with long sequences of genetic code. Occasionally, the daily journal entries would skip forward several days, as if Ambergris had recorded nothing for days at a time.

Or maybe those particular entries have been erased.

Quiz scrolled back to the first entry and started reading.

7 March—

Christian, I write these words not only for myself, but for you as well. Hopefully, you will never have to bear the burden of learning the truth contained within these pages. If you are reading this journal, then I have failed, and reluctantly pass on to you the secrets I have learned.

I have made many mistakes in my life. And as I reflect on my numerous failings, there is one mistake in particular for which I have never been able to bring myself to

ask for your forgiveness. After the death of your son,
I was unable to help you bear the burden of your grief.
The scars of my own failed relationship with my father
were still too raw after his passing. The sorrow I saw in
your eyes only served to deepen my own. As you looked
upon a bleak future filled with endless days you would
never share with your son, I saw the reflection of my own
past, filled with months and years of words unspoken and
opportunities forever lost.

I deeply regret that I waited until after my father's
death to take a proper interest in his passions. I know
now that his scholarly pursuits into the mysteries of humanity's ancient cultures created in him the same feelings that I experienced as a young man discovering the
wonders of science and genetics.

I had no faith in my father's gods, nor he in mine. For
him, the answers to life's most important questions lay
firmly entombed in the past. As for me, I looked only toward the future.

How often he tried to interest me in his newest discoveries.

How often I politely listened, with neither desire nor
intent to understand, as he tried to share with me those
insights and discoveries that constituted the most important moments of his life, those moments in which he felt
truly alive, for which he felt true purpose.

My father was a brilliant man. And in realizing my
failings as a son, I became compelled to know the inner
workings of his mind. Ironically, in my study of his
notes and the volumes, I have found a subject of common interest.

Throughout human history there have been many
myths of a great primordial language. A language that
was more than just grammar or syntax. A primordial
language that described the essential structure of life.
The Ursprache, as it has been called, was believed to be
the language that God used to breathe life into His cre-
ations.

Like my father, I have come to believe that the Ursprache is not myth at all. Rather, the mythology surrounding the Ursprache was a primitive effort by men to describe a concept that was beyond the limits of human understanding in the age in which they lived.

Fragments of truth wrapped in layers of legend.

What does the Ursprache represent? What language does the term define? To modern science, DNA is the essential language of life, the great primordial language spoken by all living things. DNA, the written instructions inscribed in the human genome, contains a written prophecy that comes to pass with each day that we draw breath.

Scattered throughout the ancient writings of human civilization are many cryptic references overlooked by modern science. References to scientific concepts far beyond the comprehension of their authors. References repeated without understanding from their original sources now lost in the mists of antiquity.

Quiz rubbed his eyes and drank deeply from his Diet Coke. A blinking icon on his computer screen indicated that the security lockdown was still in effect.

What the hell is going on?

"Is he dead?" asked Grace.

"No, he's still breathing," said Madison, wiping the blood from his hand on Crowe's jacket.

"Let's get the hell out of here," said Grace.

Madison checked Crowe's pulse. It beat a slow, steady rhythm beneath his fingertips. Madison reached down and grabbed the security badge hanging on a cord around Crowe's neck. With a quick jerk, he ripped it free.

"This will get us out," he said.

Madison folded the printout of the Magic Square and slipped it into his pocket.

"Let's go."

The halls were empty as Grace and Madison made their

way toward the elevators in the reception area. Madison's jaw throbbed with pain. He tasted blood in his mouth.

"Slow down," hissed Madison. "Walk quickly, but not too quickly."

Madison flashed a smile at Zoovas, seated behind the security desk.

"Back in a minute," said Madison. "Want an espresso?"

"Dr. Madison, we're locked down," said Zoovas. "I can't let you leave the floor."

Across the room, a set of elevator doors opened. Occam was inside. When he saw Madison and Grace, Occam drew his weapon.

Thirty-three

SECURITY STATION
34TH FLOOR LOBBY, MILLENNIUM TOWER
MANHATTAN, NEW YORK

"Run!" yelled Madison.

They darted toward a nearby stairwell. Occam and Zoovas ran after them.

"Come on," yelled Madison, dragging Grace through the door and down the first flight of stairs. They reached the next landing as Occam and Zoovas entered the stairwell above them.

"Not this floor," said Grace, panting. "The next one."

Madison took three steps at a time down the stairs to the next floor. Grace was right beside him.

"This one," she said, pushing through the door onto the thirty-second floor.

A barrage of screeching and howling assaulted their ears.

"The primate labs," she said.

The stench of urine and feces was overwhelming. A

deafening cacophony of screams and howls from the unhappy residents of stacks of metal cages filled the air. Monkeys and apes shook the doors of their small prisons and drummed their fists against the metal walls of their cages.

"This way," said Grace. "Stay away from the cages."

Small hands reached out through wire mesh, grasping at their clothing. A Colobus monkey shrieked and threw a half-eaten piece of fruit at Madison. It bounced off his shoulder and slid across the floor.

A lab technician in blue scrubs appeared at the other end of the room.

"What the hell is going on?" he demanded.

Madison charged forward, running straight at the lab tech.

"Wait!" yelled the confused tech, throwing up his hands.

Madison slammed into the man, knocking him back against a row of cages with a loud metallic bang. Small hands and fingers erupted from the wire cage doors, grasping and pawing at the tech's face and neck, cutting his skin with tiny nails.

"Christian—" said Grace.

"Go," he yelled, pointing toward an open door.

The tech screamed in pain, twisting his body away from the hostile spider monkeys. Trails of blood streamed down his face. His left foot slid on a piece of partially masticated banana and he fell in a heap on the wet floor.

Zoovas and Occam burst into the primate lab from the stairwell.

"Dr. Madison, stop!" yelled Occam.

Madison grabbed the lab tech by the leg and dragged him out of reach of the furious spider monkeys.

"Let's go," yelled Grace.

Madison dropped the tech's foot and ran toward the sound of her voice. Behind him, three small monkeys burst from their cage, the latch broken from the impact when the lab tech's body crashed into the metal door.

Zoovas froze in his tracks.

"Are those things dangerous?"

Occam sneered.

"Afraid of three little monkeys?"

"Not the monkeys," Zoovas said. "I'm afraid of what might be inside 'em."

Occam's face went white.

"Shit."

He began shouting into his radio.

They turned and ran back to the stairwell, slamming the door closed behind them. Moments later, a shrill siren began to wail.

Madison and Grace darted down a narrow hallway connecting the various Triad Genomics animal labs. The bleating sound of the alarm echoed in the corridor.

"We need to find another stairwell," said Grace.

Behind them, a shout rang out.

"Stop where you are!"

Three security guards charged around a corner twenty yards behind them, weapons drawn.

Thirty-four

TRIAD GENOMICS
32ND FLOOR, MILLENNIUM TOWER
MANHATTAN, NEW YORK

"Quick . . . this way," yelled Madison, running down a corridor that intersected with the hallway.

Grace ran after him, trying to put distance between them and the pursuing security officers. Ahead, Madison spotted a doorway marked *NE Stairwell*. He made a beeline for the door and pulled it open.

"Down!" yelled Madison when Grace hesitated.

Madison's breath came in ragged gasps as they ran down flight after flight of stairs. They could hear the pounding of footfalls above as the guards entered the stairwell and charged down after them.

"Stop!" yelled Grace, coming to a sudden halt on the landing on the eighteenth floor. Madison came to an abrupt stop behind her, grabbing the railing for support and struggling to catch his breath.

"Look," she said, peering over the railing and down the stairwell.

Three floors below, a pair of Triad security officers had taken positions on either side of the fifteenth-floor landing, weapons drawn and trained on the steps above them.

Madison grabbed Grace by the hand.

"Come on. This way. This level is hotel guest rooms."

They ran through the door at the landing and entered the hotel. The hallway was wide, with thick carpeting and rich wallpaper. Wall sconces illuminated the hall with indirect light. Lush green plants in Mediterranean clay pots filled alcoves between the numbered doors of the hotel rooms.

Thirty feet down the hallway, a housekeeping cart piled high with towels and linens was parked outside an open doorway.

"I have an idea," said Madison. He led Grace down the hallway. Madison grabbed the handle of the cart and pushed it ahead of them into the open door.

Inside, a Hispanic maid in a pale blue uniform was startled by the sudden intrusion. "*Dios mío!*"

Grace closed and locked the door behind them. Before the maid could protest, Madison grabbed her by the shoulders and spun her around, wrapping a hand around her mouth to silence her. Outside, the stairwell door banged against the wall as the Triad Genomics security guards entered the hallway.

Thirty-five

Rosa Ortiz struggled against the young man, but his grip was too strong. The plastic clip holding her long black hair snapped and fell to the floor, releasing a tumult of curls across her face and shoulders.

The man's voice was warm in her ear.

"We aren't going to hurt you. There are some men chasing us. Men who want to hurt us. Just be quiet and nothing bad will happen. This will all be over in a minute."

Rosa could hear the sounds of men running in the hallway outside. She looked at the woman leaning against the door of the hotel room. She looked genuinely frightened. Rosa could feel the heaving of the young man's chest.

She allowed her body to relax and slowly nodded her head. The grip around her loosened a bit, but still held her fast.

"Here they come," whispered the woman at the door.

A loud voice sounded in the security guard's earpiece. He recognized it instantly.

"Where are you?" demanded Crowe.

The guard raised his right hand to his face and spoke into the mike strapped to his wrist.

"Eighteenth floor. Hotel corridor. Madison and Nguyen just ran onto this floor from the stairwell."

A burst of expletives boomed from the guard's earpiece. Then a moment of silence.

"Report immediately to the atrium level. I want officers posted at every exit."

"But sir, they're on this floor. We were right behind them."

Another voice broke into the transmission.

"This is Dante Giovanni. You will break off your pursuit and report immediately to the atrium. There are hotel guests on that floor. The last thing I need is for a guest of the hotel to become alarmed and phone the police."

The guard shrugged his shoulders.

"Yes, sir. We'll be right there."

After the security officers had left the floor, Madison released his grip on the scared maid. She took a step back away from him in fear.

Madison held up his hands.

"It's okay. They've gone. We're not going to hurt you."

He reached into a pocket and removed his wallet, fishing out a hundred-dollar bill from the billfold.

"Can you help us get to the subbasement?" he asked.

"Why the basement?" asked Grace.

"We need help. Quiz's office is on the subbasement," said Madison. He turned back to the maid.

"Is there a maintenance elevator you use to take linens and things to the basement?"

"Sí," said the woman, taking the crisp bill from Madison's fingers.

"The laundry service pick up the linen from the alley behind the storeroom. I take you there."

Thirty-six

QUIZ'S OFFICE
SUBBASEMENT, MILLENNIUM TOWER
MANHATTAN, NEW YORK

Madison and Grace descended to the subbasement in the service elevator. Madison's shoulder ached and his jaw throbbed with pain.

"Let's just go," said Grace.

"Not yet. I want to see what Quiz has found."

"Are you going to tell him about Crowe?"

"No. I don't want to involve Quiz any more than we have to."

Quiz was hunched over his keyboard, stuffing a Twinkie into his mouth whole, when Grace and Madison reached his office.

Madison wiped the sweat from his forehead and slowed his breathing. He ignored the throbbing pain in his shoulder.

"Hey, Quiz."

"Mphgrph," said Quiz, choking down the Twinkie. He washed it down with a swallow of Diet Coke.

"What are you guys doing here?" he asked finally.

"We wanted to check in and see what you've found," said Madison. "Did you locate Ambergris' journal?"

"You betcher ass," said Quiz. "And Christian, the first entry is addressed to you."

"What do you mean?"

"Here, see for yourself." Quiz turned the flat-panel monitor so that Grace and Madison could read the text on the screen. He scrolled back to the first entry in the journal. Grace and Madison quickly read through the lines of text.

"Jesus," said Madison. He turned to Grace. "Did you have any idea?"

"No, Christian. He was so withdrawn. We never talked about personal things."

"Go to the next one," said Madison. Quiz scrolled down the page. Together, they continued reading.

8 March—

I have spent many hours exploring the thousands of volumes in my father's library—tomes, texts, and treatises he collected during his travels around the world. The breadth of his knowledge and the range of his interests were truly impressive. His collection is most remarkable. I have found manuscripts and scrolls from ancient Egypt, Mesoamerica, the Fertile Crescent, and the Far East.

One of his prized acquisitions was the original manuscript of a rare kabbalistic text, the *Sefer Yetzirah*. It is the oldest book in the Hebrew occult tradition, also known as the *Book of Creation*. Its fragile pages rest in a leather folio in my father's study, alongside an English translation written in his handwriting.

The *Sefer Yetzirah* describes how Yahweh created the universe and all living things within it using the twenty-two letters of the Hebrew alphabet. It explains that God "molded the letters as bits of clay into parallel and complementary strings."

Parallel and complementary strings.

Like the intertwined strands of DNA in the double helix.

The *Sefer Yetzirah* tells us that God created all living things using the twenty-two letters of the Hebrew alphabet by molding the letters as bits of clay into parallel and complementary strings. The sixty-four unique codons of our genetic alphabet are always found in groups that code for twenty-two specific genetic letters.

Shall we accept this as mere coincidence? I cannot.

The codons of DNA are made up of three genetic letters. The Hebrew language is based on root words from which nouns, verbs, adjectives, and all other grammatical variations derive. For reasons no one has been able to explain, these Hebrew root words are made up of three letters.

Like the three genetic letters in each codon within our DNA.

My father recorded in his notes that Eliphas Levi, the famous French occultist, wrote that "the *Sefer Yetzirah* is a ladder formed of truths." I cannot help but observe that the double helix of our DNA is often described as having the appearance of a twisting ladder.

Were Hebrew mystics and scholars unknowingly passing along an ancient knowledge which they could not understand?

Who taught them this knowledge?

My father once said that books are the treasured wealth of the world and the fit inheritance of generations and nations. What other secrets, hidden by ancient scholars in the writings of humanity's oldest civilizations, are waiting to be discovered, concealed in dusty volumes, slumbering, untouched, unread?

Thirty-seven

DR. JOSHUA AMBERGRIS' RESIDENCE
UPTOWN MANHATTAN, NEW YORK

Shafts of sunlight thrust through the windows of the dining room, leaving distorted squares of light on the wood floor as Arakai crept across the dining room to the kitchen. Ambergris' housekeeper was blissfully ignorant of Arakai's presence. Her back was turned as she merrily scrubbed the kitchen sink with a sponge, softly whistling the theme music from *Jeopardy*. The scent of lemons filled the air.

Arakai crept up behind the middle-aged woman, moving silently, until he was close enough to see the individual gray hairs on the back of her head. He now brandished a Taser, having placed the knife back in its hidden scabbard.

The impact of the Taser bolt against the housekeeper's back came just a fraction of a second before the first surge of electricity traveled down the thin wires connecting the bolt to the Taser. She cried out in surprise and her back arched involuntarily.

The pink sponge fell from her numb fingers and bounced once on the kitchen floor.

"You simply must stop that whistling," said Arakai.

The air crackled and popped with ozone as Arakai held down the trigger on the Taser. Arakai calmly began counting.

"One, two, three . . ."

When he reached five, Arakai released the trigger, terminating the flow of electricity, and took a step to one side.

The woman's stiff body swayed forward, then back, before crashing to the tile floor, collapsing in a heap of rubbery limbs as her muscles unlocked. The fingers on her left hand twitched twice, and then were still.

Arakai stepped over the pile of housekeeper on the floor and turned off the warm water running in the kitchen sink. He inhaled deeply, fond of the fresh scent of lemons.

Now that we've finished that untidy bit of business, Dr. Ambergris, let's see where you keep your private things.

Thirty-eight

QUIZ'S OFFICE
SUBBASEMENT, MILLENNIUM TOWER
MANHATTAN, NEW YORK

Quiz cracked the knuckles on his left hand. He rubbed the fatigue from his eyes and popped open another Diet Coke.

"Can I have one of those?" asked Grace.

Reluctantly, Quiz plucked another can from the mini-fridge beneath his desk and handed it to Grace.

"Keep going," said Madison, gesturing at the computer screen. The next entry in Dr. Ambergris' journal was dated March 10.

10 March—

As I continue my journey through the mind of my father, reflected and preserved in the treasured volumes of his private library, I am struck now by the vivid recollection of words he often spoke to me when I was a boy, words of simple yet enduring wisdom that, perhaps as a consequence of my limited perspective, failed to make a proper impact on the world of my youth.

My father often said: "A written word is the choicest of relics, something at once more intimate with us and more universal than any work of art. It is the work of art nearest to life itself. It may be translated into every language, and not only be read but actually breathed from all human lips; not be represented on canvas or in marble only, but be carved out of the breath of life itself."

I find these words of my father to be of particular importance as I contemplate the writings of the *Book of Enoch*, an ancient, fragile copy of which was preserved in a thin folio in the heart of my father's library.

The *Book of Enoch* is a ancient Hebrew religious text, banned from inclusion in the Christian Bible by those early leaders of the Christian church who took control of Christianity's doctrinal reins at the Council of Nicea. Why, you may wonder, was it banned? Enoch is a biblical figure, mentioned more than once in the Book of Genesis, one of two men taken up bodily into the presence of God, ascending into Heaven without dying. Because Enoch was enraptured, or translated bodily, into Heaven, he became the center of an apocalyptic tradition among Hebrew cabalists and early Christians.

As I have written before, I believe that there are, hidden in the ancient writings and myths of man, many cryptic references to scientific concepts far beyond the understanding of their authors, references repeated without comprehension, preserved from their original source now lost in the mists of antiquity. The *Book of Enoch* contains such references.

According to the *Book of Enoch,* the Archangel Gabriel imparted to Enoch knowledge of the secrets of creation and the cycles of events on the earth. Enoch was instructed by God to inscribe this knowledge and give the inscriptions, written in the handwriting of God, to his children so that they would be handed down from generation to generation.

I can only conclude that the "handwriting of God, inscribed for Enoch's children to be handed down from generation to generation" is a cryptic reference to the inscription of a message in the human genome, to be passed down through successive generations.

The *Book of Enoch* also describes a "chart" that God put on earth and ordered that "it be preserved, and that the handwriting of thy fathers be preserved, and that it not perish in the Deluge which I shall bring upon thy race."

If I accept that the term "handwriting of God" is a primitive reference to the human genetic code, then the "handwriting of thy fathers" must refer to the genes of our ancestors.

Madison's thoughts raced uncontrollably. His sharp intellect considered the possibilities and ramifications of Ambergris' rambling journal entries and staggering assertions.

"So what does Ambergris mean?" asked Quiz.

"He's saying that a message to humanity from God is hidden in our DNA."

Thirty-nine

QUIZ'S OFFICE
SUBBASEMENT, MILLENNIUM TOWER
MANHATTAN, NEW YORK

The trio continued reading.

12 March—

There are other considerations. The human genome is packaged in twenty-three pairs of chromosomes. The number twenty-three does not appear to have any special significance. It is actually a bit surprising that humans don't have twenty-four chromosomes. Chimpanzees, orangutans, and gorillas all have twenty-four.

Geneticists have determined that the reason humans

only have twenty-three chromosomes is that two ape chromosomes are fused together in humans. The second biggest human chromosome, chromosome two, is actually a fusion of two medium-sized ape chromosomes.

Pope John Paul II has argued that between ancestral apes and modern humans, there was an ontological discontinuity, a point at which God injected a human soul into animal evolution. Maybe this divine jump forward was manifested by the fusion of two ape chromosomes.

Can we see a reflection of the human soul in our DNA?

If we look with fresh eyes, will we find a gene for the human soul hidden in our genome, perhaps hiding in the winding proteins of chromosome two?

An alarm on Quiz's computer chimed and text scrolled up the screen.

<< SECURITY ALERT >>
<< Priority: Alpha >>
<< All security personnel are directed to immediately >>
<< conduct a level-one search of all facilities. >>
<< Lockdown in effect until further notice. >>

"We'd better go," said Madison, trying to keep his voice calm. "Quiz, can you keep reading these journal entries? I'll check in with you as soon as I can."

"No problem," said Quiz. "You better get back to your floor. Don't want to get Crowe mad at you."

"Yeah," said Grace. "No kidding."

Forty

Arakai located Dr. Ambergris' study on the second floor of the brownstone. It was large, running the entire width of the residence, and lavishly furnished.

In one corner stood a large marble sculpture of the Archangel Gabriel by Gian Lorenzo Bernini. In one hand, Gabriel brandished a sword, raised high above his head. In the other, he held a small, delicate flower. Rembrandt's *The Angel and the Prophet Balaam* hung in a gilded frame on a mahogany-paneled wall. Next to the Rembrandt, a boyish angel smiled at Arakai from a Caravaggio painting, *Amor Victorious*.

Ambergris' enormous desk occupied a large portion of the far end of the study. Two large windows allowed sunlight to filter into the otherwise darkened room. The contents of the room reflected Ambergris' eccentric nature. *And his father's,* thought Arakai.

Books lined the shelves of floor-to-ceiling bookcases along two walls of the study in sufficient numbers to seed a small library. Arakai paused to scan the titles of several leather-bound tomes.

THE BOOK OF ENOCH.

SEFER YETZIRAH.

TABULA SMARAGDINA, The Emerald Tablet.

KITAB SIRR AL-KHALIQA WA SAN'AT AL-TABIÀ, The Book of the Secret of Creation and the Art of Nature.

Arakai's eyes were drawn to the oak-paneled wall behind the mahogany desk that once belonged to Ambergris' grandfather.

There's more to this study than meets the eye, isn't there, Dr. Ambergris?

A large framed rendering of Mayan bar-and-dot numeric hieroglyphs hung on the wall.

Ah, yes.

Arakai focused his attention on the Mayan rendering and removed Ambergris' electronic key card from his pocket. He ran a finger along the top of the picture frame.

Here we are.

The frame pivoted away from the wall, hinged along its left side. Behind it was a metal plate with a small slot, just the right size for an electronic key card.

Americans and their electronic toys.

Arakai inserted Ambergris' electronic key card into the card reader recessed into the wall. There was a faint click. A small panel above the card slot slid open to reveal a numerical keypad.

Forty-one

QUIZ'S OFFICE
SUBBASEMENT, MILLENNIUM TOWER
MANHATTAN, NEW YORK

Quiz ripped the plastic wrapper off another Twinkie and continued reading. The next entry in Dr. Ambergris' research journal was dated March 25.

25 March—

A man much smarter than I once said that God does not play dice with the universe. After considerable reflection, I cannot accept the idea that a Supreme Being placed a hidden code within our DNA to convey a message to humanity. Appealing as the notion may be to those seeking solace or comfort in evidence of direct communication from our Creator, my rational mind must ultimately reject such a theory.

But there is no doubt that the Genesis Code does exist. I have as of yet been unsuccessful in my attempts to decipher the encrypted text built into the chemical structure of our genome. The question remains, who put it there and for what purpose?

The cryptic references to DNA and genetics in ancient Hebrew texts remain. I believe that Hebrew scholars of old were simply reciting fragments of advanced scientific knowledge that were beyond their ability to understand during the age in which they lived. I am expanding my review of ancient literature to include studies of writings of other ancient cultures. I have already found references in Mayan mythology and Egyptian texts similar to those in the *Sefer Yetzirah*.

I predict that the encoding of advanced scientific concepts in primitive ancient narratives will be a common theme among many of our oldest civilizations.

But if God was not responsible for the Genesis Code, who was? There is another hypothesis that warrants consideration.

Several decades ago, mathematician Johann von Neumann proposed the idea of a self-reproducing machine that would scour the universe for the existence of life.

What did von Neumann mean when he said self-reproducing? Imagine an apparatus that takes off from earth and heads for the nearest sun, Proxima Centauri. The apparatus has computers and sensors to detect the existence of planets orbiting around any stars it encounters. It finds a planet and lands, looking for signs of life. Finding none, robotic devices on board the apparatus scavenge metals and chemicals from the planet's surface.

It may take centuries, but the von Neumann apparatus builds a complete copy of itself and repairs or replaces any parts damaged during its landing on the planet. Now there are two von Neumann machines. They both take off and search for other planets. Over tens of thousands of years, the machines multiply and spread across the galaxy, searching for life.

Von Neumann was well ahead of his time, but his ideas are not inconceivable. In the future, nanotechnology could produce a machine capable of performing the functions von Neumann proposed. But why send machines into space when there is a much simpler way of accomplishing the same goal?

DNA is an organic, self-reproducing apparatus that already exists in nature. There is no need to build a von Neumann machine. The mechanism necessary to accomplish his goal already exists in the form of DNA.

Each cell in an organism contains the complete DNA necessary for reproducing the entire organism. So why use complex machine technology when microscopic DNA can do the same thing? Strands of engineered DNA could spread throughout the universe in the same fashion as a von Neumann machine. We could sow the galaxy with DNA in the same way a farmer sows his fields with seeds. Some of the DNA would find planets with chemical compounds suitable to allow the DNA to replicate itself.

Nobel Prize winner Francis Crick proposed that an alien civilization might have launched microorganisms into space hundreds of millions of years ago, spreading them throughout the universe and sowing the cosmos with life. Within the engineered DNA of these organisms, our hypothetical alien civilization could have encoded messages, or even an entire universal language, to pass on their knowledge to other civilizations.

When these genetic messengers encountered life, they could insert the Genesis Code into its DNA, much in the same way that gene therapy inserts new sequences of genes into the DNA of living patients. The messages hidden in the Genesis Code would be preserved and passed on from generation to generation, awaiting discovery by intelligent life.

Is this the origin of the Genesis Code? A truly ancient message delivered to us across time and space? A communication from a distant civilization?

Quiz picked up the phone and dialed Madison's extension. Five rings passed before Madison's voice mail picked up.

"You've reached Christian Madison. I'm either on another call or away from my desk . . ."

Why isn't Madison back in his office?

Quiz waited impatiently for the beep.

"Christian, it's Quiz. Call me as soon as you get this message. You're not going to believe this."

Forty-two

MILLENNIUM TOWER SUBWAY STATION
MANHATTAN, NEW YORK

Madison breathed a sigh of relief as the subway car began to pull away from the platform. The subway car was only a quarter full. An assortment of well-dressed businesspeople, teenagers in baggy jeans and T-shirts, and tourists with cameras and fanny packs were spaced in clumps along the hard plastic seats.

Madison and Grace took a relatively private bench at the rear of the car where they could talk without being overheard. Newspapers littered the aisle. The air in the subway car was warm and stale.

Madison winced as he rubbed his right shoulder. He removed the printout of Ambergris' e-mail from his pocket, unfolded it, and spread the page across his lap.

"Maybe we should go to the police . . . or the FBI," said Grace.

"And tell them what?" asked Madison. "We almost killed the chief security officer of Triad Genomics. Crowe thinks you were involved in the murder of Dr. Ambergris."

"I wasn't there last night," said Grace. "I swear I wasn't there. Either someone made a mistake or evidence was deliberately fabricated implicating me in Ambergris' murder."

Grace tapped a finger on the printout of Ambergris' e-mail.

"Dr. Ambergris sent this to you before he was killed. In code, to protect the message from someone inside Triad Genomics who might try and read it. Maybe the same person who planted false evidence about me."

Madison was silent.

"And maybe the same person who plans to detonate a bomb during the Biogenetics Conference," said Grace. "We can't just run away from this. We have to tell someone."

"Do you want to walk into FBI headquarters and claim that Dr. Ambergris was killed because he discovered an encrypted code hidden in human DNA? And that we got a phone call from some anonymous person telling us that Ambergris' killers are going to blow up the Millennium Tower?"

"It does sound absolutely crazy . . ."

"No one is ever going to believe us. We'll be locked up in an interrogation room while Ambergris' killer is free to cover up his tracks and, God forbid, follow through on his plans to blow up the Millennium Tower."

"I suppose you have a better idea?"

Madison closed his eyes and thought for a moment.

"We need some tangible proof to take to the authorities."

"What about the journal?" asked Grace.

"That doesn't prove anything. We need Ambergris' raw data. His research notes. The genome sequences he was working with. Would Dr. Ambergris have kept any of his research at his residence?"

"I'm not sure."

"Sooner or later, either Triad Genomics security or Ambergris' killer is going to search Ambergris' house."

"If they haven't already," said Grace. "If there are any documents at his house—"

"We need to get to them first," concluded Madison.

Forty=three

DR. JOSHUA AMBERGRIS' RESIDENCE
UPTOWN MANHATTAN, NEW YORK

The subway station closest to Dr. Ambergris' brownstone deposited Grace and Madison on a trendy block of newly renovated historic buildings with elegant brick facades and wrought-iron balconies. Shops and restaurants filled the first floor of each building along the street. Small bistro tables spilled out onto the sidewalk from cafés with European names featuring "fusion cuisine." After the close of business, the cafés and restaurants would begin to fill with small crowds of young professionals mingling and networking—young administrative assistants sipping dirty martinis, flirting with accountants and lawyers drinking imported beer from glass bottles..

Madison and Grace walked at a brisk clip, avoiding eye contact with the few people they passed on the sidewalk. The second and third floors along the block were filled with offices of accountants, real estate agents, designers, and lawyers. Lofts and condos occupied the upper floors. The neighborhood was typical of the multi-use "new urbanism" developments gentrifying older downtown neighborhoods in cities across America.

"Down this block," said Grace.

She led Madison into a quiet neighborhood still untouched by the rash of urban redevelopment only two blocks away. The small enclave of ancient brownstones was nestled beneath a canopy of tall oaks that lined the narrow street.

"This is it," said Grace, stopping in front of an impressive four-story residence.

"Is there a back door?" asked Madison. "There's no way I can kick in that front door without drawing attention."

"I know where the spare key is hidden," said Grace.

Madison raised an eyebrow.

"Oh, stop. It's nothing like that. Ambergris sent me here two or three times to pick up books or journal articles he needed at the office."

"Sure he did."

"Fine. Think what you want."

She walked along the wrought-iron fence enclosing the small front yard. At the fourth fence post, she stopped and knelt down on the sidewalk, reaching beneath the bottom railing.

"It's still here," she said, producing a small magnetic box. Inside was a single shiny key.

Grace removed the key and slipped the magnetic box back into its hiding place.

"The front gate was never locked," she said, raising the iron latch. The gate groaned as she pushed it open.

Madison followed Grace through the gate and closed it behind them. He scanned the street for curious neighbors and saw none.

"I kept telling him to get an alarm system," said Grace, inserting the key into the lock on the front door and giving it a clockwise twist.

"Wait a minute . . . ," cautioned Madison.

Grace opened the front door.

Forty-four

DR. JOSHUA AMBERGRIS' RESIDENCE
UPTOWN MANHATTAN, NEW YORK

A black streak shot out through the doorway as Grace pulled the door open. The overweight black cat darted straight at Madison, who jumped to one side to avoid the feline projectile. Never losing speed, the cat darted through a narrow opening beneath the gate, executed a ninety-degree turn, and dove into the bushes.

Grace cried out as she lost her balance, falling backward off the top step. Madison stepped forward with his arms outstretched, neatly catching Grace in his arms as she fell.

"Nice catch," she said.

Madison set her down on the brick walkway. "Come on," he said, walking up the steps to the door. "Let's get inside before we alert the entire neighborhood."

The house was dark and quiet. The faint smell of lemons lingered in the air downstairs. Grace led Madison through the first floor and up the stairs to Dr. Ambergris' study.

"It doesn't look like anyone has been here," said Grace.

"Just keep your eyes open," said Madison.

The door to the study was ajar. Madison crept up to the doorway and peered inside the study.

"I don't see anyone."

"Look," said Grace, pointing.

On the far wall, a framed picture was swung away from the wall on hidden hinges. Exposed behind the frame was a hidden safe and a small numeric keypad.

"Have you ever seen that before?" asked Madison.

"No."

"The door to the safe is closed. Maybe Ambergris didn't swing the picture frame back into place the last time he opened it. Or if someone else was here searching, maybe they weren't able to get into the safe."

They crossed the room and inspected the keypad.

"Any ideas?" asked Madison.

Grace considered the possibilities.

"The total of each row and column in the Magic Square in the e-mail Dr. Ambergris sent you was two hundred sixty," she said.

"Give it a shot."

Grace punched the three digits into the keypad. There was a small electronic whirr behind the panel.

"Try it."

Grace grasped the handle on the safe and pushed

down. With a loud clank, the door swung open. Inside were three leather-bound ledgers and a sheaf of handwritten letters. Grace gingerly removed the stack from the safe and spread out the individual items on Ambergris' desk.

"These letters are all addressed to Ambergris' father. The return address is Dr. Georgia Bowman. Yale University. New Haven, Connecticut."

"I know that name," said Grace. "Dr. Ambergris spent a lot of time with her over the past few months. She's a history professor at Yale; teaches graduate courses on ancient civilizations. She was a friend and colleague of Ambergris' father—"

Grace stopped midsentence and froze. Footsteps echoed from the ground floor.

"Someone's coming," whispered Madison.

Hidden inside the small closet in Dr. Ambergris' study, Arakai watched Madison and Grace through the keyhole in the door. Alerted to footsteps on the first floor below, they scrambled to gather the contents of Dr. Ambergris' safe.

Arakai grasped the doorknob and tensed the muscles in his legs, preparing to strike.

Forty=five

DR. JOSHUA AMBERGRIS' RESIDENCE
UPTOWN MANHATTAN, NEW YORK

In rapid succession, footfalls echoed from the stairway leading to the second floor. Grace struggled to reassemble the pile of letters from the safe.

"Leave them," hissed Madison.

Madison ran to a large window in the west wall of the study. He unlocked the metal latch and strained to lift the window. As it popped free and slid upward, Crowe stormed through the doorway into the study.

"Christian!" yelled Grace.

Madison spun around to see Crowe burst into the room with his gun drawn.

Crowe raised the 9mm and aimed directly at Grace.

"Get down!" yelled Madison.

Without warning, the door to the small closet in the study burst open, slamming into Crowe and knocking him backward. As the door crashed into Crowe's body, the gun discharged, sending a round speeding across the room, narrowly missing Grace and splintering the wall behind her.

"Grace, come on! Out the window!"

Grace reached out and took Madison's hand as they climbed onto the broad windowsill. There was a loud noise behind them. Without looking back, they jumped, falling from the open window and crashing into a tangle of thick shrubbery. Madison cried out in pain as his ankle twisted beneath him.

Madison extricated himself from the dense foliage and jumped to his feet.

"Are you hurt?"

"No," said Grace, surveying her body. "I don't think so."

Madison pulled her to her feet. Together, they ran across the yard to an adjoining alley. Madison limped as he ran, gritting his teeth against the shooting pain in his ankle.

Grace looked back over her shoulder at Ambergris' brownstone. She gasped as a wiry Asian man leapt from the window, landing neatly in a crouch on the green grass below.

Forty-six

The cool air-conditioning on the city bus was a godsend. They had run seven blocks from Dr. Ambergris' brownstone before catching the bus at a busy intersection. Madison chose a seat near the back and collapsed onto the hard plastic. Grace plopped down next to him.

When Grace finally caught her breath, she leaned over and whispered to Madison.

"Did you see him? The Asian guy that ambushed Crowe?"

"Yes," said Madison, as he massaged his injured ankle.

"Who the hell was that? And why did he just watch us from the closet until Crowe showed up?"

"I have no idea."

Grace chewed on her bottom lip.

"And he jumped out the window after us, but I didn't see him chasing us once we hit the street. What was that about?"

"Grace, I don't know. I have no idea."

"I should have taken those letters. What a waste."

Grace slouched in her seat and laid her head against Madison's shoulder.

"Let me see the e-mail again."

He dug in his pocket and retrieved the folded page. Grace took the paper and unfolded it on her lap, smoothing the creases with her fingers. She contemplated the grid of numbers in silence for several minutes.

"Okay, what do we know so far? Dr. Ambergris was trying to tell us something. Sixty-four numbers arranged in a grid. But not just any grid. These numbers form a Magic

Square. And we know that the root of this Magic Square is two hundred and sixty. One year on the Mayan calendar."

"But now we're stuck," said Madison.

"We must be missing something."

"I just don't know much about the Maya."

"Neither do I. But the letters in Ambergris' safe," said Grace. "All from Dr. Bowman. Ambergris spent a lot of time with her. And I know she's an expert on ancient civilizations. Maybe those letters were left for us to find."

Madison nodded. He looked down at his watch.

"Ever been to Yale?" he asked.

Crowe wiped the blood from his broken nose and dialed a number on his cell phone. A male voice answered the line.

"Security."

"This is Crowe. I want you to pull Dr. Joshua Ambergris' phone logs for the last eight weeks."

"Shall I take a number and ring you back?"

"No," he said. "I'll wait."

Crowe kicked Ambergris' desk chair with a savage spinning blow. It crashed against the wall. Blood again trickled from his nose and dripped onto the floor.

The voice came back on the line. "Okay, I have it. What are you looking for?"

"Any calls to persons outside the facility other than his home or relatives. Look for anything out of the ordinary."

The security officer muttered to himself as he scanned the list of names and numbers.

"Here's an unusual one. Multiple calls to a Dr. Georgia Bowman. Yale University."

"Any others?"

"Yes. Also multiple calls to Dr. Alberto Vasquez. University of Chicago."

"Anything else?"

"No. Other than those, just the usual stuff."

"Give me the numbers. And I need addresses as well."

Forty-seven

QUIZ'S OFFICE
SUBBASEMENT, MILLENNIUM TOWER
MANHATTAN, NEW YORK

Quiz twisted the white cap off the pill bottle, tipped the bottle to one side, and coaxed a small blue pill onto the palm of his hand. He popped "Quiz's little helper" into his mouth and swallowed hard, chasing down the bitter anticonvulsant with a shot of Diet Coke. He rubbed the cool aluminum can across his forehead.

Madison was nowhere to be found. Out of ideas, Quiz had also tried to check in with Grace. No luck. Quiz was completely frustrated. And now he was down to his last Diet Coke.

Dammit.

A tinny, disembodied voice echoed from speakers overhead.

"Attention, please. May I have your attention, please. The level one lockdown has now been lifted. The security drill has concluded. External communications have now been restored. Thank you for your cooperation."

His computer beeped and displayed an incoming systemwide communication from Triad Security.

<< PRIORITY COMMUNICATION >>
<< From: TRIAD GENOMICS SECURITY >>
<< Priority: BETA >>
<< To: ALL >>
<< Level one security lockdown is now lifted. >>
<< External communications restored. >>
<< Security drill complete. >>

Thank God.

From beneath the computer desk, Quiz's chihuahua barked in agreement.

Part II

The oldest Egyptian or Hindu philosopher raised a corner of the veil from the statue of the divinity; and still the trembling robe remains raised, and I gaze upon as fresh a glory as he did, since it was I in him that was then so bold, and it is he in me that now reviews the vision.

—Henry David Thoreau

Who in his own skull confiding,
Shall with rule and line
Mark the borderland dividing
Human and divine?

—H. W. Longfellow, *Hermes Trismegistus*

Forty-eight

BEINECKE RARE BOOK AND MANUSCRIPT LIBRARY
YALE UNIVERSITY
NEW HAVEN, CONNECTICUT

Yale University, originally called the Collegiate School, was founded in 1701 in the home of its first rector, Abraham Pierson. The fledgling institution was renamed Yale University in 1719, in honor of benefactor Elihu Yale, who made a gift to the university consisting of nine bales of goods, a portrait and arms of King George I, and about four hundred books.

Since that time, Yale has added a few volumes to its collection.

The Beinecke Rare Book and Manuscript Library, its edifice faced with translucent slices of marble to protect the collection from damaging sunlight, is one of the largest buildings in the world devoted entirely to rare books. The library's central tower and underground stacks now contain over five hundred thousand volumes and several million manuscripts.

A friendly inquiry at Yale's Department of History revealed that Dr. Georgia Bowman had spent the afternoon engaged in research at the Beinecke Rare Book and Manuscript Library. The department receptionist politely suggested that she might still be found there, pondering obscure volumes from the library's expansive collections, in her usual corner of the fourth-floor reading room.

A short stroll brought Grace and Madison to the center of the Yale campus. As they approached, the Beinecke Library appeared to hover over the granite plain of

Beinecke Plaza in proportions of Platonic purity: the structure was exactly twice as deep as it was high, and three times as long. The cool gray granite and white marble of the library contrasted with the warmer stone and red brick of the adjacent Yale Law School and Berkeley College.

"Christian," said Grace, reaching out and taking Madison's hand as they neared the revolving door in the library's facade. "Thank you for what you did back there."

Grace stopped, turning to face Madison, still holding his hand.

"When Crowe grabbed me, I was so scared. I don't know what would have happened if you hadn't been there. If you hadn't been there to stop him . . ."

Her eyes welled up with tears.

"You're welcome," said Madison. "I never liked him anyway."

Grace choked out a laugh, wiping the tears from her eyes with her free hand.

"Hey, it's the least I could do. You were there for me. Even if I didn't appreciate it at the time. When Justin . . ."

The memory breached the walls in his mind, pouring into his consciousness.

Justin was a ghost of a child, lying thin and frail under the starched white sheets of a hospital bed. A tangle of tubes and wires crisscrossed his chest, connecting his dying body with IV bags, monitors, and machines.

The monotonous beep of a heart monitor ticked off the passage of seconds. Christian Madison sat at his bedside, gently holding Justin's hand.

Madison struggled to find words.

"After Justin was gone, and Kate left, I didn't think I was going to make it. I never told you how much . . . how much that time with you meant to me."

Grace blinked away another tear. "Then why? Why did you run away from me?"

"I don't know, Grace."

His face clouded with emotion.

"You never told me why. Never considered my feelings when you ended it," she said.

"Do we have to do this now?" He closed his eyes. "I don't think I can do this now."

Grace looked away, wiping her cheek with the back of her hand. She turned her back to Madison and started walking toward the Beinecke Library.

Madison wanted to tell her how he really felt. Wanted to reach out, take her into his arms, and tell her everything would be okay.

Wait. Come back.

But the words wouldn't come.

Forty-nine

THE PALAIS DES NATIONS
GENEVA, SWITZERLAND

Housed in the Palais des Nations overlooking Lake Geneva, the United Nations Office at Geneva (UNOG) is the second largest United Nations center after the United Nations Headquarters in New York. Unbeknownst to the UN staffers working on the premises, it also serves as the unofficial headquarters of the Order's European membership.

The secretary politely excused himself from a meeting of the United Nations Conference on Trade and Development, exited the Palais des Nations' E-Building through the first floor's northern portico, and strolled through the forty-five-hectare Ariana Park toward the Villa le Bocage. Originally converted into office space for use by the United Nations, the nineteenth century villa had been quietly appropriated by the Order to serve as its European base of operations.

The secretary was soon joined by a prominent member of the trade delegation from Italy.

"Buon giorno," said the Italian diplomat.

The secretary inclined his head in greeting.

A cooing peacock strutted across the stone path in front of them, its iridescent emerald tail feathers spread in a display of courtship.

They walked together in silence.

As they neared the villa, the secretary caught sight of the Celestial Sphere, a monument encircled by stands of hundred-year-old cedar trees. Its spherical frame was adorned with sixty-four gilded constellations and 260 silvered stars. A motor hidden in its base turned the sphere in slow revolutions around an axis aligned with the Pole Star.

The secretary and the Italian trade delegate were the last to arrive at the villa. Inside, they joined four other well-known European officials who had also been inducted into the secret ranks of the Order. A luscious fresco depicting *The Triumph of Venus* looked down upon the group as they assembled around a rectangular conference table.

The secretary convened the meeting.

"I trust we are all well aware of the nature of the actions we are taking here today. We have a decision to make. Once this line has been crossed, there can be no turning back."

A French industrialist folded his hands on the table.

"It is time," he said. "Under Tanaka's leadership, the Order has become reckless. His aggressive tactics pose a great threat to our plans. We cannot allow this madness to continue."

The secretary tipped his head back, staring up at the vaulted marble ceiling.

"Yes," he sighed. "I fear you are right."

The deputy consul from Russia banged on the table with a hairy fist. "I, for one, have had enough. It is time for a change in leadership."

Fifty

The Beinecke Rare Book and Manuscript Library is, in essence, a box within a box. Contained within thick exterior walls of stone and glass, bronze and marble, a glass-walled tower of books rises upward through the heart of the library. From the mezzanine below, Madison and Grace ascended a stairway that encircled the interior glass walls, spiraling upward through the core of the central tower.

A lone female figure occupied the fourth-floor reading room.

Seated at an oak table between the thick stone of the library's exterior wall and the transparent panes of the glass book tower, Dr. Georgia Bowman communed with the dead. Immersed in the depths of an ancient Greek text, Bowman was oblivious to her surroundings, unaware that those few students who had occupied the tables around her had abandoned their studies as the afternoon drew to a close, leaving her in sole possession of the room.

The scene brought the words of Henry David Thoreau to Grace's mind: *To read well—that is, to read true books in a true spirit—is a noble exercise . . . Books must be read as deliberately and reservedly as they were written.*

"Dr. Bowman?" asked Grace. Her voice sounded loud in the silence of the reading room.

"Yes?" she answered, lifting her eyes from the page.

"I'm sorry to interrupt. My name is Grace Nguyen. I'm a geneticist. And this is Dr. Christian Madison."

Bowman looked around the room before fixing her gaze on the pair of scientists in front of her. Her eyes flitted back and forth between Grace and Madison as she examined their faces.

"We work with Dr. Joshua Ambergris at Triad Genomics," Grace offered.

Bowman leaned back in her chair and folded her arms across her chest.

"You're a long way from home, Ms. Nguyen."

"Dr. Nguyen, actually. But please call me Grace."

"What do you want, Dr. Nguyen?" asked Bowman.

"Dr. Ambergris suggested that you might be able to answer some questions for us," offered Madison.

"I find that to be highly unlikely," said Bowman.

She closed the vellum tome on the table in front of her and removed her reading glasses, placing them gently on the leather cover of the Greek manuscript.

"I'm afraid you've made a mistake. I will not be able to help you. And I have work to do. You are intruding. Good day."

"But Dr. Bowman—"

"I said good day, Dr. Nguyen."

Grace was at a loss for words. She looked over at Madison.

"Let's go, Grace," he said. "We've taken up enough of Dr. Bowman's time.

"But—"

Madison took her by the hand and led Grace away from the table.

"Something's not right here," he said when they were out of earshot. "We need to try a different approach."

Madison stopped near the stairway. Looking back toward the reading room, he could still see Dr. Bowman through a gap in the bookshelves lining the interior glass wall. She appeared deep in thought. After a moment, she rose from the table, leaving her glasses and briefcase, and walked toward the restrooms at the far end of the room.

"I have an idea," said Madison.

He removed the printout of Ambergris' e-mail from his

pocket and unfolded the paper. When the door to the ladies' restroom closed behind Dr. Bowman, he turned to Grace.

"Wait here," Madison said.

"But what—"

Grace watched as Madison jogged around the perimeter of the room. When he reached Dr. Bowman's table in the reading room, Madison laid the printout of Ambergris' e-mail on top of the book Bowman had been reading.

"Now let's wait," Madison said when he returned to their partially hidden vantage point behind the glass-walled stacks.

Three minutes later, Dr. Bowman returned to her table. She noticed the printout immediately, picking it up as she took her seat. Bowman retrieved her reading glasses, perching them precariously toward the end of her nose, and scanned the page.

Her stern expression faded as she studied the grid of numbers.

52	61	4	13	20	29	36	45
14	3	62	51	46	35	30	19
53	60	5	12	21	28	37	44
11	6	59	54	43	38	27	22
55	58	7	10	23	26	39	42
9	8	57	56	41	40	25	24
50	63	2	15	18	31	34	47
16	1	64	49	48	33	32	17

Her lips silently voiced the words as she read the single line of text beneath the grid.

"This is the beginning of the ancient word."

Bowman's eyes darted across the rows and columns of numbers, her brow knitted in concentration. After a moment, she looked up. Her eyes searched the room. Finally, she spotted Madison and Grace watching her through the gap in the bookshelves.

She sighed, and then reluctantly waved them over.

"Where did you get this?" she asked when they reached the table.

"It's an e-mail from Dr. Ambergris. He sent it to me this morning. At four-thirty A.M."

Bowman gestured to two empty chairs at the table. Grace and Madison took their cue to sit.

"Do you know what this is?" she asked.

"We believe it's a Magic Square," said Madison. "Other than that, we really don't have a clue."

"What happened to . . ." she began. Then she held up a hand. "No, wait. I don't want to know."

She thought for a moment. Then, having reached a decision, Dr. Bowman rotated the paper so that the numbers were right-side up to Grace and Madison.

"Magic Squares are very interesting," said Bowman. She offered neither an apology nor an explanation for her initial behavior.

Grace took a chance. "What can you tell us?"

Dr. Bowman's expression softened. Madison thought he detected sadness in her face.

"Joshua was quite enamored with Magic Squares," she said. "Variations and derivations of the Magic Square have been around for thousands of years. The oldest known Magic Square is contained in an ancient Chinese text, the *Yih King*."

Bowman tapped a finger on the grid of numbers.

"But the architect of this particular Magic Square appears to have an interest not only in ancient China, but in other ancient civilizations as well," she said.

"We suspected that," said Madison. "The rows and columns of this Magic Square all total two hundred and sixty. Grace recognized the significance of that total—the number of days in one year of the Mayan calendar."

"Yes, but I believe the Mayan reference is only part of it," Bowman said. "And to be precise, two hundred sixty is not the number of days in one year of the Mayan calendar. The Mayan calendar actually used three distinct, parallel dating systems—the Long Count, the Tzolkin, and the Haab. The length of the Tzolkin year was two hundred sixty days and the length of the Haab year was three hundred sixty-five days."

"Three parallel calendars? That sounds pretty sophisticated for a pre-Columbian culture," said Madison.

Dr. Bowman leaned back in her chair.

"The Maya were a truly remarkable civilization," she said. "While Europe was still in the midst of the Dark Ages, the Maya built a remarkable civilization spanning much of southern Mexico and Central America. Let me give you some background."

Her speech took on the pedantic rhythm of one accustomed to the art of lecture.

"The Maya mapped the heavens and were masters of mathematics. Without metal tools, they constructed vast cities with an amazing degree of architectural perfection."

"I had no idea they were so advanced," said Madison.

"Unfortunately, that seems to be a common misconception. There were several sophisticated cultures in Central and South America that predated the arrival of European influence—the Maya, the Aztec, the Inca, and the Olmec, for example."

"Olmec?" asked Grace.

"Yes. The Mayan civilization followed the Olmec. Mayan priests freely admitted in their writings that much of their scientific and mathematical knowledge came from the Olmec."

"And where did the Olmec come from?" asked Madison.

"That's a real enigma," said Dr. Bowman. "Archaeologists have never been able to find any signs indicating a developmental phase of the Olmec culture. It's almost as if they appeared one day, fully developed as a society. Their knowledge and technological skills, which should have taken hundreds or thousands of years to develop and evolve, appeared almost overnight."

Bowman plucked the reading glasses from her nose and laid them on the table.

"According to the admissions of their own sacred writings, the Maya built on the inherited inventions and ideas of the Olmec, developing advanced knowledge of astronomy, calendrical systems, and hieroglyphic writing. They built stone pyramids that rival the biggest Egyptian pyramids, and linked their cities with roads almost as extensive as those of the Roman Empire."

"Before their civilization collapsed," countered Madison.

"Yes, the disappearance of the great Mayan empire is one of history's most intriguing puzzles," said Bowman. "At the peak of its glory, Mayan civilization suddenly vanished. The Maya abandoned their sacred temples and pyramids. They fled from thriving cities. Modern-day archaeologists can offer no solutions to this ancient puzzle."

Dr. Bowman looked up from the printout.

"But, as I'm quite sure you must be wondering, what does any of this have to do with solving the mystery of your Magic Square?"

She paused.

"I believe the key to the solution is this," she said, pointing to the line of text beneath the grid of numbers.

This is the beginning of the ancient word.

Fifty-one

"Have you ever heard of Gematria?" asked Dr. Bowman, still contemplating the eight-by-eight grid of numbers on the printout of Dr. Ambergris' e-mail.

Madison shook his head.

"No, I haven't," said Grace.

"Gematria is a method originally used by Jewish mystics to discover hidden meanings in words. Numbers are assigned to the letters of the Hebrew alphabet and the letters are organized into tables according to mathematical arrangements," said Bowman.

She uncrossed her legs and leaned forward.

"And Jewish scholars weren't the only ones to use Gematria. Isopsephy is the ancient Greek system of Gematria based on the numerical values of the Greek letters. We also find references to Gematria in Roman texts."

"I'm not sure I understand," said Madison. "Is Gematria some sort of code?"

Bowman nodded. "The kabbalists of the thirteenth century believed that the Old Testament was written in a hidden code inspired by God. They used Gematria as one of the chief methods to decipher this code. In the medieval mystical text called *Sefer Yetzirah, The Book of Creation,* the letters of the Hebrew alphabet are described as the stones used to build a house. They are called the 'twenty-two letters of foundation.' Kabbalists believe that this reference is a metaphor for the divine code hidden in religious texts."

Madison sat forward in his chair. "Twenty-two?"

"Yes," said Dr. Bowman. "The Hebrew alphabet

contains twenty-two letters. Is that number significant to you?"

"It is." Madison's eyes moved to Grace, then back to Dr. Bowman. "The sixty-four codons in human DNA are always found in groups that code for twenty-two specific genetic letters."

Bowman folded her hands on the table. "That's a remarkable coincidence," she said, smiling.

Grace thought she detected a note of amusement in Dr. Bowman's voice, but it vanished as quickly as it had appeared. She glanced at Madison.

"Gematria can also be used to encode messages. It's a very old form of cipher. Numbers are substituted for words or letters in a grid," said Bowman.

"So these numbers may actually represent Hebrew letters?" asked Grace, pointing to the grid of numbers from Ambergris' e-mail.

"Or Greek letters?" said Madison.

"Neither Hebrew nor Greek, I suspect. That's where this line of text comes into play: *This is the beginning of the ancient word*."

"You recognize that sentence?" asked Grace.

Bowman smiled. "Come with me. I'll show you."

Fifty=two

BEINECKE RARE BOOK AND MANUSCRIPT LIBRARY
YALE UNIVERSITY
NEW HAVEN, CONNECTICUT

Dr. Bowman escorted Grace and Madison to a glass-walled gallery on the mezzanine level of the Beinecke Rare Book and Manuscript Library. Inside, climate-controlled glass enclosures housed the rarest and most valuable items of the library's collections. As Bowman led them toward the center of the gallery, she pointed out a particular glass display, fixed in a thin white beam from a spotlight above.

"One of our treasures," she said. A hint of institutional pride crept into her voice. "The first book in Western civilization printed using movable type."

Grace and Madison dutifully admired the Gutenberg Bible.

"And here we have Audubon's *Birds of America*," Bowman said. Next to the seven rare volumes, a beautiful watercolor rendering captured the image of two drake mallards taking flight above a broad meadow.

"But this is what I want you to see," said Dr. Bowman.

In the center of the gallery, a large stone monument inscribed with columns of hieroglyphs and pictographs towered above a mahogany metal and glass display case.

"The stone monument is a Mayan stela. Just a reproduction, actually," said Bowman. "But the manuscript is an original."

Beneath a pane of thick glass, a long sheet of coarse paper, folded accordion-style, rested on the mirrored deck of the display case.

"The *Popul Vuh*."

Bowman pointed to the double-sided bark pages of the Mayan text, rich with detailed glyphs painted over a smooth surface of hardened lime paste.

"The *Popul Vuh* is a Mayan religious text that details their creation mythology," said Bowman. "Until about ten years ago, the oldest manuscript of the *Popul Vuh* was from the sixteenth century, a copy made by an unknown author from an earlier text. Ten years ago, two archaeologists discovered this copy, dating back two thousand years."

"Is this the original?"

"We'll probably never know. But it's surely much closer to the original text of the *Popul Vuh* than any other copy found to date. Do you want to take a guess at who made this discovery?" asked Bowman.

Madison thought for a second.

"Maximillian Ambergris," he said.

Bowman smiled. "Exactly. And who else?"

Grace raised an eyebrow. "You?"

"Yes. I was quite the adventurer in my youth."

She pointed to the first line of hieroglyphs on the first page of the screenbook.

"The *Popul Vuh* begins with this line: *This is the beginning of the ancient word.*"

Fifty-three

BEINECKE RARE BOOK AND MANUSCRIPT LIBRARY
YALE UNIVERSITY
NEW HAVEN, CONNECTICUT

"So the Mayan *Popul Vuh* is the source that was used to encode this grid of numbers using Gematria?" speculated Grace.

"I believe so," said Bowman. "I've made a copy of this grid. I'm going to translate the Gematria tonight."

Madison opened his mouth to protest, but Grace kicked him under the table.

"Will you share the translation with us?" asked Grace, ignoring Madison's glare.

Bowman's eyes narrowed for a moment. "I suppose I can't really refuse, since you brought this to me. If you meet me here tomorrow morning, I'll tell you what I've learned."

Grace frowned. "There's something I still don't get. All of the rows and columns in the Magic Square total two hundred and sixty. We know that two-sixty is an important number in the Mayan calendar system, but why was it so important to Dr. Ambergris to include two-sixty in this coded message to us?"

"Perhaps it represents additional information he was trying to convey to you," said Bowman.

Madison watched Bowman closely. He was certain that she knew more than she was telling.

"Mayan priests were some of the first astronomers," said Bowman. "And charting time was an important concern of ancient Mesoamerican sky watchers. The Maya made detailed astronomical observations well over two thousand years ago. Much of their knowledge of astronomy is set forth in the *Popul Vuh*."

"And what does this have to do with anything?" asked Madison.

Bowman frowned at him, then turned to Grace and continued.

"The Mayan religious framework embraced a concept they called the 'Ages of Man.' Essentially, Mayan priests believed that time was divided into distinct epochs based on astronomical cycles such as the precession of the equinoxes. The *Popul Vuh* speaks of eras of 5,125.40 years, equaling thirteen 'baktuns' of 144,000 days each. Each cycle of thirteen baktuns was reckoned as an Age or Great Cycle, a specific historical epoch."

"Why was that important? Why did the Maya expend so much effort calculating these Ages of Man?" asked Madison.

"The Maya believed that the end of each epoch marked drastic and sometimes cataclysmic changes in the history of the human race. Naturally, there was a great interest in when the current Age of Man would end."

"How does the Mayan calendar tie into all that?"

"The Mayan Long Count system is related to certain astronomical cycles. Priests used the Mayan Long Count calendar for recording important events. An event was dated according to the number of days that had passed since the beginning date of the current Age of Man."

"Beginning date?"

"Yes," said Bowman. "August thirteenth, 3113 BC. Judging by archaeological evidence, 3113 BC was well before the emergence of the Mayan civilization. No one knows for sure why they chose this date, but I believe that to the Mayan priests, 3113 BC marked the beginning of the current Age of Man."

Madison digested the information.

"When does the next Age of Man begin?"

"That's a very interesting question. Dr. Ambergris thought so as well. He was quite interested in this subject. It seems that we are living in the last Age of Man."

"The last age?" asked Grace.

"The current Mayan Age of Man, the fifth, was said to be a synthesis of the last four Ages. It is symbolized by the heiroglyph *Ollin*, meaning movement or shift. The glyph for the last katun of this Age, which began in 1992 on our calendar, is Storm followed by Sun—a period of darkness followed by one of light."

"Meaning what? The apocalypse? The end of humanity?"

"No one knows for sure what the Maya believed would happen at the end of the last Age of Man."

"When does the Mayan calendar end?"

"On the Mayan calendar, it's 13.0.0.0.0."

Bowman paused.

"On our calendar, the date is December twenty-first, 2012."

Madison was stunned. "December twenty-first, 2012?"

"How much do you know about astronomy?" asked Bowman.

"A little," he replied.

"I mentioned the term 'precession of the equinoxes' before. Do you understand what that means?"

"No, not really."

"The earth spins on an axis, with the northern end at the North Pole. The spinning action is like that of a top; and, like a top, the earth wobbles as it spins. But it wobbles very slowly, with one wobble taking approximately twenty-five thousand eight hundred years. This 'precession of the equinoxes' takes twenty-five thousand eight hundred years to complete one cycle. With me so far?"

"I'm with you."

"Precession causes the location in space that the North Pole points at to gradually change. At present it points to Polaris, the North Star. In twelve thousand years' time it will be pointing close to Vega. As the Pole Star changes, so does the position in the sky of all the other stars, relative to our wobbly spinning earth. If you read the *Popul Vuh,* it becomes very evident that the Maya understood precession."

"Okay, but why is 2012 significant?"

"I'll tell you why. The Milky Way has a galactic center around which all the stars in our galaxy revolve. It's located in the starriest part of the Milky Way. Only four times during the twenty-five-thousand-eight-hundred-year precessional cycle does the galactic center align with the sunrise of a solstice or equinox."

"And?"

"The next galactic alignment occurs in December of 2012."

Grace was shocked. "The same year that the Maya predicted would be the end of the current Age of Man."

Fifty-four

BEINECKE RARE BOOK AND MANUSCRIPT LIBRARY
YALE UNIVERSITY
NEW HAVEN, CONNECTICUT

Madison's head was spinning. He needed time to digest and process everything Dr. Bowman had told them. A massive paradigm shift loomed on the far edges of his thoughts.

"I'm having a hard time getting my mind around all of this," he said. "I need to let it marinate in my brain for a while."

Dr. Bowman nodded.

"There's someone else you should speak with about this when you're ready. Dr. Alberto Vasquez, at the University of Chicago. Dr. Ambergris spent a lot of time talking with him in the past few months. These days he teaches a class or two at the university and spends a lot of time as a curator at the Field Museum of Natural History."

Grace rubbed her tired eyes and yawned.

"For now, why don't you take a room at the bed and breakfast across from the art gallery on Chapel Street?" Bowman suggested. "It's just a couple of blocks from here. We can meet again in the morning when I've finished the translation."

Grace realized how exhausted she actually felt.

"Sounds good," she said.

"What time shall we meet?" asked Madison.

"I'm an early riser. How about eight o'clock in the reading room?"

Madison nodded his assent. "We'll see you then."

Fifty-five

POP'S DINER
NEW HAVEN, CONNECTICUT

Pop's Diner was down the street from the Colony Inn Bed and Breakfast. Acquiescing to the rather vocal demands of her growling stomach, Grace insisted that they eat dinner before checking in to the bed and breakfast.

Grace consulted the sticky menu.

"I'll have the three-egg omelet," she said. The forty-something waitress wiped her sweaty palms on her apron, then adjusted the name tag on her bright yellow shirt. She searched in vain for a pen in the pocket of her apron before finally locating a yellow pencil poked through the hair bun on the top of her head. She licked the dull point of her pencil, then jotted down Grace's order.

"Toast or biscuit, hunny?"

"Toast, please, Irma," said Grace, reading the waitress's name tag. "Rye. And bacon. Coffee to drink."

"How 'bout you, hun?" asked Irma, scribbling on her small notepad with the stubby pencil.

Madison squinted at the specials.

"*Scungilli fra diavolo,* please. And a glass of the house merlot."

"Huh?"

"Just a joke."

"Right," said Irma. Grace rolled her eyes.

"BLT," said Madison. "And a Coke."

Irma collected their menus, refilled Madison's ice water, and wandered off toward the kitchen. Elvis crooned about blue suede shoes from the jukebox in the corner.

"So according to the Maya, the world is coming to an end in 2012. Maybe I should start running up my credit cards," said Madison grimly.

Grace chewed her lip, lost in thought.

"Grace?"

She looked up. "Sorry. I was just thinking . . ."

"About?"

"Christian, have you ever heard of the Bible Code?"

He hadn't.

"Ambergris actually turned me on to the concept a couple months ago," she said. "He gave me a book on the Bible Code from his father's library. I was reminded of it when Dr. Bowman started talking about Gematria. And then when she told us that 2012 was the end date of the Mayan calendar, the hair stood up on the back of my neck."

"Okay," said Madison. "Lay it on me."

"The Bible Code started with Jewish scholars who were searching the Hebrew text of the Torah for hidden meanings. They came to believe that there are secret codes hidden within the Bible, mostly confined to the first five books."

"Sounds like a lot of hooey."

"Maybe. But one set of Bible Codes has even been published in a scientific journal, *Statistical Science*. The article claimed that the names of famous rabbis, together with their dates of birth and death, were encoded in the book of Genesis."

Genesis?

"Believers in the Bible Code find these codes using equidistant letter sequences, or ELSs. In other words, you take letters at equal intervals in the Bible text you're interested in, and see if they make a meaningful word. Most of these equidistant letter sequences will be nonsense, but some will make up real words."

"Give me an example."

"Okay. Here's an example from the Book of Genesis. Take the first letter *Y* that occurs in the text of Genesis, and then count forward seven letters but ignore any spaces between words. You will find the letter *H*. Count seven more letters and you will come to *W*, and then count a further seven letters to find another *H*. These Hebrew letters spell the name of God, 'YaHWeH,' sometimes also translated 'Jehovah.' At the beginning of Exodus, the next book in the Bible, this same pattern is repeated."

"And people actually believe this?"

Grace sighed. "Just once try and keep an open mind? Just listen for a minute. Bible Code researchers have also found lots of clusters of related words in the same areas of biblical text."

"Like what?"

"Phrases have been found relating to the Holocaust, the Gulf War, the assassinations of Yitzhak Rabin, Anwar Sadat, and John F. Kennedy, and earthquakes in Japan and Los Angeles. Researchers have also found references to biblical characters, like Aaron and Abraham, and religious objects, such as trees in the Garden of Eden."

"Are you suggesting some connection to Dr. Ambergris' e-mail and the year 2012?"

"Well, Bible Code researchers found a code in the Book

of Genesis that supposedly predicts the end of the world. Hidden in the text, they found the words *earth annihilated, it will crumble,* and *comet.* In this same cluster, they found a specific date predicting when this catastrophe will occur."

"When?"

"In the year 2012."

Fifty-six

BEINECKE RARE BOOK AND MANUSCRIPT LIBRARY
YALE UNIVERSITY
NEW HAVEN, CONNECTICUT

The storm hit shortly after dark. Swollen black clouds rode in on restless winds, breaking upon the campus with drenching fury. Sheets of driving rain assaulted the library. Deafening cracks of thunder followed brilliant flashes of lightning.

In the gallery of the Beinecke Library, Dr. Bowman carefully removed the Mayan screenbook from its display case. Holding it delicately in her wrinkled hands, she admired the faded colors of the richly detailed hieroglyphs of the *Popul Vuh.*

Her mind drifted back through years of memories to the expedition she'd made with Maximillian Ambergris to Central America in search of lost Mayan history. Bowman vividly recalled the first time she saw the jungles of Belize.

Their plane had just broken through a thick layer of white clouds when the pilot announced they had entered Belizean airspace. Far below, the Caribbean Sea was a deep azure blue crested with white rolling waves. A short distance offshore, a chain of barrier islands and a long winding coral reef separated the calm coastal waters from the blue-black waves of the Caribbean.

From Bowman's vantage point twenty-five thousand feet above the earth, the jungles of Belize were a vast emerald-green carpet, transected by snaking brown rivers. Ridges of barren mountains pierced the monochrome green canopy of the rain forest.

Hidden beneath the unbroken expanse of lush vegetation, hundreds of Mayan ruins gave silent testament to an ancient civilization. Infrequent dirt roads crossing the pristine jungle were sharp red ocher brushstrokes on a field of deep green.

Bowman allowed her thoughts to linger in the pleasant memory for a moment before returning to the task at hand. Moving with deliberation and care, she carried the fragile, ancient text in her hands to the reading room. She carefully unfolded the accordion pages across the broad expanse of the table. The musty smell of the coarse paper again triggered the vivid memories of the expedition into the jungles of Central America.

The Mayan tomb where they found the *Popul Vuh* had been discovered by a young Mayan boy, Pakal Q'eqchi, and his sister Aluna. The boy had died in the caves beneath the tomb, and Dr. Ambergris learned of the discovery through an acquaintance, a physician from Doctors Without Borders who treated Aluna at the small, primitive medical clinic in her village.

AUGUST 11, 1983
BELIZE, CENTRAL AMERICA
35.13' N, 84.23' W

Deep in the maze of caverns beneath the Temple of the Jaguar, Georgia Bowman and Maximillian Ambergris found a wooden door fitted into the rock wall. Around it, handprints were stamped onto the rock in bright pigments.

Through the doorway was a corridor leading into the tomb's interior. Particles of dust floated in narrow beams of sunlight that pierced the corridor's ceiling and created circles of light on the stone floor.

Bowman cautiously stepped through the door.

"Come on. We'll be careful."

When Ambergris hesitated, she reached back and took his hand.

The air in the cavern was hot and still. On the left wall, an elaborate stucco relief depicted life-sized representations of Mayan priests in ceremonial costumes. Two of them stood in rigid solemnity, holding plumed scepters and flanked by female attendants.

The right wall opened into three narrow vaulted chambers divided by thick partitions. Set in the interior wall of each chamber was a stone tablet covered with finely etched Mayan hieroglyphs. Very little light filtered into the three chambers.

"It's too dark to make these out, but it's very rare to see glyph tablets preserved in this fashion. I can't wait to read these," said Bowman.

Ambergris sneezed loudly. The noise echoed though the interior of the temple.

"Bless me," he said. "It's really dusty in here."

Startled by the noise, a long green lizard darted from one of the alcoves and fled down the corridor into the pyramid's interior.

"Let's go a little farther. The structure looks pretty stable. I don't think we're in any danger of a cave-in," said Bowman.

They crept forward another fifteen feet along the gradually darkening corridor. The distant echo of dripping water was the only sound penetrating the silence. Stucco reliefs of Mayan warriors and priests peered at the pair of scientists from the corridor walls.

"This is getting a little eerie," said Ambergris.

Bowman stopped abruptly.

"What's the—"

"Shhh," whispered Bowman.

She crouched down and stared into the darkness. In the

blackness ahead, a pair of glowing eyes stared back. A wet, wheezing growl emanated from the shadows.

"What is that?"

Bowman began to slowly back up.

"Slowly. Move very slowly."

As they inched slowly backward, a shape emerged from the darkness and stopped just at the edge of their vision.

"Keep moving," whispered Bowman.

A large, muscular jaguar stepped into view. Reflecting the meager sunlight, the jaguar's eyes shone like gold in the dark passageway. Long and sleek, its pelt was a light brown marked with a distinctive rosette pattern. The predator weighed at least two hundred pounds and stood three feet tall at the shoulder.

Oh, shit.

The jaguar bared its sharp, curved teeth. Its tail slashed angrily from side to side.

"Keep your head down. Don't make eye contact," hissed Bowman. "No sudden movements. Just back out slowly."

Ambergris didn't reply. His heart pounded in his ears. Adrenaline surged through his body. The jaguar opened its jaws and snarled aggressively.

"Nice kitty," pleaded Bowman.

The jaguar hesitated for a moment, its whiskers twitching. Then it began to trot down the corridor toward them, ears flattened against its head. The jaguar's claws clicked on the stone floor. Its rumbling growl grew louder.

Ambergris started to panic. His breathing was quick and shallow. The muscles in his stomach clenched involuntarily.

"Go, go!" he urged. His backward pace quickened, pushing Bowman along behind him. She started stumbling, trying to keep her balance.

The jungle cat froze in a low crouch. Its eyes narrowed, glaring at the intruders. The jaguar opened its powerful jaws and roared: a high-pitched, throaty scream that echoed down the corridor.

Fifty-seven

"Would you be interested in getting a shot that prevents cancer? What about a pill to cure diabetes or heart disease? Or an injection that adds twenty extra years to your life?"

Flavia Veloso, speaking with clearly articulated words and careful pronunciation, wore the television reporter's uniform—bright, solid colors and an appropriately professional smile.

"Questions like these, and scores of others just like them, will be discussed at the Ninth Annual International Biogenetics Conference that begins in just two days here at the Millennium Tower convention center in lower Manhattan. Over three hundred of the world's leading scientists in the fields of genetics, bioinformatics, and human genomics will gather here to announce breakthrough discoveries and to discuss cutting-edge research."

The camera pulled back for a wider shot.

"Behind me is the Millennium Tower, where the International Biogenetics Conference will take place."

Flavia made a sweeping gesture with her right arm.

"The Millennium Tower is also the home of Triad Genomics, a global biotech conglomerate that has made billions in the genetics revolution. In June of 2000, scientists at Triad Genomics triumphantly announced they had won the race to decipher the human genome. In mapping out the three-point-two billion units of our DNA, geneticists sparked a firestorm of discovery and ushered in a new age of science."

Flavia brushed away a silky strand of hair that danced across her face in the breeze. She looked straight into the camera.

"Triad Genomics, and legions of other biotech companies around the globe, claim that the genetics revolution offers boundless potential to humanity, ranging from discovering cures for diseases like cancer and Alzheimer's to dramatically extending the human life-span and choosing the genes of our children. The genomic revolution is changing the way we see ourselves and all life on planet earth."

Flavia's image was replaced by video footage of a small crowd of protesters holding signs and placards. Her voice continued in the background.

"But the genetics revolution has also created a firestorm of controversy. Many people, like this group protesting the Biogenetics Conference in a show of opposition to stem cell research, believe that scientists are now playing God. In their view, human DNA is sacred, a special province of the divine, that should be off limits to human tampering."

On the screen, video footage taken that morning showed Grace Nguyen approaching the group of protesters. Flavia continued to narrate.

"In the Bible, verse 16:18 of the Book of Proverbs says that 'pride goes before destruction.' Earlier today, a heated disagreement between opponents of the genomic revolution and a geneticist from Triad Genomics turned into an ugly confrontation."

An edited version of the encounter between Grace and the protesters unfolded in vivid detail. As Grace approached the Millennium Tower, a young female protester, holding a large sign with small hands, gave voice to her convictions.

"Stop stem cell research now!"

On camera, Grace's face reddened with anger as she approached.

"You're blocking my way."

Flavia's voice continued. "Dr. Grace Nguyen of Triad Genomics verbally assaulted this young protester early this morning outside the Millennium Tower."

Grace walked directly toward the protester.

"We're here to protect the unborn, those who can't protect themselves!"

"How nice for you. Now step out of my way."

Grace squared off with the protester. Her eyes narrowed and her hands clenched into fists.

"People like me? Listen to me, you ignorant girl."

The camera angle shifted.

"Don't you dare say another word to me."

The young woman shrank from Grace's burst of anger.

"Now step out of my way before I knock you to the ground."

The young woman lowered her sign, looked dejectedly at the ground at her feet, and moved to the side. Without uttering another word, Grace walked defiantly through the small crowd of protesters.

The video footage was replaced with a tight shot of Flavia Veloso's solemn face.

"A sad display of rage and arrogance," said Flavia. "It has been said that when we see ourselves as the creators of life, we lose our reverence for life. Perhaps nowhere has this loss of reverence been more evident than this morning in lower Manhattan. This is Flavia Veloso, reporting from outside the Millennium Tower."

Within an hour, Flavia's report was picked up by the national media. Across the country, millions watched as Grace Nguyen verbally attacked the young protester. In living rooms from Los Angeles to New York, righteous anger flared and activists began to mobilize.

Fifty-eight

Lost in her memories, Dr. Bowman stared vacantly out the window of the reading room. The lighting flashed almost continually, creating a strobelike effect against the dark backdrop of the surrounding buildings.

In her mind's eye, Maximillian Ambergris stumbled and fell, landing heavily on his right shoulder. He rolled onto his back and turned just as the jaguar burst out from the doorway, running full speed directly at him.

Before Ambergris could react, the jaguar was almost upon him. Ambergris threw his arms in front of his face and pulled his knees up toward his chest.

The jaguar was a blur of motion.

Ambergris squeezed his eyes shut and yelled out in terror. With a rumbling snarl, the jaguar leapt over the quivering form of Dr. Ambergris, its back claws raking the skin on his forearms.

The jaguar bounded down the corridor and disappeared into the shadows.

For a moment time was suspended. Slowly, Ambergris' brain began to comprehend that the jaguar hadn't attacked him. He exhaled slowly, letting out a deep sigh of relief. His arms and legs felt like rubber. Ambergris let his body collapse, lying spread-eagled on the cool stone floor.

Bowman ran to Ambergris' side, kneeling down beside him.

"Are you okay? Are you hurt?"

Ambergris took inventory of his aches and pains.

"I think I'm okay," he said. "Twisted my ankle and banged up my shoulder pretty good."

Ambergris turned his arms to get a clear view of the outer side of his forearms. His hands shook. Four narrow cuts sliced into each arm.

"Caught me with his back claws, but the cuts aren't very deep," he observed.

Ambergris rolled into a sitting position and put his head in his hands, trying to calm his nervous system. An adrenaline storm still raged in his body.

"Wow, that'll sure get your heart pumping!" he said, quickly and loudly. "I've never seen a jaguar in the wild. It was so *fast*! Did you see how fast it moved? It was like one of those dreams where you try to run but your feet feel like they're stuck in molasses. I thought I was a goner for sure! And good Lord, did you see those teeth?"

Bowman eyed Ambergris curiously.

His shirt collar poked up haphazardly and his hair stuck out in several different directions. A streak of black dirt ran down the side of Ambergris' face and several leaves were stuck in his hair. There was a wild, elated look in his eyes.

Fear and tension drained from Bowman's body and she began to giggle. Ambergris grinned.

"I just remembered something. Did you really say 'nice kitty' back there?" he said.

Bowman giggled louder.

"You aren't a cat person, are you?" he asked. Bowman's laughter was contagious and soon they were both giggling hysterically.

When the laughter finally subsided, Bowman and Ambergris investigated the chamber that the jaguar had taken as its lair. Inside, they found the small body of a young boy. In his pocket were several Belizean twenty-dollar bills and a tiny jade carving.

"Now we know what happened to Pakal Q'eqchi," said Ambergris.

Clutched in his left hand, Pakal held a faded Mayan text.

The *Popul Vuh*.

A tear slid down Georgia Bowman's face and fell onto the marble floor of the reading room in the Beinecke Library. Her fingers traced the edge of the Mayan text.

Engrossed in her memories, Bowman failed to notice the dark shadow that moved silently across the floor of the Beinecke Library reading room. Rain pelted against the window. Outside, the storm raged, casting jagged bolts of lightning against the earth and howling with terrible fury.

Fifty-nine

LILY'S MOTOR LODGE
NEW HAVEN, CONNECTICUT

Much to their disappointment, the Colony Inn Bed and Breakfast had no rooms available. In fact, advised the plump clerk at the reception desk, Madison and Grace were likely to have a difficult time finding a room at all. The West Haven Apple Festival had begun that day and attracted families from across New England, filling most of the available hotels and motels in the area.

Soaked from the thunderstorm howling outside, Grace was on her last nerve when they finally found a vacancy at Lily's Motor Lodge several blocks from campus. The faded sign in front of the motel advertised *Free cable!* and *New Management!* for the bargain price of only $34.95 per night.

Madison paid cash for the room and in return received a single silver key attached to a bright yellow plastic square emblazoned with their room number: lucky 13. He led a wet and irritated Grace up the concrete steps to their room overlooking the asphalt parking lot. After three attempts, Madison managed to unlock the door.

The small room smelled musty, and held only one queen-sized bed, covered with a threadbare wool blanket and dingy white linens. A boxy air-conditioning unit rattled in the window. Plastic sunflowers in a vase on the nightstand were apparently intended to give Lily's Motor Lodge that cozy New England "B&B" feel.

The expression on Grace's face spoke volumes.

"Hey, at least it's clean," said Madison.

The word "clean" was still lingering on his tongue when Madison caught a glimpse of something small and black with lots of legs darting across the carpet to seek refuge beneath the battered dresser. Fortunately, Grace failed to notice the presence of their tiny new roommate.

Madison retrieved two threadbare towels from the bathroom, threw one to Grace, and tried in vain with the other to dry his wet clothes and hair.

"We need to call Quiz," he said, reaching for the rotary-dial phone. "See what's been happening at Triad Genomics."

"Go ahead and call him. I'm getting out of these wet clothes," said Grace, padding across the worn green carpet toward the adjoining bathroom.

Madison watched her as she walked away, then picked up the phone and dialed Quiz's number. Quiz answered his cell phone on the first ring.

"Yello."

"Quiz, it's Christian."

"WHERE THE HELL HAVE YOU BEEN?"

Madison yanked the phone away from his ear.

"Take it easy. It's a long story. This will take a minute to tell you."

Madison gave Quiz the condensed version of the confrontation with Crowe, their exploration of Ambergris' brownstone, and their conversations with Dr. Bowman.

Quiz let out a low whistle.

"I knew something wasn't right," said Quiz. "And no one here has mentioned a peep about Dr. Ambergris. Why are they keeping this under wraps?"

"I'm not sure, but I have some suspicions. What happened with the security lockdown?"

"The lockdown was released in the afternoon. Must have been after you and Grace escaped from the building. They told us it was just a security drill."

Madison thought for a moment.

Grace returned from the bathroom. She had shed her clothes and was wrapped in a white bathrobe. Her dark silky hair was damp. As she sat on the bed beside Madison, her robe parted slightly, revealing an expanse of tanned skin and the round curve of a small breast.

Grace caught his roving eyes. "Eyes on your own paper," she said.

"Christian, are you there?" asked Quiz.

"Yeah. Sorry." He forced his thoughts back to the conversation. "There's something else I haven't told you."

Madison told Quiz about the strange phone call and bomb threat.

"Do you think it's for real?" asked Quiz.

"No way to know for sure. But whoever it was, they got a call through the security lockdown. That makes me believe we have to take it seriously."

"What are you going to do? We have to do something."

"I know. We need to find some answers and then go to the police. And if we come up empty, I can call in a bomb threat to the NYPD or the FBI a few hours before the conference is scheduled to begin. I know enough details about the conference and the Millennium Tower that they'll have to take me seriously."

"Why don't we call the cops now? Or the FBI?"

"I thought about that. But they might sweep the building for explosives and come up with nothing. The police might decide it was a hoax. Then there's nothing to stop these people from smuggling a bomb into the Millennium Tower just before the conference starts."

"I guess so . . ."

"Plus, we still have some time before the conference begins. It's apparent that Giovanni and Crowe haven't told the authorities about Ambergris' murder. The last thing we need right now is for the FBI to start hunting us. Not when we still have a chance to find out what's going on and gather enough evidence to show that Grace had nothing to do with Ambergris' murder."

"What should I do?" asked Quiz.

"You need to act like you're completely in the dark about all this. Don't give anyone a reason to be suspicious of you."

"Okay, but I'm not going to like it."

Grace put a hand on Madison's arm. "The journal?"

"Quiz, were you able to read through the rest of Dr. Ambergris' journal?"

Madison tipped the phone away from his ear and gestured to Grace to listen in. She tucked her damp hair behind an ear and leaned in to hear. The soft contours of her left breast pressed against Madison's arm. He struggled to keep his attention focused on the telephone.

"Yes, most of it. You're not going to believe this."

Quiz gave them an abbreviated version of Dr. Ambergris' journal entries. As he recounted Ambergris' rambling discourses, pieces of the puzzle began to snap together in Madison's mind.

"This is unbelievable."

"Ambergris really found a code hidden in human DNA?" asked Quiz.

"Yes," said Grace. "His greatest discovery."

"And tomorrow," said Madison, "we're going to find out what it says."

Sixty

As the morning sun rose over lower Manhattan, the street in front of the Millennium Tower became a combat zone. They arrived by subway, taxi, bicycle, and bus. They had signs, T-shirts, bullhorns, and flyers.

And they were angry.

Zealots, neocons, right-wingers, and pro-lifers faced off against libertarians, angry college students, fringe advocacy groups, and pro-choicers. Verbal taunts turned into shouting matches. Tempers flared.

"What the hell happens to people when they join together in a group?" Zoovas asked the female NYPD officer standing beside him in the lobby of the Millennium Tower.

Sergeant Lori Peters looked out at the sidewalk where uniformed cops were coralling the two opposing camps behind police barricades and yellow tape on opposite sides of the front entrance to the building.

"Mob mentality. Crowd psychology," she said. "People think and act differently in a hostile crowd than they would on their own."

She turned to Zoovas.

"Probably a good thing you called us before this got out of hand. How did you get stuck being the liaison between Triad Genomics and the NYPD for this little party?"

"Liaison? That's a nice way of putting it. Gofer is more like it. My boss isn't very pleased with me at the moment."

Peters made a pouty face. "Don't care for my company?"

Zoovas grinned. "Take it easy, Officer. I'm a married man."

"Well, in that case, how about marching your married ass over to Starbucks and getting us some coffee?"

Zoovas chuckled at his former partner. "As I recall, I always got the coffee when we rode together."

"Tell you what," she said. "You fetch it and I'll pay."

The radio clipped to Zoovas's belt squawked.

"Mr. Zoovas. Report, please."

Zoovas rolled his eyes. "Speak of the devil."

Zoovas hoisted the radio to his face and replied.

"NYPD is setting up police barricades. They're in the process of cordoning off a section of the sidewalk for the protesters. And another section for the anti-protesters."

"Anti-protestors?" said Crowe with a snort.

"Well, what would you call them?"

Crowe ignored the question. "Things still tense?"

"They've calmed down a little. Policemen with guns tend to have that effect on people."

"Who's in charge for NYPD?"

"Sergeant Peters."

"Peters is the ranking officer on the scene?"

"Yes."

"How many cops?"

"Five. Six including Peters."

"Okay. I want you down there with the cops for now. You're the point person to deal with the NYPD. The lawyers are telling us we can't have the crowd dispersed if they don't break any laws. Free speech, freedom of assembly, and all that bullshit."

"Spoken like a true patriot," said Zoovas in a whisper to Peters.

"Understood," he said into the radio.

"Keep me informed, Mr. Zoovas."

Sixty-one

Madison and Grace rounded the corner of the Yale Law School building, heading toward the Beinecke Rare Book and Manuscript Library. The sun was still low on the horizon. The air was rich with the smell of morning.

Grace yawned, covering her mouth with a small hand. Her back was sore from sleeping on the lumpy mattress at Lily's Motor Lodge, and the muscles of her legs ached from the physical exertion of the previous day.

Madison and Grace had slept little, lying side by side in the uncomfortable bed discussing the astounding possibilities of the Genesis Code, trading tearful memories of Dr. Ambergris, and each of them for reasons of their own trying to ignore the strong chemistry between them.

Madison had almost succeeded in falling asleep, lying next to Grace on the uncomfortable mattress, when she abruptly broke the dark silence.

"I never even gave her a name," said Grace in a strained voice.

Madison listened for a moment to the rhythm of her breathing, watching in silhouette the steady rise and fall of Grace's chest as she stared at the ceiling.

"Never gave who a name?"

"My daughter," she said.

Madison's breath caught in his throat.

"When?" asked Madison.

"When I was an undergrad. I had only been dating the guy for a few months. After I told him I was pregnant, I never heard from him again."

She paused.

"It's strange to hear myself say that word—daughter. She only lived for a few minutes after she was born," said Grace.

She began to cry.

"I guess I tried not to think of her as a real, whole person. She should have had a name. I should have given her a name."

"Grace, it's okay. You have nothing to feel guilty about. You were coping as best you could."

She began to weep.

Madison struggled to find the right words to comfort her. His mind was blank. He could think of nothing that didn't sound trite or hollow. Finally, he just reached out in the darkness, took Grace in his arms, and held her as she cried.

"Something's wrong," said Madison, stopping suddenly.

Stripes of red light flickered on the stones, wood carvings, and stained-glass medallion windows of the Sterling Law Building.

"Look," said Grace, pulling on his sleeve.

In front of the Beinecke Library, an ambulance and police cars were parked at haphazard angles, their sirens spinning silently. A young woman wandered aimlessly around the stone terrace in front of the library.

"Oh, no," said Grace, covering her mouth.

"Come on," said Madison, taking her hand.

They quickly covered the distance to the terrace. Grace recognized the young woman—she had manned the reception desk the previous evening.

"What happened, Jessica?" Grace asked, reading her name from the small name tag pinned to Jessica's denim shirt.

"It's just awful," said Jessica. A wave of dark hair highlighted with red streaks nearly covered her red-rimmed eyes. A tiny diamond poked out from the side of her nose.

"Dr. Bowman is dead. The police said it looked like a

burglary. Dr. Bowman must have surprised them in the act. They shot her. And looted the gallery. Took everything— the Gutenberg Bible, the *Popul Vuh* . . ."

Grace's face went pale.

Jessica peered closely at Grace.

"Wait a minute. Didn't I see you on TV last night?"

"What . . ."

Jessica looked back and forth between Grace and Madison. "And weren't you two here late last night with Dr. Bowman?"

A beat of silence.

"Well, yes," said Grace. "But she was fine when we left her."

Jessica started toward the revolving door. "Wait right here. The police are going to want to talk to you."

Madison grasped Grace's arm. "Grace, I have a bad feeling about this . . ."

She nodded quickly. "Let's get out of here."

They turned and began walking quickly away from the library. When they were halfway across the Beinecke Plaza, a shout rang out.

"Hey, you two. Stop right there."

Madison threw a glance over his shoulder. A beefy cop stumbled out of the revolving door, hitched up his belt, and broke into a jog toward them.

Not again.

"Run!"

Grace and Madison sprinted away from the library toward the law school. Madison's twisted ankle screamed in protest. The fat cop ran after them, yelling into his radio as he lumbered across the granite plaza.

Sixty-two

Grace walked down the jetway connecting Delta Flight 613 to the terminal at O'Hare International Airport. Madison trailed just behind her.

The flight to Chicago had been packed, full of business commuters toting briefcases and laptops, jetting to the Windy City from New York.

Grace checked her watch. It read 10:42 A.M.

After fleeing from the police at the Beinecke Library, Madison and Grace quickly decided that remaining in New Haven was probably not the wisest course of action. Their only other lead was Dr. Bowman's suggestion that Dr. Alberto Vasquez at the University of Chicago might prove to be a valuable resource.

Dr. Vasquez had reluctantly agreed to a meeting once he learned that Grace and Madison worked with Dr. Ambergris, and that Dr. Bowman had suggested they speak with him. After Vasquez extended an invitation to visit him at the Field Museum of Natural History, Madison booked them on the morning shuttle to Chicago.

Rushing through the terminal, Grace found herself scanning the crowd for threatening faces. The incident at the Beinecke Library had left her more shaken than she'd initally realized. Fear and paranoia haunted her thoughts. A cold lump had taken up residence in the pit of her stomach.

Her eyes welled up with tears.

Madison caught the look in her eyes and saw that Grace was struggling with her emotions. He reached out and took her hand.

"I could use a toothbrush. How about you?"

Grace smiled through her tears, but the tension in her face remained.

"And some deodorant," said Grace, pinching her nose.

Gripping her hand tightly, Madison led Grace through baggage claim, out the automatic doors, and toward a long line of yellow taxicabs.

Sixty-three

THE FIELD MUSEUM OF NATURAL HISTORY
CHICAGO, ILLINOIS

The African bull elephant, its trunk raised in alert, stood proudly in the center of the Stanley Field Hall in the Field Museum of Natural History. Enormous ivory tusks jutted from its upper jaw, each the length of a man. A leathery gray hide stretched taut over sinewy muscle. With coal-black eyes, it silently surveyed the small knots of tourists meandering across the marble floor toward the museum's exhibit halls.

In the distance, at the south end of the hall, a pack of wide-eyed schoolchildren craned their necks upward to gaze in fear and awe at the bottomless eye sockets and razor-sharp teeth of an enormous *Tyrannosaurus rex* skeleton.

"There," said Grace, pointing toward the east end of the Stanley Field Hall.

Red silk banners, draped across iron grillwork, rippled and flowed from the second-floor balcony to the marble floor of the rotunda. The facade of an ancient Mayan temple, partially obscured by snaking vines and deep green foliage, framed a set of double doors leading to the special exhibit area directly across from the museum's main entrance.

Hand-sculpted from Styrofoam and meticulously painted,

the ancient ruin appeared completely authentic. Illuminated by theatrical lighting, a massive sign above the faux temple announced the exhibit's title:

MYSTERIES OF THE ANCIENTS

Barring entry to the exhibit, a red velvet rope drooped between two metal stanchions in front of the double doors.

"That must be Dr. Vasquez," said Grace, pointing.

A silver-haired man in a tweed blazer was speaking to a small group of college students assembled near the entrance to the exhibit. He gestured wildly as he spoke, jabbing at the air with a fountain pen.

Madison and Grace skirted around the group and parked themselves against the wall within earshot of Dr. Vasquez's talk.

"The consensus view of modern anthropology," said Dr. Vasquez, "is that modern man emerged in Africa approximately one hundred thousand years ago, spread outward into Asia as a primitive hunter-gatherer, and migrated into Europe some thirty-five thousand years ago. He started farming around the end of the last Ice Age, about 8000 BC, and began building cities a few thousand years later. But—"

"There's always a but," said a young coed.

Laughter rippled through the group.

Vasquez smiled. "Quite. And the 'but' in this case is this: just because scientists have reached a consensus does not necessarily mean that they have reached the truth."

Vasquez retrieved his leather backpack from the floor at his feet, opened it, and withdrew a white human skull. A ragged hole on the crown of the skull suggested that the life of this particular *Homo sapiens* had met with an untimely end. He held it up for everyone to see.

"Most college textbooks on anthropology categorically state that the first modern humans appear in the fossil record about a hundred thousand years ago. But this claim, that no anatomically modern humans existed prior to a hundred thousand years ago, is contradicted by numerous finds."

Dr. Vasquez paused and contemplated the skull.

"John—heads up . . ."

Without warning, Vasquez tossed the skull like a softball at a male student in the group. Startled, John managed to raise his hands in time to catch the flying fossil.

"Nice catch," said Dr. Vasquez.

John grinned nervously. He held the skull at arm's length as if it might bite.

"Now pay attention," said Dr. Vasquez. "A human skull fragment was unearthed at Vertesszollos, Hungary, which carbon-dated to between two hundred fifty thousand and forty-five thousand years ago. Two skeletons found in England, at Ipswich and Galley Hill, and a human jaw and paleoliths found at Moulin Quignon in France, were carbon-dated as at least three hundred thousand years old."

Dr. Vasquez saw that he had captured the group's attention. He noticed Grace and Madison standing next to the wall and smiled.

"A human footprint was discovered at Terra Amata, France, that dates back four hundred thousand years," said Dr. Vasquez. "This obviously suggests that modern man was in Europe more than a hundred thousand years before he was supposed to have left Africa.

"Even Louis Leakey, whose towering reputation and famous African discoveries serve as the bedrock for much of the consensus view, reported finds of human skull fragments and paleoliths in Kenya, and in the Olduvai Gorge in Tanzania, dated between four hundred thousand and seven hundred thousand years ago. Astoundingly, the clear implications of these finds have been ignored. The consensus view holds that since these incredible discoveries contradict the established view of human evolution, they *must* be misdated or inaccurate."

Vasquez called out to Grace and Madison.

"Please, join us," he said, waving them over.

"The evidence gets even more interesting," said Vasquez, as Madison and Grace joined the group.

"If we look closely, we begin to see cracks in the foundation of the consensus view," said Dr. Vasquez. "Consider the existence of a fossil record suggesting the existence of modern humans *one million years ago!*"

One million years ago?

"An anatomically modern human skull was discovered in Buenos Aires and was carbon-dated at between one million and one-point-five million years old. Eoliths at Monte Hermoso, Argentina, are believed to be between one and two-point-five million years old. A human tooth at Trinil in Java was dated at one to one-point-nine million years old."

John was incredulous. "I'm sorry, but are you suggesting that modern humans were around over a million years ago?"

Dr. Vasquez smiled.

"I'm not suggesting anything. Not yet, anyway. I'm just asking you to consider the evidence with an open mind. These discoveries raise some very interesting questions, don't they?"

He jabbed in the air with his fountain pen.

"Followed to their logical conclusion, these findings would seem to suggest that our entire view of human evolution is remarkably off base."

He paused.

"They would seem to suggest that humans have been around for a very, very long time."

Dr. Vasquez addressed the young man holding the skull. "John, could you toss our friend back to me, please?"

John hefted the skull and pitched it in Dr. Vasquez's direction. Dr. Vasquez deftly snatched it out of the air and held the fossil aloft in a macabre display.

"This interesting skull is actually a replica of a find which is even more staggering than the ones I've already articulated. According to current thinking, the ancestors of modern humanity, the hominids, diverged from apes somewhere between five and eight million years ago. The Miocene Period, an extremely ancient geological period, began some twenty-five million years ago. Consensus science says that no human beings, in any form, walked the planet during the Miocene."

Dr. Vasquez patted the skull and grinned.

"But our friend here is a replica of a skull that was discovered with a *Homo sapiens* skeleton at Table Mountain, California, that dates back *at least thirty-three million years ago*. A human skeleton found in Switzerland has been carbon-dated to *thirty-eight million years ago.*"

"Thirty-eight million years ago?" asked John. "That's almost as old as the dinosaurs. How can that be possible?"

Dr. Vasquez held up a hand.

"Hold on a second. We know that dinosaurs became extinct about sixty-five million years ago. There is no fossil record of dinosaurs, not even the slightest trace, more recent than sixty-five million years old. Clearly there is no way that humans could have evolved on this planet more than sixty-five million years ago. Right?"

"Why do I have the feeling you're going to tell us otherwise?" asked John.

Dr. Vasquez held up a finger.

"One. In 1938, Professor W. G. Burroughs, head of the Department of Geology at Berea College, Kentucky, reported the discovery of human footprints 'sunk into the horizontal surface of an outcrop of hard massive gray sandstone' at the O. Finnel farm in Kentucky. Dr. C. W. Gilmore, curator of Vertebrate Paleontology at the Smithsonian, confirmed the discovery. The footprints were made on what was once a sandy beach."

Vasquez held up a second finger.

"Two. In 1960, H. L. Armstrong wrote in the prestigious scientific journal *Nature* about fossilized human footprints found near Glen Rose, Texas. Dinosaur footprints were found in the same strata."

He held up a third finger.

"Three. In 1968, a fossil collector named William J.

Meister split open a block of shale near Antelope Springs, Utah, and found a fossilized human *shoe* print. There were trilobite fossils in the same stone. Dr. Clarence Coombs of Columbia Union College and geologist Maurice Carlisle of the University of Colorado confirmed that the find was a genuine fossil."

A fourth finger joined the previous three.

"And four. In 1983, the *Moscow News* reported the discovery of a fossilized human footprint next to the fossil footprint of a three-toed dinosaur in the Turkmen Republic, part of what was then the southwestern USSR."

Dr. Vasquez paused.

"What do these four discoveries have in common? They all date back well beyond the watershed of dinosaur extinction. Some of them date back very, very far. The Turkmen print is from the Jurassic Period. The Meister's shoe print is Triassic. And the Kentucky find dates back to the Carboniferous, which makes it more than two hundred and eighty-six million years old."

He smiled.

"Clear evidence that human beings walked the earth two hundred and eighty-six million years ago."

Sixty-four

THE FIELD MUSEUM OF NATURAL HISTORY
CHICAGO, ILLINOIS

As the students dispersed, Grace and Madison approached the professor.

"Dr. Vasquez? I'm Grace Nguyen. This is Christian Madison. We spoke on the phone?"

Dr. Vasquez tugged open the flap on his leather backpack and slid the skull inside.

"Yes, of course," said Vasquez.

"We're interested in learning more about the ancient Maya. Dr. Bowman suggested that you would be an excellent resource."

"Joshua Ambergris' father and I were colleagues, you know. Joshua developed quite an interest in the Maya and other ancient cultures this past year. His enthuisiasm must be contagious."

Madison forced a smile.

"I assume you are interested in the same lines of inquiry that Joshua pursued?" asked Vasquez.

Grace and Madison exchanged a glance.

"Yes, we are," said Grace.

"I thought you might," said Vasquez. "Actually, I believe that our new exhibit may be of great interest to you. It is titled 'Mysteries of the Ancients.' "

Sixty-five

THE FIELD MUSEUM OF NATURAL HISTORY
CHICAGO, ILLINOIS

"I've developed a reputation for working at the fringes of my field," said Vasquez, as he led them through the set of double doors beneath a sign that read:

MYSTERIES OF THE ANCIENTS

"I've always had a keen interest in the more unconventional schools of thought in archaeology and anthropology. I think that most people are far too willing to blindly accept whatever version of facts are spoon-fed to them by mainstream academia."

Madison raised an eyebrow.

"The University of Chicago and the Board of Trustees of the Field Museum tolerate me provided that I don't publicly discuss the more radical notions I've explored. They don't want to be embarrassed, you see," said Vasquez.

Beyond the set of double doors granting entrance to the Mysteries of the Ancients was a darkened hallway about forty feet long. Along each wall, recessed display cases housed relics from thousands of years of human history. Overhead spotlights illuminated each artifact.

"According to them, such unconventional theories are the exclusive domain of conspiracy theorists and crackpots. Not an appropriate line of inquiry for a proper scholar."

Toward the far end of the hall the room became a jungle. The design was elaborate, even by world-class-museum standards. The artificial tropical jungle was filled with towering trees, rising into the darkness above. Branches overhead were densely covered with exotic plants and tied together with liana vines.

"This is amazing," said Grace.

On either side of a raised central walkway was the jungle floor—a bright green carpet of broad ferns on a thin layer of fallen leaves, seeds, fruits, and branches. Simulated sunlight filtered through the dense canopy above. The howls of monkeys and screeches of macaws echoed through the air.

Madison shook his head. "I don't recall field trips to any museums like this when I was a kid."

"Thank you," said Vasquez. "Dr. Madison, these days museum exhibits have to pack a punch to draw the crowds. Sterile displays behind glass just can't compete with the multimedia entertainment of the modern world. To draw in a fickle public, museums are becoming entertainment venues as well as centers of learning."

Ahead were the crumbling remnants of a moss-covered faux stone wall, barely visible under dense jungle foliage. Behind it, the entrance to a cave yawned like a black hole in the jungle.

"Perhaps a bit overdramatic, but overall a nice effect," Vasquez said with a chuckle. "The ancient Maya believed that caves were entrances to Xibalba, the underworld," said Vasquez.

He led them through the cavern's wide mouth.

Vasquez smiled.

"Our cave, however, leads only to the first gallery of the exhibit."

The first room was a wide gallery ringed by tall glass display cases containing fully articulated human skeletons. The room was dark. Narrow beams of light illuminated the grinning skeletons from above in pools of ghostly white light. The effect was quite dramatic.

"Before our ancestors invented the written word," said Vasquez, "early humans, like the ones in this room, passed information from one generation to the next by telling stories. Each new generation learned the accumulated knowledge of those that lived before through the oral histories told to them as children. Do you know what the scholars of today call those oral histories?"

"Myths," said Grace.

"Precisely. Myths and legends. Modern scholarship doesn't consider myths and legends to be historical evidence. References to human experience prior to the invention of writing around five thousand years ago are largely omitted from what we consider history."

Vasquez looked around the gallery, pleased with his work.

"But there are many examples of myths we dismissed as fantasy that were later proven to be entirely accurate. The city of Troy from Homer's *Iliad* is one example. Homer based the *Iliad* on stories he was told as a child. Until the late nineteenth century, scholars dismissed Troy as a mythical city, a figment of Homer's imagination. But in 1871, the German explorer Heinrich Schliemann followed the geographical clues contained in the *Iliad* and discovered the remains of the city of Troy in western Turkey, exactly where Homer had said it was."

"That's one of the problems with the modern world," said Madison. "There's so much information out there that we tend to specialize in very narrow areas of expertise. As a geneticist, I'm completely ignorant when it comes to ancient history or archaeology. No one can be an expert in everything, so we never see any synthesis across different disciplines."

"I've got another example," said Vasquez. "Before British archaeologist Sir Arthur Evans came along, historians thought that the Minoan civilization on Crete existed only in legend. Then Evans excavated the remains of a highly advanced ancient culture on Crete, now firmly identified as that of the Minoans."

Vasquez led them toward a door across the room.

"Dr. Ambergris believed," he said, "that many ancient myths show evidence of advanced knowledge that should have been unknown to humans at that point in our development. Myths that can be found in a wide range of ancient cultures that presumably had absolutely no contact with one another."

"What sort of advanced knowledge?" asked Madison.

"This line of thought was actually the inspiration for this exhibit. I'll give you some examples," said Vasquez, leading them into the next room.

"Ancient Egypt."

The recreation was tremendous in its scale. A winding walkway snaked across the room through dunes of desert sand. Enormous scale models of Egyptian pyramids from the Giza Plateau rose high above their heads. Columns and obelisks rose from beneath the sand. Near the center of the room, a broad stone plaza displayed statues of Isis and Ra, an elaborately decorated sarcophagus, and a complete Egyptian mummy.

Dr. Vasquez stopped and turned to face Grace and Madison.

"Are you familiar with the precession of the equinoxes?"

Grace's eyes grew wide. "As a matter of fact, we were recently discussing that very topic. As I understand it, precession is basically the wobble of the earth as it spins. Once every twenty-five thousand years or so."

Madison felt a strong sense of déjà vu as he recalled their conversations with Dr. Bowman about the Mayan calendar and its prediction that the current Age of Man would end in 2012.

"Good. Then you may also know that precession through sixty degrees along the ecliptic takes 4,320 years."

"I'll take your word for it," said Grace.

"It does—4,320 is a very significant number, astronomically speaking."

"Okay."

"What if I told you that the number 4,320, and derivations of that number such as 43,200, 432,000, and 4,320,000, also appear in ancient mythological accounts throughout the world?"

"I'd say you were crazy," said Madison.

"But it's true," responded Vasquez. "The number 432,000 occurs in both the Babylonian and Christian great flood stories. In the Babylonian story, there were ten kings who lived very long lives from creation to the time of the great flood—a total of 432,000 years.

"In the biblical account, there were ten patriarchs between Adam and Noah, who also lived long lives. Noah was 600 years old at the time of the landing of the Ark on the mountains of Ararat. The total years add up to 1,656, or 86,400 weeks. Half the number of weeks is 43,200."

"I find this very difficult to believe," said Madison.

"Your closed-mindedness does not become you, Dr. Madison. Variations of the number 43,200 pop up in other mythological belief systems too. Viking Ediotic poems found in Iceland tell the story of the Day of Ragnorook, the Doomsday of the Gods. Eight hundred Divine Warriors will come out of each of the 540 Doors of Valhalla. Eight hundred times 540 equals 432,000.

"In India, the number of years assigned to a Great Cycle, or Mahayuga, of cosmic time is 4,320,000.

"A Chaldean priest, Berossos, writing in Greek around 289 BC, reported that according to Mesopotamian belief,

432,000 years elapsed between the crowning of the first earthly king and the coming of the deluge.

"The Chinese Imperial Library is said to contain a vast work consisting of 4,320 volumes handed down from ancient times," said Vasquez.

Madison shook his head in disbelief.

"Kind of hard to get your mind around, isn't it?" asked Vasquez. "Clearly, these numbers were of great importance to all of these civilizations long before they should have had any advanced knowledge of astronomical concepts like precession. And it was evidently very important to them to communicate these numbers to future generations."

He paused.

"Joshua Ambergris, like his father, wanted to know why," said Vasquez.

He walked over to the scale recreation of the Great Pyramid of Giza.

"Some ancient civilizations, like the Egyptians and the Mayans, also encoded advanced knowledge into their architecture."

"What?" exclaimed Madison. "That isn't possible. I've never heard that."

"This is a scale model of the Great Pyramid of Giza," Vasquez said, pointing.

"The Great Pyramid is gigantic. It weighs about six million tons and covers over thirteen acres. Napoleon's surveyors calculated that the three pyramids on the Giza Plateau contained enough stone to build a wall three meters high by one meter thick around the entire perimeter of France. Now, let's assume that we have measured both the height of the Great Pyramid and the perimeter around its base."

Vasquez gave them the pyramid's dimensions.

"If you divide the pyramid's perimeter by twice the value of its height, you get an interesting result."

"What?" asked Grace.

Madison did the calculation in his head.

"Jesus Christ—3.1415. The value of pi."

"The Egyptians knew about pi?" asked Grace.

"Not according to any textbook or modern-day historian," said Vasquez. "According to the mainstream view taught on every college campus, Archimedes was the first man to calculate pi correctly at 3.14. In the third century BC."

"But this can't be a coincidence," said Madison. "It's statistically impossible. I just can't believe that the ancient Egyptians understood pi and deliberately encoded its value in their architectural calculations."

"Your disbelief does not erase the evidence, Dr. Madison. You can also find advanced mathematics and astronomy encoded in Mayan structures. The Mayan Temple of the Sun, the structure I've recreated as the entrance to this exhibit, is a great example."

Madison again recalled the evidence that the Maya had incorporated an understanding of precession into their Long Count calendar, and used it to calculate the end of the current Age of Man in 2012.

"Let's assume that we've taken the same measurements of the Temple of the Sun that we took of the Great Pryamid of Giza. If you divide the measurement of the perimeter around the base of the temple by four times the value of the temple's height, you get—"

"Pi," finished Madison.

"Precisely. But wait. If you take the temple's perimeter and multiply that number by two, you get a length that is precisely equal to the length of one minute of latitude as measured at the earth's equator."

"I don't believe it," said Grace.

"Do the calculation yourself," said Vasquez. "These structures have been measured thousands of times. The measurements are verifiable. Do the math yourself, and you'll see I'm right."

Grace was speechless.

"Ready for more?"

Grace nodded.

"You'll recall that 4,320 is an important number related to precession. It and its derivations appear in the mythology of many ancient civilizations. Now, if you take the height of the Temple of the Jaguar and multiply it by 43,200, you get 20,796,260 feet, 3,938.685 miles, which is a pretty close estimate of the polar radius of the earth."

"No way."

"Likewise, if you take the temple's perimeter at the base and multiply by 43,200, then you get 130,600,483 feet, or 24,734 miles—a result that is within 170 miles of the true equatorial circumference of the earth. That's a minus-error of only three quarters of a single percent."

Madison struggled to digest what he was hearing.

"This is what Dr. Ambergris was studying," said Vasquez. "Knowledge that our ancient forefathers never should have possessed. Where did it come from? How was it obtained? Joshua Ambergris picked up his father's work where Maximillian left off. He had two questions."

He paused, then stuck up a finger.

"One, how did these relatively primitive ancient cultures, with no contact between them, learn these advanced concepts?"

A second finger joined the first.

"And two, why was it so important to them to preserve this knowledge in their mythology and architecture?"

For a moment, Madison and Grace stood in silence.

"Dr. Ambergris figured it out, didn't he?" asked Madison.

Vasquez smiled.

"Yes, Christian," he said. "I believe he did."

Sixty-six

"The most important revelations are often revealed in giant leaps of sudden insight. Dr. Ambergris made his leap of insight when he read an article one morning in the newspaper," said Vasquez. "The *Washington Post* reported that the U.S. Department of Energy commissioned a study about creating warnings for nuclear waste storage. Nuclear waste will remain deadly to humans for over ten thousand years. The problem they were trying to solve is this: How do you warn future generations, perhaps ten thousand years in the future, that the nuclear waste contained inside is deadly?"

Vasquez paused to let them ponder the issue for a moment, then continued.

"Most likely, the cultures that exist today will be gone in ten thousand years. The languages that we speak today will be incomprehensible ten thousand years in the future. After all, how many people do you know that can speak Sanskrit or read Aramaic? Do you remember how difficult it was in college just to read Shakespeare in the Old English translation?"

Madison took a seat on a wooden bench next to a statue of Osiris.

"Professor Thomas Sebeok, of the University of Indiana, headed the study. Care to guess what he recommended? Sebeok's recommendation was *the placement of large symbolic signs and the creation of a myth and legend,* based on his observation that the oldest known human messages were oral traditions passed down verbally from one generation to the next."

Grace took a seat next to Madison.

"What if Sebeok's ideas had already been employed by ancient humans? Sebeok recommended the placement of large symbolic signs. How about the monolithic stone pyramids and temples of Egypt, China, and Central America?"

Madison nodded, his mind struggling to keep up.

"Sebeok recommended the creation of myths and legends to preserve the knowledge of grave danger," said Vazquez. "How about literally dozens of references in the mythologies of dozens of ancient civilizations to the same advanced mathematical and astronomical concepts?"

But how does this relate to the code Ambergris found hidden in the genome?

Madison had a moment of clarity. The puzzle pieces came together in his mind.

"That's what all of this is about. That's what Dr. Ambergris discovered. Someone in our ancient past went to incredible efforts to send us a warning from tens of thousands, or maybe hundreds of thousands of years ago."

A warning hidden in the mythologies and architecture of humanity's oldest civilization.

Grace felt a sudden chill.

"A warning about what?" she asked.

Sixty-seven

THE FIELD MUSEUM OF NATURAL HISTORY
CHICAGO, ILLINOIS

"Dr. Vasquez, is there anything else you can tell us? Any other pieces of the puzzle?" asked Madison.

"There's one more thing I can show you," said Vasquez. "Let's go into the next room. It's a recreation of the interior of the Mayan Temple of the Sun."

He escorted them through a large door into the next room. Madison was stunned by the sheer size of the gallery.

The ceiling rose fifty feet overhead, supported by mock-ups of wide corbeled arches. Intricate stone carvings of celestial imagery adorned the walls.

Near the doorway, on a waist-high platform, stood the fearsome form of Chac, the Mayan Rain God, chiseled in white stone. In his right hand, Chac brandished a feathered staff adorned with two intertwined serpents coiled along its length.

Xenon floodlights mounted on steel tripods were spaced around the room, pointing inward toward the chamber's principal occupant. A massive stone monument dominated the center of the room.

"Pretty impressive, isn't it?"

The xenon lamps illuminated the twelve-foot-tall Mayan stela, bathing it with an eerie blue light. The stela was covered with a series of glyphs and pictographs.

"Are these Mayan glyphs?" asked Madison.

"Yes and no. They're a hybrid of Mayan and Olmec. The top portion is historical. It says that the city where this stela was discovered was modeled on the original capital of a lost homeland."

"Interesting."

"Dr. Ambergris was most interested in this portion of the heiroglyphs. Look at these lines of text here in the middle."

Vasquez pointed to a line of inscriptions resting on the Mayan symbol for the water goddess, Chalchiutlicue.

"It says, *In the fourth age of man, destruction came in the form of torrential rains and floods.*"

Vasquez moved his finger down to the next sequence of glyphs, adjacent to a carving of the face of Chac, symbolic of the current Mayan Age of Man. His tongue was depicted as an obsidian blade, signaling his need for the nourishment of human blood. Chac's features were wrinkled, representing his advanced age.

"This sequence says: *In the fifth age, there will be a movement of the earth and fire in the heavens and we shall all perish.*"

"The end of the current Age of Man," said Grace. "In 2012."

"And look at this," said Vasquez.

He pointed to a detailed pictograph carved into the stone. It depicted a tall, bearded figure holding a feathered staff. Coiled around the staff were two intertwined serpents.

"Look familiar to you at all?"

Grace considered the image. "It actually looks a lot like the staff of Aesculapius."

Vasquez nodded. "Dr. Ambergris thought so too."

"Who, or what, was Aesculapius?" asked Madison.

"Aesculapius was a Roman physician who was such a skilled healer that he became a god," said Vasquez. "The image of his wooden staff with a snake coiled around it was adopted as the symbol of the medical profession by the American Medical Association."

"But the staff of Aesculapius only had one serpent," said Grace. "This looks a more like the caduceus."

"Exactly what Dr. Ambergris said. The caduceus, which was probably the prototype for the Roman version," said Vasquez. He turned to Madison.

"The caduceus consists of two intertwined serpents encircling a wand or rod. It was carried by Hermes in Greek myths and Mercury in Roman mythology, the messenger of the gods."

The messenger of the gods.

Madison scrutinized the intertwined serpents.

"Remind you of anything else, Grace?" asked Madison.

Grace was struck by a sudden insight.

"It looks like the double helix of DNA," she said.

"Damn right it does."

"My god," said Grace.

"Intertwined serpents are common images in the mythology of ancient cultures," said Vasquez. "They appear everywhere. Ancient China, Egypt, Sumeria. They were also used by the Olmec, the Maya, and the Aztecs."

Madison struggled to fit together the various pieces of this historical puzzle in his mind.

Fossil evidence that humans walked the earth hundreds of thousands, if not millions of years ago.

Evidence of advanced scientific knowledge scattered throughout the writings of our ancient past.

References to advanced scientific knowledge encoded in ancient mythologies and architecture, warnings to future generations.

A coded message hidden in human DNA.

"Dr. Vasquez," asked Madison, "does Mayan mythology tell us what happened to end the previous Ages of Man?"

Sixty-eight

QUIZ'S OFFICE
SUBBASEMENT, MILLENNIUM TOWER
MANHATTAN, NEW YORK

Quiz had completely lost track of time. His stomach growled a reminder that he hadn't eaten since yesterday.

Quiz popped open another Diet Coke and pulled open a bag of chips.

Stuffing a handful of chips in his mouth, Quiz scrolled to the next entry in Dr. Ambergris' journal.

3 April—

These strange common elements of mythology and symbolism have been studied by many of history's most famous scholars, the wisest men of their age, including Aristotle and Nostradamus. The mythologies of many apparently unrelated cultures contain stories of global catastrophes that have wiped out human civilization, leaving only a few survivors to carry on the human race.

In a Sumerian account, King Utnapishtim told Gilgamesh of a decision by the gods to destroy mankind. One of the gods took pity on Utnapishtim and instructed him to build a large boat and put aboard the seed of all living things. A global torrent flooded the earth, wiping out all living things. The parallel with Noah and the flood story of the Bible is unmistakable.

Aztec mythology reveals that a great deluge covered the entire earth and ended the age of the Fourth Sun. Only two human beings survived, who escaped in a huge boat that came to rest on the peak of a tall mountain.

Chinese myths tell of the destruction of mankind when waters rushed upwards with violence and overflowed the earth. Similar accounts appear in the folklore of many cultures.

Stories of a terrible deluge also appear in the Mayan *Popol Vuh*. Even the word "Maya" is revealing.

In Aramaic, the word "Maya" means "water."

Sixty-nine

THE FIELD MUSEUM OF NATURAL HISTORY
CHICAGO, ILLINOIS

"Take a look at these," said Vasquez. At the opposite end of the gallery, four enormous stone slabs stood upright behind a wall of glass.

"What am I looking for?" It appeared to Madison that they were bare stone, painted a dull greenish brown.

"Take a closer look," said Dr. Vasquez.

Madison walked over to the glass. On closer inspection, he realized that the earthy coloration was a thin layer of mold that covered almost the entire surface of each slab.

"Paint," said Dr. Vasquez. "The Olmec and the Maya sometimes used ground-up plant and animal tissues to make colored pigments. There's a bas-relief mural of Chac, the Mayan god of rain and lightning, on these stones. It was found in the Temple of the Jaguar. We had it crated up and shipped here. The surfaces of the slabs are covered by mold that was attracted to the organic compounds in the paint."

Without warning, Vasquez switched off the lights, plunging the chamber into complete darkness.

"Hey, what gives?" asked Madison.

"Just wait," said Vasquez's voice from the darkness.

He turned on an ultraviolet lamp near the center of the room. Instantly an intricate mural sprang into existence on the stone slabs.

"Nice trick," said Grace.

"The UV light picks up the contrasts of the pigments. Unfortunately, I can't take credit for the idea. Archaeologists have been using this technique for years."

On the elaborate mural, Mayan artists had painted a fierce manifestation of Chac seated on a throne. Above him, renditions of stars and constellations portrayed the complex cosmology of the heavens. The constellation of Orion was centered above the throne.

Priests wearing jaguar masks engaged in ritual bloodletting, piercing the tongues and lips of slaves with obsidian blades and long thorns. Offerings of crocodiles, turtles, peccaries, and jaguars were arrayed at Chac's feet. To the left of the throne, a naked young woman, her body painted blue, was stretched over a stone altar. A jaguar priest had torn open her chest with a flint knife and removed her heart, holding it high above his head in sacrificial offering. Within the mural were long lines of Mayan hieroglyphs and dot-and-bar numerals.

"Let me read this to you," said Vasquez. "It says: *The first men were the People of the Serpents who came from the east with their leader Quetzalcoatl, the Serpent of the East, who could cure by laying on hands and who revived the dead. Quetzalcoatl possessed great wisdom and spoke the language of life and the stars.*"

Vasquez moved to another set of hieroglyphs.

"*The First Men were endowed by Quetzalcoatl with great intelligence. They saw far. They succeeded in discovering great wisdom. They examined the four corners of the heavens, the four points of the arch of the sky, and the round face of the earth.*"

Madison arched an eyebrow.

"*Then the Heart of Heaven blew mist in their eyes and clouded their sight. Their eyes were covered and they could see only what was close. In this way, the wisdom and knowledge of the First Men were destroyed.*"

"Sounds a little like the Adam and Eve story in Genesis," said Grace. "Expulsion from the Garden of Eden after eating from the Tree of Knowledge."

"And don't forget who lived in the Tree of Knowledge," said Madison. "A serpent."

Vasquez began reading the next set of hieroglyphs.

"*Quetzalcoatl came to the aid of man after the flood that ended the fourth Age of Man. Together with Xolotl, the twin, he descended into the underworld and retrieved the remains of men killed by the deluge. He milled their bones like corn on a grindstone. Upon it, he released his own blood and wrote in the language of the gods, thus creating the flesh of the current Age of Men.*"

"Quetzalcoatl took the bones of men and regenerated human life," said Madison. "He wrote in the blood of man using the language of the gods. Grace, could this be the origin of the Genesis Code?"

Seventy

The faint murmur of voices echoed from the next room. Crowe paused and listened intently.

Madison. Grace. And another man.

That must be Dr. Vasquez with them.

Crowe stuck a hand inside his blazer and gripped the handle of his 9mm, pulling it from the leather shoulder holster beneath his left arm.

The metal was cold against his fingers.

Crowe crept to the double doors leading to the room where Madison and Grace were engrossed in conversation with Dr. Vasquez. He pushed the door open ever so slightly, peering through the crack to gauge the location and distance to his quarry.

Excellent.

Their backs were turned.

Madison made large gestures in the air with his hands as he talked. Dr. Vasquez stood with a hand on one hip, his head cocked to one side as he listened intently to Madison's speculations.

The lighting in the room was dim and the overhead spots cast a faint blue glow over everything in the gallery. The unsuspecting trio stood no more than sixty feet away.

He mentally repeated the strategic mantra taught to British special forces during combat training.

Observe.

Orient.

Decide.

Act.

Crowe removed a silencer from his breast pocket and screwed it tightly onto the barrel of his 9mm.

Seventy-one

"That's it," said Madison, gesturing wildly at the Mayan stela in excitement. "That's the connection!"

"What, Christian? What is it?" asked Grace.

"All of these cryptic references in ancient mythology. Dr. Ambergris believed that they were attempts by someone in our ancient past to communicate to future mankind from tens of thousands, perhaps hundreds of thousands of years before what we think of as the dawn of civilization. To communicate a warning to us."

"And the Genesis Code?"

"Dr. Ambergris believed that there are many examples in ancient texts and mythologies that seem to refer to DNA and genetics."

He pointed to a pictograph on the stela.

"Two intertwined serpents that resemble the double helix of human DNA. That's what the Genesis Code must be. Another way to send us a message from the distant past. A coded message hidden in our genome that would survive as long as humans survive. Even if the pyramids of Egypt were swept away and our ancient mythologies were forgotten, a message in our DNA would still survive, passed down from generation to generation, awaiting discovery."

His mind churned with the possibilities.

"An encoded message hidden in human DNA, waiting for the time when humanity developed, or should I say regained, the ability to read our own genetic code!"

The thought took his breath away.

"The ultimate secret message. Carried with us within our own bodies until we discovered the means to unlock it."

Seventy-two

Dr. Vasquez placed his hand on Madison's arm. "I have a confession to make," he said. "Even before you phoned, I knew that you would be coming to see me."

Madison tried to conceal his alarm.

"How could you know that?"

"He told me," said Vasquez.

"He?"

"Joshua. Dr. Ambergris."

Grace took a step back. "Dr. Ambergris told you that Christian and I would come to see you?"

"Yes, he did. Joshua told me that one day soon, the two of you might come to see me, asking the same sorts of questions that you have asked me today."

Dr. Vasquez smiled as he stuck his hand into his jacket pocket.

"Joshua asked me to provide you with the answers to your questions."

Vasquez withdrew a small CD-ROM in a plastic cover from his pocket. He leaned forward to hand the disk to Madison.

"He also asked me to give you this."

Suddenly Vasquez's head jerked violently to the side. The disk fell to the floor.

A spray of crimson painted a mist of red across the right side of Grace's face. The muted thump of a silencer barely reached Madison's ears.

Before Madison could react, Vasquez's body fell backward, carried by the momentum of the bullet's impact. His arms hanging limply at his sides, Vasquez fell against the massive Mayan stela, the full weight of his body slamming into the towering monument.

"Goddammit," yelled Crowe from across the room.

Grace's scream split the air. She wiped frantically at the blood on her face.

The stone stela shuddered from the impact of Vasquez's falling body. A cracking, splintering noise echoed from the platform beneath the stela as its weight shifted.

The massive stone began to sway.

Madison reacted without conscious thought, taking Grace by the wrist and yanking her away from the teetering monument. Throwing a backward glance over his shoulder, Madison thought for a moment that the stela would regain its balance. And then it began to fall slowly and gracefully backward, gathering momentum as two tons of carved rock toppled silently toward the marble floor.

"Move!" yelled Madison, dragging Grace by the arm away from the center of the room and shoving her toward the door. Diving to the ground, he lunged across the floor on his hands and knees toward the computer disk that had fallen from Vasquez's lifeless fingers.

The impact of the enormous monument against the marble floor was deafening, thundering through the gallery like the roar of a cannon. The top of the falling stela caught the edge of a tall glass display case, shattering the glass and crushing its wooden frame beneath the stela's tremendous weight.

The stela shattered as it struck the floor, sending spinning slabs of rock hurtling across the smooth marble. Fragments of stone and shards of glass cut through the air, showering the gallery with a storm of debris.

A billowing plume of dust and pulverized stone engulfed the fallen stela like a mushroom cloud from a nuclear explosion. Knocked off their feet by a hail of bits of glass and rock, Madison and Grace fell in a heap on the floor, the backs of their shirts soaked with the blood of a hundred tiny gashes.

Madison twisted in pain, his eyes searching through the cloudy haze in the room for the shooter. In his bloody fingers, Madison clutched the computer disk.

Grace's crumpled body lay still.

Seventy-three

THE FIELD MUSEUM OF NATURAL HISTORY
CHICAGO, ILLINOIS

Madison breathed a deep sigh of relief when Grace finally stirred. Her eyelids fluttered open. She gingerly touched the grape-sized lump on the side of her head with an index finger.

"Come on, Grace," hissed Madison, rising to his feet. "We have to get the hell out of here."

Grace struggled to stand up, cringing against the sharp pain that felt like an army of needles piercing the skin of her back. Fifty feet to the south, Crowe banged open the double doors leading into the gallery.

"Grace!"

Raising his arm, Crowe took aim.

Seventy-four

THE FIELD MUSEUM OF NATURAL HISTORY
CHICAGO, ILLINOIS

Madison and Grace charged forward as Crowe prepared to fire a second shot, reaching the double doors leading to the next hall only an instant before Crowe pulled the trigger. The bullet whined like an angry wasp as it sliced through the air and slammed into the doorframe with a loud crack, mere inches from Grace's head.

As they burst through the dooway into the next room, Grace saw an etched glass sign suspended from the ceiling above.

BABYLON.

Madison's eyes roamed wildly around the large room, searching for an exit. The rectangular exhibit hall was a recreation of the ancient city of Babylon. Along each wall, facades of mock stone created the illusion of stone buildings lining a long street.

Directly ahead, a recreation of the Ishtar Gate rose twenty-five feet into the air, framing the entrance to Processional Way through the center of the imperial city of Nebuchadnezzar, ruler of the second great Babylonian empire. The clay bricks of the gate were painted a vivid blue and decorated with rows of bulls and dragons.

Grace grabbed Madison's hand.

"We can't just leave Dr. Vasquez in there," said Grace. Her voice trembled.

Madison stopped and looked at Grace. The crimson spray of Vasquez's blood on her face had become a smear of dark red. Grace's eyes darted about.

"Grace . . . Dr. Vasquez is dead," said Madison. "He was shot in the head."

She trembled.

"Y-you can't be sure," she stuttered. "What if he's still alive?"

Madison took both of Grace's hands and held them tightly.

"Grace, Dr. Vasquez is dead. I saw it. I'm sure."

A tear ran down her cheek.

"It was Crowe," said Madison. "I saw him at the other end of the hall after he shot Dr. Vasquez. He took another shot at you. He'll be coming after us. We can't stay here."

Grace absently chewed on her bottom lip. She swayed gently on her feet, her expression vacant.

"Come on. I'm going to get us out of here."

He led Grace by the hand through Nebuchadnezzar's gate and onto the cobblestones of Processional Way. As they ran down the avenue, the fog in Grace's mind began to lift.

On the south side of the hall, a scale model of the Temple of Marduk jutted high above the surrounding buildings. A glass display case held a facsimile of Hammurabi's Code carved into a diorite pillar. On the north side of the hall, the biblical Tower of Babel towered above. The great ziggurat was a narrow, stepped tower reaching upward toward heaven.

Grace took deep, ragged breaths as they ran. "Why would Crowe shoot Dr. Vasquez?"

"I don't think Crowe was aiming for Vasquez," said Madison. "He just got in the way."

The imperial palace of Nebuchadnezzar stood at the end of Processional Way. The palace was an impressive stone edifice, guarded by a mock moat and wooden bridge. Two imperial Babylonian guards stood immobile at the foot of the bridge, garbed in leather armor and brandishing sinister-looking weapons, curved blades affixed to long stout poles. Where the entrance to the palace should have been, a pair of doors led into the next exhibit.

"MADISON!" yelled Crowe, his voice ringing out from the Egyptian gallery.

Madison and Grace ran toward the imperial palace, skirting around a large etched-glass map of Hammurabi's Babylon of the Old Kingdom. Eight feet tall and ten feet wide, the transparent glass diagram was intricately etched with the winding streets of Old Babylon sitting astride a branch of the Euphrates River. In the upper-left corner of the pane, two intertwined serpents were carved into the thick glass.

Crowe appeared at the entrance to the Babylonian exhibit hall behind them. Madison and Grace had almost reached the small bridge spanning the shallow moat around the imperial palace.

As Crowe raised his pistol, they ran behind the freestanding etched-glass diagram of Old Bablyon.

Crowe squeezed the trigger, sighting down the length of his right arm. The bullet smashed into the glass panel with a loud crack. For a fraction of a second, Crowe could see a spidery web of cracks radiate outward from the point where the bullet impacted the glass. Then it imploded, raining shattered glass onto the cobblestones beneath.

Madison and Grace dashed across the moat, barreling through the doors in the center of the palace facade.

Seventy-five

THE FIELD MUSEUM OF NATURAL HISTORY
CHICAGO, ILLINOIS

Anger boiled behind his eyes as Crowe watched Madison and Grace escape from the Hall of Babylon. With great effort, he tried to still the raging storm in his mind, forcing his frustration to subside. His eyes scanned the room.

Observe.
Orient.
Decide.
Act.

Crowe slowed his breathing, drawing upon his military training to control the adrenaline coursing through his veins. With cold, calculating determination, Crowe crossed to the room in pursuit of his prey.

Drops of blood dotted the stone floor.

One of them is injured.

Crowe silently cursed himself for allowing emotion to hinder his abilities. He fingered the trigger of his pistol. He would not miss again.

With quick, long strides, Crowe rapidly covered the distance across the hall. He passed between the silent imperial guards, their weapons raised in warning. Passing beneath a mock stone arch above the entrance to the imperial palace,

Crowe cautiously pushed open the pair of double doors and stepped through into the Tomb of Tutankhamen.

Come out, come out, wherever you are.

Dark and shadowed, the chamber contained an exact replica of the tomb of King Tutankhamen just as it was discovered by British archaeologist Howard Carter beneath the desert sands of the Valley of the Kings.

Illuminated in a circle of white light, stylized lettering on a sheet of papyrus anounced, *Tomb of Tut-ankh-Amen: The Living Image of Amen.*

A quick visual survey of the interior of the chamber revealed no movement.

The room was heavy with the smell of damp earth and the faint perfume of spices. Crowe increased the pressure on the laser grip of his pistol, and a razor-thin beam of red light cut through the gloom. A small red dot appeared on the far wall.

Crowe swept the ghostly red line of laser light in a slow arc around the chamber, probing the dim interior of the room.

Behind glass to his left, a plaster casting that had once sealed the entrance to Tutankhamen's burial chamber was displayed against a backdrop of black velvet. Impressed in the plaster were seven cartouche seals, showing depictions of Anubis engaged in different ritualistic activities. One of the seals showed Anubis above nine captives kneeling with their wrists bound behind them.

The pinpoint of red laser light raked across divine lotus blossoms sprouting from the bindings of the nine captives.

Crowe listened intently.

There was only slience.

If Madison and Grace were running through one of the adjacent rooms, he should be able to hear them.

They're hiding somewhere.

As his eyes adjusted to the dim light, Crowe realized that he was standing in some sort of antechamber. It was packed with objects lining the walls from floor to ceiling.

Four finely decorated chariots lay dismantled against the southeast wall.

Three large gilded platforms with handles used to transport sarcophagi lined the west wall, each adorned with the image of a goddess.

Sekhmet, daugher of Ra, the Sun God.

Hathor, the Mother-Goddess.

Thoueris, the patron Goddess of Women in Childbirth.

Stacks of wooden boxes against the wall contained dried meats. A pair of life-sized wooden figures stood guard on either side of an open door.

Hanging above a tarnished brass lantern, a hand-lettered wooden sign was written in the simulated handwriting of archaeologist Howard Carter.

On the sign were two words.

BURIAL CHAMBER.

Seventy-six

THE FIELD MUSEUM OF NATURAL HISTORY
CHICAGO, ILLINOIS

The gallery was a complete recreation of King Tutankhamen's burial chamber and treasury. The thick stone wall that orginally separated the burial chamber from the treasury had been replaced with a Plexiglas partition, providing a panoramic view of both chambers.

An opening in the partition allowed museum guests to walk between the two rooms.

The burial chamber was dominated by Tutankhamen's elaborate sarcophagus. When it was originally discovered, the mummified body of Tutankhamen was entombed within the smallest of four sarcophagi, placed one inside another. The museum exhibit displayed a cross-section cutaway of the tomb, permitting guests to view each of the nested sarcophagi as they were originally stacked.

A plaque near the door caught Crowe's eye as he passed. It indicated that 144 objects were discovered interlaced and woven in the layers of bandages wrapped around Tutankhamun's mummified corpse.

One hundred and forty-four.

The same number found inscribed on the forehead of the Mayan Lord Pakal lying in his tomb in Central America.

The same number of millennia in one baktun of the Mayan calendar—a hundred and forty-four thousand days.

Crowe recalled a Bible verse from the Book of Revelation he had memorized as a teenager under the strict supervision of a particularly cranky Catholic nun.

> *And I saw an angel ascending from the east, holding the seal of the living god, and he cried with a loud voice to the four angels, saying "Hurt not the earth until we have sealed the servants of our God." And I heard the number of them which were sealed: a hundred and forty-four thousand.*

In the center of the nested sarcophagi, in a solid gold coffin, the mummified remains of King Tutankhamem were bound in long strips of gray cloth. The mummy wore a golden mask, made from solid gold inlaid with opaque pieces of blue glass.

Around Tutankhamen's neck was a beaded necklace, woven in a complex pattern of six tiers resembling the rays of the sun. On his breast was an intricately crafted brooch of a scarab pushing a solar disk.

A gold placard near the mummy stated that the necklace contained 400 beads, and lines radiating from the center of the solar disk to its outer edge divided the disk into 360 degrees.

$400 \times 360 = 144,000$.

On the north wall of the burial chamber, a colorful mural depicted Tutankhamen commencing his journey to the stars, where he would be reborn.

Crowe moved silently through the burial chamber and into the treasury.

Come out, come out, wherever you are.

Seventy-seven

THE FIELD MUSEUM OF NATURAL HISTORY
CHICAGO, ILLINOIS

Grace's legs cramped as she crouched behind a row of wooden boxes and coffers in King Tutankhamen's treasury, hidden in the shadows of the darkened chamber. The air was musty and still. Kneeling beside her, Madison barely fit within the narrow alcove between the head-high stack of funereal offerings and the rear wall of the treasury.

Beads of perspiration traced lines down the small of Grace's back beneath her shirt.

Madison's breath was hot in her ear.

"Here he comes."

Through a narrow crack in the wall of painted crates, Grace peered out into the chamber. Facing the doorway to the treasury was the most beautiful shrine she had ever seen. Egyptian hieroglyphs covered a grand canopic chest, gilded in gold and decorated with a canopy of solar disks and intertwined serpents. An ostrich-feather fan with an ivory handle rested atop a casket of ivory and wood inlaid with gold and blue. An eight-foot-tall carved ebony statue of the Jackal God Anubis kept vigil over the boy-king's treasures.

A dark, hulking shadow passed through the entrance to the treasury.

Crowe.

Muted footfalls whispered on the rough stone floor. A thin beam of red laser light pierced the darkness, searching.

Grace felt a hand on her shoulder, a light touch of warning. Madison's eyes spoke to her in the silence, darting toward a door at the opposite end of the treasury.

Someone else is coming.

Grace pressed her lips tightly shut and held her breath, fearful of making the smallest noise that might betray their hiding place behind Tutankhamen's treasures.

Crowe paused, hearing the same small noises that reached Grace's ears a moment later. Someone else was walking toward the treasury.

Crowe froze, and the red laser beam vanished.

Seconds passed.

The doorway swung open.

The beam of a flashlight swept across the floor.

A museum security guard stepped cautiously into the treasury, his sillouette neatly framed in the open doorway.

He's just an old man, thought Grace.

The aging guard peered nervously into the room, wielding his flashlight with a shaky hand. Flickering light reflecting from gilded gold painted the guard's anxious expression with an unearthly pale hue.

Grace watched the light of the guard's searching beam slowly inch across the room toward the shadows where Crowe stood motionless in the dark.

The flashlight beam stopped its forward advance.

Grace looked back at the guard. The flashlight momentarily forgotten, he appeared puzzled, brushing at a pinpoint of red on his chest with a sweaty hand.

"No!" Grace yelled.

There was a small puff of light from the dark shadows across the room, a muzzle flash from Crowe's silenced weapon.

The impact of the bullet spun the guard around, clutching at his chest. His knees buckled and he dropped to the floor.

Crowe stepped from the shadows, turned, and focused his gaze on the stacks of wooden boxes that concealed Grace and Madison. He raised his weapon and began advancing across the room.

Seventy-eight

THE FIELD MUSEUM OF NATURAL HISTORY
CHICAGO, ILLINOIS

A storm of anger swept through Madison's mind.

Anger at Grace for revealing their hiding spot to Crowe by yelling out a warning.

Anger at himself for thinking such a selfish thought, knowing that Grace had called out in a desperate attempt to save the life of the security guard.

The security guard who now lay dead or dying on the cold stone floor.

Like Dr. Ambergris, lying dead in a pool of his own blood on the floor of his office.

Like Justin, lying dead beneath a dingy white sheet in his hospital bed.

Madison's anger turned to rage, emotion overpowering reason.

The footsteps were close now. Red laser light flashed through cracks between the crates, searching for a target as Crowe neared. Madison placed his right shoulder against the towering wall of crates.

Wait.

Panicked, Grace's body tensed as she helplessly watched Crowe through the narrow slit in the wall of boxes. Madison nudged her leg with his foot.

"How close?" he asked in a barely audible whisper.

Grace's eyes flashed with understanding. She held up a hand, indicating that he was still out of range.

Wait.

Footsteps. A flash of red light.

"Now," hissed Grace.

Madison threw his weight against the stack of crates, pushing against the rear wall of the chamber with his right foot for leverage.

The wall of boxes creaked and groaned, and then began to fall.

Realizing his mistake, Crowe threw his arms above his head as the first crate slid from the toppling wall and fell, striking him a glancing blow across the shoulder.

"Door!" yelled Madison, pointing in the direction of the lifeless body of the guard and the open door behind him.

The wall of crates collapsed on top of Crowe, knocking him to the ground beneath its weight in a tremendous crash.

Grace bolted toward the door. Madison was only a step behind her.

Crowe's weapon clattered across the floor, dropped from numb fingers as he was knocked unconscious by Tutankhamen's falling coffers.

It slid across the stone, coming to rest at the feet of the ebony statue of Anubis.

Seventy-nine

JOHN F. KENNEDY EXPRESSWAY
CHICAGO, ILLINOIS

Grace closed her eyes and leaned into the wind that streamed in through the open window of the taxi, allowing the cool breeze to wash over her face. She rubbed her fingers in small circles over her temples, willing the wicked headache behind her eyes to subside. The abraded skin on her back stung like a bad sunburn. Her muscles ached from exhaustion.

She opened one eye, squinting at Madison. He was staring out the window, deep in thought. His fingers nervously massaged his knuckles.

"Hey," said Grace. Her voice was soft.

Madison shifted his gaze from the space beyond the window to Grace's blue eyes.

"You okay?" she asked.

Madison forced a half smile. "I'm not sure."

The narrow escape from Crowe at the Field Museum had left Madison and Grace physically and emotionally exhausted. After fleeing from the museum through a delivery entrance behind the exhibit hall, they took temporary refuge in a nearby transit authority station. Grace washed up in the public restroom while Madison wolfed down three chili dogs he bought from a Jamaican hot dog vendor.

"I just can't watch anyone else die," said Madison in the backseat of the taxi. He closed his eyes.

Justin was a ghost of a child, lying thin and frail under the starched white sheets of a hospital bed. A tangle of tubes and wires crisscrossed his chest, connecting his dying body with IV bags, monitors, and machines.

The monotonous beep of a heart monitor ticked off the passage of seconds. Christian Madison sat at his bedside, gently holding his son's hand.

Most of the time, Justin didn't seem to know what was happening. He stared straight ahead, his eyes glassy and vacant. His breathing was labored. At times, the rise and fall of his chest would stop completely. He would make a small gurgling sound, swallow, and then his breathing would start again.

Madison was utterly powerless. He worshipped science like a religion, but science refused to perform any miracles for one of its most faithful disciples. He prayed to a God he didn't believe in, bargaining for the life of his dying son.

Grace squeezed his hand, bringing Madison back to the present. He opened his eyes.

"I will not watch anyone else die," he said.

Madison sat up in his seat. He allowed his anger to give him strength.

"We have the disk. With a little technical assistance from Quiz, we should be able to translate the Genesis Code. We have to get back to New York."

Part III

Our doubts are traitors,
And make us lose the good
We oft might win,
By fearing to attempt.

—William Shakespeare

A man's character is his fate.

—Heraclitus

Eighty

Quiz's loft was near the edge of Chinatown on Manhattan's Lower East Side. As their taxi rolled down the street, Madison peered through a grimy window, searching for Quiz's building. From the tinny speakers of a battery-powered radio on the cab's front seat, the voice of an obnoxious talk radio host berated the show's hapless callers and proselytized about the New York Mets.

"Can you turn that down?" asked Grace.

The greasy cabdriver grunted. He reached over and lowered the volume on the radio, but only slightly.

On the sidewalk, a Chinese teenager with slicked-back hair and an irritating sneer argued with a small, feisty elderly man in loud Cantonese. The sidewalk was filled with ice-filled boxes of fish, buckets of fresh-cut flowers, and tables filled with knockoff designer handbags. Smoked ducks and featherless poultry hung by their necks behind cloudy windows. Faded signs written only in Chinese jutted out from the densely clustered brick and stone facades that lined the street.

Halfway down the block, Madison spotted the building.

"Right here is fine," he said to the cabdriver. Madison fished two twenties from his pocket and handed them to the sullen cabbie, who eyed Grace's backside in his rearview mirror as she climbed out of the taxi.

A shop window on the first floor of the building was filled with a variety of gnarled roots and dried herbs. Through the herbalist's open door, soothing traditional Chinese music mixed with the bustling sounds of the street. The sharp odor of ginseng and incense mingled with the strong smell of yeast emanating from a small bakery selling tea buns and rice cakes.

Madison consulted a directory beside the entrance to the upper floors of the Earnhardt Building. He picked out Quiz's name from a list dominated by Li's and Chung's and Chow's, and pressed the buzzer next to the peeling label. Within seconds, the lock of the door clicked open. Grace grabbed the door's brass handle and swung it open.

Quiz met them at the landing on the fourth floor and led them into his small loft.

"I'm so glad to see you guys," he said, throwing an arm around Madison's shoulder and grasping Grace's hand. "Anyone want a beer?"

"Absolutely," said Grace.

"Christian?"

"Sounds good."

Quiz twisted the caps off three bottles of light beer and distributed them to Madison and Grace, reserving one for himself.

They sat around Quiz's coffee table beneath fourteen-foot ceilings and sipped their beers in silence, watching the activity on the street through oversized windows.

Madison and Grace took turns bringing Quiz up to date on their experiences in New Haven and Chicago. Then Quiz recited what he could remember from the remainder of Dr. Ambergris' research journals.

The trio sat in silence as they tried to assimilate the new information that had been exchanged. Quiz was the first to break the silence.

"So what now?" he asked.

Madison shifted in his chair. "I think that we can translate the Genesis Code," he said. "Dr. Vasquez gave us a disk that contains the rest of the encryption key that Dr. Ambergris encoded in his e-mail to me."

Grace picked up his train of thought. "Dr. Bowman told

us that it's a type of substitution cipher called Gematria. Each of the sixty-four different codons in our DNA corresponds to a unique Mayan hieroglyph. It should be simply a matter of running the encryption key against the intron sequence Dr. Ambergris was studying."

"Do you know which sequence of introns he was using?" asked Quiz.

"No, but the data must be in Ambergris' research journal or his notes. Did you see any DNA sequences in the computer files you found on the Triad Genomics server?"

Quiz considered. "I did. I didn't pay much attention to it at the time, but one of Ambergris' files was just a long sequence of genetic code."

"That must be it," said Grace.

"Can we access Ambergris' files on the server remotely?" asked Madison.

"No," said Quiz. "The security server that Ambergris hid his files on is not interconnected with the Triad Genomics mainframe. It's an independent network, secure from outside access."

"So we need to get back inside the Millennium Tower," said Madison.

"How the hell can we do that?" asked Grace. "We'll never get past security."

Quiz drummed his fingers on the table.

"I may be able to get to the subbasement without passing any cameras or security stations. There's a maze of corridors and hallways down there. And there are several maintenance entrances at street level and in the parking structure that lead into portions of the subbasement. It's risky, but not as risky as trying to bluff our way through security."

"And how do we get into the subbasement?"

"With my security pass, I can open the doors. Triad Genomics has no reason to lock out my security clearance. We just have to try to avoid any areas or entrances with security cameras."

"And you can get us through the subbasement?"

"I don't know. But I think it's our best shot. There are some remote terminals in the server farm with access to the network. We can tap into Ambergris' data from one of those terminals."

Quiz drained the last of his beer and pushed his chair back. "Let me show you something."

Madison and Grace followed Quiz into a small bedroom that Quiz had converted into an office. The room was a miniature version of his office at Triad Genomics. Racks of computer components lined one wall and an overabundance of equipment filled every available space.

Quiz dropped into a rolling office chair and toggled the mouse sitting next to a modified keyboard. Three large flat-screen monitors sprang to life.

"Give me a second," he said, punching the keys on the keyboard and entering Triad Genomics' remote access Web address into his Internet browser.

When the Triad logo appeared, spinning on the monitor, Quiz keyed in a password.

"I always leave a back door," said Quiz. "Never know when you might need it."

"But I thought you said we couldn't access Ambergris' data remotely," said Grace.

"We can't, but this will help us find a way into the building."

Quiz navigated through several menus and pecked at the keyboard. On the monitor, a three-dimensional rendering of the Millennium Tower appeared.

"Building schematics," said Madison.

Quiz smiled. "Watch this."

Quiz toggled the mouse and the solid surfaces of the image of the Millennium Tower vanished, revealing the details of the building's interior framed in thin lines like a three-dimensional blueprint.

"Let's find the subbasement."

As Quiz maneuvered the mouse, the image on the screen moved in response.

"This software allows you to virtually move through the

inside of the building, almost as if you were there. It allows architects and designers to do a virtual walk-through of their designs before the building is ever built."

On the screen, the building rotated in cyberspace.

"This is parking garage number three," said Quiz, pointing to the monitor. "And this is a maintenance access to the HVAC system below the parking structure. That's our way in."

"But that parking garage is locked down at night. The gates don't open until 7:00 A.M.," said Grace.

Madison nodded.

"Tonight we'll study the specs for the subbasement. We'll leave for the Millennium Tower first thing in the morning."

Eighty-one

TRIAD GENOMICS SECURITY OFFICE
34TH FLOOR, MILLENNIUM TOWER
MANHATTAN, NEW YORK

Crowe paced back and forth across his office, absentmindedly rubbing his right shoulder as he barked instructions to his security officers.

"Not one of you can tell me where Dr. Madison and Dr. Nguyen might be?"

No response.

"Listen closely. You are going to find them for me. Now. I want surveillance teams on their residences. And their families."

Crowe pointed to one of the security officers.

"You, make it happen."

The officer sprinted from the room. Crowe fixed his gaze on a second officer.

"Interview every Triad Genomics employee that interacted with either Dr. Madison or Dr. Nguyen on a regular basis. Call them at home. Pull their personnel files and phone records. I want to know who Madison's and Nguyen's friends are, and where they might go when they need help."

Crowe stopped pacing and closed his eyes, thinking.

"And I want security doubled in the building. Everyone pulls extra shifts."

Crowe picked up his 9mm and popped out the clip. He unlocked the ammunition locker next to his desk and retrieved a small box.

"And deploy the mobile security cameras. I want every inch of this building secured."

He refilled the clip with hollow-point bullets from the ammunition locker.

"They can't hide forever."

Eighty-two

8:00 A.M., JUNE 13
LEVEL TWO, UNDERGROUND PARKING GARAGE
MILLENNIUM TOWER
MANHATTAN, NEW YORK

The white van arrived at precisely eight A.M., noticed by passersby but dismissed from their conscious minds without a second thought, as the driver carefully maneuvered the van through the entrance of the underground parking structure beneath the Millennium Tower.

The driver wore denim overalls, had a closely trimmed beard, and was of average height and physical appearance. He was not the type of man who would stand out in a crowd or in the minds of people who caught a glimpse of him that morning and would later be questioned by law enforcement.

He drove slowly around the parking garage to the second level, where he pushed the gearshift into neutral and waited for exactly three minutes and thirteen seconds. At exactly 8:05 A.M., a nondescript tan Cadillac backed out of a parking space located a few scant yards from one of the building's main structural support columns.

With a quick but calculated glance, the driver of the Cadillac confirmed the presence of the van and then drove away without looking back.

The van turned into the parking space. With a slow and determined manner, the bearded driver climbed out, turned and locked the driver's-side door, pocketed the keys, and walked to the stairwell. Exiting at street level, he quickly disappeared into the bustle of the morning crowd.

Two minutes before the white van arrived at the Millennium Tower, Omar Crowe answered the ringing telephone in his office.

"Crowe."

"Sir, I have a call from the police commissioner."

"Very well. Put him through."

The phone clicked as the call was transferred to Crowe's extension.

"Hello, Commissioner. This is Omar Crowe, head of security. What can I do for you?"

"Hello, Mr. Crowe. Our 911 emergency center and the local NYPD precinct have received several bomb threats directed at the Millennium Tower. I felt that I should communicate these threats to you personally."

Crowe smiled.

"Thank you for your concern, Commissioner. As I'm sure you know, the Millennium Tower is equipped with the best security technology money can buy. We have highly sensitive detectors and X-ray equipment deployed at every entrance to the building. It is quite impossible for anyone to smuggle an explosive device into the Millennium Tower. Our sensors detect hazardous chemical, biological, and radioactive materials in the air at concentrations as low as two parts per million. That's as good as the Department of Defense technology deployed at the Pentagon."

"Yes, Mr. Crowe. I've been to the demonstrations. It's quite impressive. Your state-of-the-art security technology is the only reason that the NYPD hasn't dispatched Haz Mat and Bomb Disposal teams to the Millennium Tower in response to these threats. Well, that and the phone call I received from the governor about how important it is that the International Biogenetics Conference take place as scheduled. Triad Genomics sure does have some serious political pull."

"I'm afraid that part of the operation is well above my pay grade, Commissioner. But yes, it does seem that our board of directors has many friends in high places."

The commissioner's voice took on a conspiratorial tone.

"I'm certainly not interested in questioning the powers that be. They say leave you alone, that's what I'm going to do."

"Commissioner, I appreciate the call," said Crowe.

"My pleasure. Please give Mr. Giovanni my regards."

As Crowe hung up the phone, a program discreetly inserted into the Millennium Tower's security system disabled the detectors arrayed at the east entrance to the Millennium Tower's parking garage. The detectors remained off for three minutes as a white van entered the parking garage, and then silently switched back on.

Eighty-three

"No, there's a security camera up that way. Take the next left. We'll circle around," said Quiz.

So far, everything had gone according to plan. Madison, Grace, and Quiz had covertly entered the Millennium Tower's subbasement through a maintenance access in the parking structure. But security cameras were plentiful, and avoiding the Triad security guards making their rounds through the facility tested their nerves and will.

Quiz, his face creased with nervous tension, guided Madison and Grace through the maze of tunnels. After several wrong turns, Quiz finally navigated a circuitous route that he hoped avoided the hidden security cameras placed throughout the subbasement.

It felt as though several hours had passed when the trio finally emerged in a hallway adjacent to the Triad Genomics server farm.

"We can use one of the terminals in the server farm to access the security server."

Quiz led them to a recessed computer terminal hidden among the towering black servers. The machinery gave off considerable heat, and oscillating fans streamed cool air down the alleys between the rows of equipment. The odor of hot plastic and circuitry hung in the air.

Quiz took a seat at the workstation and began typing.

"I can pull up Dr. Ambergris' data files from here. If that disk does contain an encryption key, I can run an algorithm on the intron sequences Ambergris was analyzing."

"Meaning?" asked Grace.

"Meaning that with a little help from the Cray-2 super-computers that drive Triad Genomics' genetic sequencers, we should be able to translate the Genesis Code."

Dante Giovanni stood in front of the large window in his corner office, staring silently at the Manhattan skyline. Morning mist lingered over the green expanse of Central Park. He looked at the Rolex on his left wrist.

A cup of Earl Grey tea sat half-empty on the conference table. Giovanni absently toyed with the silver cufflinks at his wrist. The cellular phone in the breast pocket of his Armani suit chirped.

"Yes."

"Sir, the face-recognition protocol just acquired your targets. The hidden security cameras in the subbasement picked up Dr. Madison and Grace Nguyen headed through the subbasement toward the Triad Genomics server farm and the gene sequencers."

Giovanni shifted the phone to his other ear.

"And Quiz was with them?"

"Yes, sir. As you suggested he would be."

"Loop the recording of the video feed to my terminal." Giovanni opened a new window on his desktop computer.

"Streaming video now," said the voice on the phone. The grainy digital video clearly showed the faces of Quiz, Madison, and Nguyen.

Giovanni sighed. "Very well. And you've told no one else?"

"No, sir. Your instructions were quite clear. I've alerted only you. And I am the only security officer monitoring the face-recognition protocol at this time."

"Let's keep it that way."

Giovanni started to press the end key on his cellular phone. Then he put the phone back to his ear.

"Mr. McLain?"

"Yes, sir?" asked the security officer.

"Purge the data from the face-recognition protocol and the cameras in the subbasement for the past thirty minutes. Then shut off the feed from the cameras below the second floor."

"Yes, sir. Purging now."

"And Mr. McLain? When you've finished, I want you to leave the building and walk six blocks west. Wait at the corner until you receive further instructions."

Or until all hell breaks loose.

"I beg your pardon, sir?"

"Just follow my instructions."

"Yes, sir."

Giovanni ended the call and slipped the phone back into his jacket pocket. Then he walked to his oversized mahogany desk and unlocked the bottom drawer. He pulled open the drawer, retrieved a .38 revolver, and stuck the weapon in his belt in the small of his back, concealing it beneath his jacket.

It's time.

Giovanni adjusted his jacket, drained the last of his lukewarm tea, and headed toward the elevators.

Crowe leaned back in the spartan wooden chair behind his desk. With his eyes closed, he sat pefectly still, feeling the rise and fall of his chest with each breath. He imagined the oxygen filling his lungs and flowing into his bloodstream, feeding each cell in his body as his heart pumped the oxygenated blood through his veins and arteries.

The phone on his desk rang.

Crowe sat motionless.

The phone rang agan. And then a third time.

Crowe opened his eyes, leaned forward, and grabbed the receiver.

"Yes."

"Sir, we just got a hit on the tap on Mr. Giovanni's cellular phone."

Crowe rubbed the bridge of his nose between a thumb and forefinger.

"Play it back."

Crowe listened intently to the playback of Giovanni's last call.

"Got it," he said. "Alert me immediately if he receives any other calls."

"Very well, sir."

"And don't leave your station. For any reason. Clear?"

"Yes, sir."

Crowe checked the magazine of his 9mm, then replaced the gun in his shoulder holster. He adjusted his jacket, spit once on the floor, and headed toward the elevators.

Eighty-four

SUBBASEMENT, LEVEL C
MILLENNIUM TOWER
MANHATTAN, NEW YORK

"Okay, I've found the data files with the intron sequences," said Quiz. He looked up toward a large flat-screen display on the adjacent wall.

"Let me put it up there on the screen."

Quiz clicked several keys, and the plasma display sprang to life, showing line after line of genetic code, streaming endlessly across the screen.

```
GTACCATATGCGCATATACACGACAT
TACAGCTGTACTAGCCATATACACGA
CATCATATGCGCATATAGTACTAGCC
ATATATTTCAGGACCAAAGTATACAC
GCATATGCGCATATAGTACTAGCATA
TATTCCATATCACCACATCATATGCG
CATAGTACTAGCCATGTGACCATG
```

"Let me have the disk."

Madison removed the disk from his pocket and handed

it to Quiz, who promptly inserted it into one of six DVD-ROM drives at the workstation.

"This will take a minute."

"Okay," said Madison. "It's time to make the call."

He dialed three digits into his cellular phone.

"Nine-one-one emergency," said a voice after the second ring.

"Listen to me carefully," he began. "There is a bomb in the Millennium Tower . . ."

Eighty-five

63RD FLOOR, PETRONAS TOWERS
KUALA LUMPUR, MALAYSIA

Tanaka absently drummed his fingers on the desk as he studied a report from the Order's top geneticist. He was not pleased. He did not look up as his personal valet entered the room carrying a covered dinner tray. The aroma of lobster tails wafted through the air.

"Wine this evening, sir?" asked the valet, placing the tray on Tanaka's desk. He folded a white linen napkin and placed it on the desktop.

"Red. Caymus Cabernet, Special Select."

"Very good, sir," said the valet, bowing deeply at the waist. He placed a sterling silver fork and knife on the crisp linen napkin.

Tanaka pressed a button beneath his desk. A significant section of the west wall of his office slid open to reveal a private wine cellar. Rows of fine wines were lined up side by side in floor-to-ceiling oak racks.

The valet selected the appropriate wine and gingerly lifted it from its cradle. He peeled the foil from the neck of the bottle, exposing the cork beneath.

"Late night tonight, sir?" asked the valet.

"Perhaps."

The valet removed a corkscrew from a pocket of the small apron tied at his waist.

As he placed the tip of the corkscrew against the soft cork, his shirtsleeve slid up his forearm, revealing a small tattoo of two intertwined serpents.

Eighty-six

SUBBASEMENT, LEVEL C
MILLENNIUM TOWER
MANHATTAN, NEW YORK

"I'm feeding the data from the disk into an encryption algorithm. In a minute, we'll be able to run the program on Ambergris' intron sequence."

"We're running out of time," said Madison. "How much longer is this going to take? We have to find out what the Genesis Code says."

Behind them, a voice echoed from the darkened recesses of the server farm.

"I'll tell you what it says."

Madison spun around, searching for the source of the voice.

"Who's there?"

Grace and Quiz scanned the room, searching for a figure hidden among the rows of servers and gene sequencers.

Dr. Joshua Ambergris stepped out from the shadows.

Eighty-seven

Christian was stunned at the apparent resurrection of his former mentor.

"Dr. Ambergris?"

Grace was speechless. Her hands covered her mouth in shock. Quiz stared at Ambergris as if he had risen from the dead.

Dante Giovanni stepped from the shadows to stand by Dr. Ambergris' side.

"This will take quite a bit of explanation," said Giovanni.

Grace snapped out of her momentary shock at seeing Ambergris alive. She ran to him and threw her arms around his neck in a tight hug. Tears streamed down her face.

"I'm sorry, so sorry, for what you must have suffered as a result of my charade," said Ambergris. "But I believe you will forgive me once I make it clear to you what was at stake."

Madison stepped forward and grasped Ambergris' outstretched hand.

"Christian. So good to see you," his former mentor said.

Ambergris turned to Quiz.

"And Mr. Quiz, it seems we owe you a debt of gratitude as well."

Madison, Grace, and Quiz all began to speak at once.

"How did you—"

"You were both in on this—"

"Why did you have to—"

Dr. Ambergris held up a shaky hand.

"Please. I will explain everything. But I think you will understand better if I first share with you the secret of the Genesis Code."

Eighty-eight

SUBBASEMENT, LEVEL C
MILLENNIUM TOWER
MANHATTAN, NEW YORK

Zoovas stood at the urinal, humming quietly to himself. When Sergeant Peters walked into the men's room, the humming stopped.

"What the hell . . ."

The worried look on her face stopped him midsentence.

"Zoovas, we have a problem. I just got a call from the 911 center. A bomb threat to the Millennium Tower was phoned in a couple of minutes ago."

"Yeah, we've had four of those so far today. Crackpots and hoaxers. What's the big deal?"

"This one is different. The caller said to contact you directly. He identified himself as Dr. Christian Madison."

Holy Jesus.

"We can't find Omar Crowe," said Peters. "But he did designate you as liaison to the NYPD. Somebody has to make a decision. You've got to make the call."

Zoovas didn't hesitate.

"If I lose my job, so be it."

He grabbed his radio and keyed in a three-digit code.

"Security," said the voice on the radio.

"This is Zoovas. We have a credible threat of a bomb in the Millennium Tower. I'm ordering an immediate evacuation of the entire building. Implement evacuation protocols immediately."

The voice hesitated.

"Yes, sir."

Two seconds later, all security officers were ordered to begin implementing evacuation protocols. Two minutes later, red emergency lights throughout the building began to blink. A voice was broadcast throughout the Millennium Tower.

"Attention, please. May I have your attention, please. All persons in the Millennium Tower are asked to proceed immediately to the emergency exits at the stairwells located near the center of each floor. Security officers are positioned throughout the building to provide assistance and to direct you to the nearest exit. There is no immediate threat to your safety, but we ask that you proceed in a safe and orderly manner to the nearest emergency exit."

Eighty-nine

SUBBASEMENT, LEVEL C
MILLENNIUM TOWER
MANHATTAN, NEW YORK

The room was silent with anticipation. All eyes were on Dr. Ambergris.

"That disk does, in fact, contain the encryption key for the Genesis Code. After considerable trial and error, I was successful in translating the code," said Ambergris.

"The code was based on a substitution cipher? Gematria? With Mayan hieroglyphs?" asked Madison.

"Yes," said Ambergris. "My father's research, his life's work, started me down the right path. The key to translating the code was hidden in the text of the *Popul Vuh*. But I've discovered that the key was also hidden in the Hebrew alphabet by ancient Jewish scholars. The encryption cipher can be found in the text of the *Sepher Yetzirah*. Either can be used to translate the Genesis Code. And there may be other encryption keys hidden in texts of other ancient civilizations. I suspect there may be similar keys to breaking the Code in Chinese, Hindu, and Assyrian manuscripts."

"Unbelievable," said Quiz.

"The intron sequence that I translated tells the story of the origins of the Genesis Code."

Madison held his breath. The weight of the moment was overwhelming. They were about to learn mankind's oldest secrets.

"The first section of the Genesis Code says essentially this: An advanced human civilization flourished on the earth in the distant past, hundreds of thousands of years ago, only to be wiped out by a global cataclysm. This lost civilization is the common ancestor of what we consider earth's most ancient cultures."

"That explains the remarkable similarities in the mythologies of ancient cultures around the world, the recurrence of astronomically significant numbers and mythological themes," said Grace.

"Yes. Passed along through oral tradition by the survivors of the cataclysm that destroyed this lost civilization. Before their destruction, they discovered a pattern of global cataclysms that periodically afflict our planet. These worldwide catastrophes coincide with the precession of the equinoxes and the alignment of the earth in relation to other astronomical bodies."

"So what are you saying?" asked Quiz. "That every couple hundred thousand years, the earth goes through a period of cataclysmic changes? And one of these cataclysms destroyed this lost civilization?"

"Precisely," said Ambergris. "My speculation is that as the earth revolves through the galaxy, it periodically passes through a region of space that has a devastating impact on the earth. Perhaps it's a field of tremendous gravitational pull. I don't know."

"They knew it was coming, but had no way to stop it," said Madison.

"Yes. Our ancient forefathers were powerless to stop the catastrophe, but they devised a way to warn future human civilizations of the pattern of cataclysms."

"They created the Genesis Code," said Grace.

"Ingenious, isn't it? Mankind's first advanced civilization evolved hundreds of thousands of years ago. They attained a high level of technological achievement and scientific knowledge. Knowing that it would be tens of thousands of years or more before the next cycle of global cataclysm struck, they had to allow for certain possibilities: that when the next cataclysm occurred, mankind could be speaking entirely new languages, or using any sort of numbering system. How could they pass along this knowledge in a way that would be discovered?"

Ambergris paused and pointed to the plasma screen displaying the intron sequence.

"They decided to send us a warning by inserting a coded message into human DNA."

The intron sequence scrolled across the plasma screen.

"A warning to be discovered when humankind again became advanced enough to find it and read it. A warning that could never be erased or lost, because it was written into the essential structure of our bodies. As long as there are humans, the message will survive."

"But they couldn't save themselves."

"No. Apparently that was beyond their ability. The global cataclysm struck and decimated most of humanity. The disaster was so terrible that most humans perished. Those that did survive were forced to live like animals while the earth recovered over tens of thousands of years."

"Mankind basically had to start over," said Madison.

"Humanity lost tens of thousands of years of advancement. We almost didn't survive at all. Over hundreds of generations, memories of the past faded and knowledge was lost. Society began again from scratch, returning to pagan beliefs and simplistic lives. But there were some who remembered more, who retained some of the advanced techniques and ideas that others had forgotten.

This ancient knowledge appears in the mythologies and architectures of ancient cultures, placed there to preserve it for future generations."

"Like the mathematics encoded in the architecture of the Egyptian pyramids and the Mayan temples," said Madison.

"And the recurring numbers relating to precession and astronomical cycles in ancient mythologies," added Grace.

"Yes," said Ambergris. "But you must ask yourself, why did those who retained this ancient wisdom keep it secret from the rest of humanity?"

Ninety

MILLENNIUM TOWER
MANHATTAN, NEW YORK

Groups of people began streaming out of the Millennium Tower and spilling into the street. The crowd of protesters, now in their second day of protesting the Biogenetics Conference, stopped chanting and watched the exodus with concern.

Zoovas and Sergeant Peters climbed up on a concrete planter on the sidewalk, elevating themselves above the crowd. Peters handed Zoovas a bullhorn.

"Listen up, everyone. I'm Michael Zoovas from Triad Genomics security. This is Sergeant Peters from the NYPD. We have begun an evacuation of the Millennium Tower due to a bomb threat phoned in to 911 just a few minutes ago. For your safety, we are asking that you proceed in a safe and orderly manner away from the area immediately."

Protesters began dropping their signs, collecting their friends and family, and walking at a brisk pace away from the Millennium Tower. But a small group of them remained rooted in place.

Jennifer looked up at Zoovas, considering the possibility of another terrorist attack in Manhattan. Her concerns about stem cell research suddenly seemed trivial. Her eyes were drawn to an American flag flapping in the wind above the entrance to the atrium of the Millennium Tower.

She dropped her sign to the ground. "Is there anything we can do to help?"

Ninety-one

SUBBASEMENT, LEVEL C
MILLENNIUM TOWER
MANHATTAN, NEW YORK

"Over time, those who preserved this ancient knowledge became a secret society of global elites. They have been among us for thousands of years," said Ambergris.

"They call themselves the Order," said Giovanni. "But they have been known to the rest of the world by many names—the Rosicrucians, the Bildeburgers, the Trilateral Commission, and many others."

"The Order has kept the ancient knowledge hidden from the rest of humanity. They are fearful that if the masses learned of the coming cataclysm, and the probable death of human civilization in the next global catastrophe, there would be a complete collapse of the institutions of civilized society. A collapse that would plunge the world back into a state of barbarism and chaos."

"But they couldn't possibly have kept such secrets hidden for so long," said Grace.

"To maintain their conspiracy of silence, the Order co-opted or killed those who discovered the truth throughout our history. Many have been killed to keep mankind ignorant of its dark future."

Madison thought for a moment. "They were going to kill you too."

Ambergris nodded somberly. "Yes."

"How did you find out?" asked Grace.

"There is dissension within the Order. Some of its members oppose the acts of murder and violence that perpetuate the conspiracy. A splinter faction of the Order decided that the threat of societal collapse did not justify a policy of premeditated murder. Secretly, they began to warn those targeted for assassination."

Ninety-two

STREET LEVEL
MILLENNIUM TOWER
MANHATTAN, NEW YORK

Thick streams of people surged out of the Millennium Tower onto the sidewalk. Security officers posted on each floor tried to control the flow of evacuees into the stairwells to avoid a panicked mass rush for the exits. Jennifer and the small band of protesters who volunteered to help stood near the entrance to the atrium of the Millennium Tower directing the human traffic.

"Triad Genomics security has trained for this type of situation," Zoovas had said to Jennifer and the volunteers. "But things are going to happen quickly. Hopefully, most of the evacuees will stay calm and follow the directions of the security officers in the building."

Zoovas was struck by the bravery of the volunteers. They were risking their lives to help.

"But some of them won't. Some of the evacuees will be confused, exhausted from climbing down the stairs, or agitated. Some of them may be physically infirm and will need assistance. Here's what I need from each of you. I need you to help escort those people away from the building as quickly as possible. It is essential that we stop any panic from spreading. Try to keep them calm."

Jennifer and the others nodded. Zoovas began handing out orange vests marked with word *Security* on the front and back.

"Wear these. Sergeant Peters has informed the NYPD that anyone wearing this vest will be assisting in the evacuation effort. If you take it off, the police may try to forcibly remove you from the area."

Jennifer slid the vest over her head and cinched it around her waist. The others followed her example.

"Questions?" asked Zoovas.

There were none.

"Okay," said Zoovas. "Let's get to it."

Just minutes after the evacuation order was announced, Flavia Veloso began a live broadcast across the street from the Millennium Tower.

"We have just received word of a bomb threat at the Millennium Tower here in lower Manhattan. Minutes ago, police officers and security personnel began an evacuation of the entire building. Law enforcement sources speculate that the bomb threat was intended to disrupt the International Biogenetics Conference that was scheduled to begin this morning."

Panic was beginning to rise as the stream of evacuees became a flood. Caught in the throngs of people that rushed out of the Millennium Tower, a diminutive elderly gentleman struggled to stay on his feet.

As he was buffeted by shoulders and elbows, his strength was quickly failing after the long descent from the thirty-fourth floor. He started to hyperventilate.

I'm going to be trampled to death.

Just as he began to lose all hope, a young man in an orange vest muscled his way through the human exodus and threw his arm around the old man's waist. He used the bulk of his body to shield the stooped man from the rush of the crowd.

"Not to worry," said the young man. "Let's get you out of this crowd to a safer place."

He tried to calm the elderly gentleman, to distract him from the increasingly agitated mob of people rushing out from the building.

"My name is John. John Vedder. What's yours?"

"Edward," said the old man. "Dr. Edward Sullivan. I'm a geneticist. Here for the Biogenetics Conference."

Sullivan noticed a tattoo on Vedder's forearm. It was a colorful depiction of Jesus Christ.

"I recognize you," said Sullivan, suddenly concerned. "I saw you on television. You were part of the protest this morning." Worry clouded his face.

Vedder nodded. "Yes, I was. But that's not important right now."

Sullivan searched the young man's face for signs of malice. He saw only compassion.

"Thank you," said Sullivan.

Vedder smiled as he lifted the elderly scientist in his arms and carried him out of the surging crowd.

Ninety-three

SUBBASEMENT, LEVEL C
MILLENNIUM TOWER
MANHATTAN, NEW YORK

"I was approached by an agent of this splinter faction of the Order. He warned me that my death had been ordered by the Council, the governing body of the Order," said Ambergris.

"And Dr. Ambergris came to me for help," said Giovanni.

"There was only one solution," said Ambergris. "The

Order is incredibly powerful. I couldn't fight them. So I had to make them believe that they had succeeded in murdering me. If the Order thought I had been killed, I could continue on, in hiding, living under an assumed identity."

"So you staged your own death," said Madison.

"Yes, with the help of an assassin in the Order also allied with the splinter faction. He agreed to assist in staging my death."

"But why did the finger get pointed at me? I was framed for your murder," said Grace.

"We were unaware of that part of the Order's plan. It was kept from those who warned me of the assassination. The Order took steps to frame you for the murder to divert the suspicions of any law enforcement agencies who might investigate my death."

"But that means the Order had another agent inside Triad Genomics," said Madison. "Someone with the access to plant the false evidence."

"Yes. We already suspected that the Order had infiltrated Triad Genomics. It could have been anyone. But it had to be someone close to me. Someone with access to my work. It could have been you, Christian. Or you, Grace. We couldn't be sure."

Grace interrupted. "And that's the reason for the clues you sent to Christian by e-mail."

"Yes," said Ambergris. "If you or Christian were working for the Order, you certainly wouldn't need to try and solve the mystery I left behind. You would already know why I had been murdered."

He turned to Madison. "It was too late to stop them from framing Grace for my murder. This was the only way we could be sure that you weren't acting as an agent of the Order. If you tried to solve the puzzle I left behind, then we knew that you could be trusted."

Madison nodded, his mind digesting what Ambergris had told them.

"We don't have long before the Order carries through on their plan to blow up the Millennium Tower. I gave the police enough time to evacuate the building and search for the bomb," said Madison.

"I'm not inclined to rely on the Order's timetable," said Giovanni. "We need to get out of here."

Suddenly a shot rang out.

Ninety-four

63RD FLOOR, PETRONAS TOWERS
KUALA LUMPUR, MALAYSIA

Tanaka stretched his arms over his head to relieve the tension in his shoulders and neck. He rubbed his eyes, tired from staring at the computer screen. Behind him, he could hear the pop of a cork as his valet opened a bottle of his favorite wine.

Perhaps I won't stay late tonight.

His thoughts turned to a young call girl he had visited twice in the last week. A fine end to a long day.

Tanaka turned his attention back to the reports he was reading on the computer monitor. He tuned out the sounds of the valet decanting the bottle of cabernet sauvignon.

The Order's geneticists were simply moving too slowly. He would have to devise a way to motivate them. Perhaps a "visit" to some of their family members?

A shadow crossed the computer screen.

The valet bumped the back of his chair.

"Dammit! How many times have I told you—"

Tanaka's mind exploded in a burst of fiery pain. The valet twisted his wrist violently as he drove the corkscrew into the base of Tanaka's skull.

He tried to scream, but the only noise that escaped his lips was a small gurgling sound.

Then everything went black.

* * *

"Get down!" yelled Madison, shoving Ambergris to the floor.

Madison turned to see Crowe walking toward them from across the room, his 9mm raised.

"He shot Giovanni!" screamed Quiz.

Dante Giovanni toppled over backward, falling to the floor. A bullet wound perforated his forehead.

As Crowe readjusted his aim, sighting down the barrel of the 9mm at Dr. Ambergris, his torn shirtsleeve fell away from his wrist. Madison could barely make out the faint image of a tattoo of two intertwined serpents on the inside of Crowe's wrist.

Ninety-five

SUBBASEMENT, LEVEL C
MILLENNIUM TOWER
MANHATTAN, NEW YORK

"No!" yelled Madison. *Not again! I will not allow it!*

He reacted instantly, running across the room and leaping at Crowe. For an instant, Madison thought he might reach Crowe before he could pull the trigger.

Then he heard the crack of a gunshot.

The slug from the 9mm caught Madison in the flesh of his right biceps, passing through the muscle and leaving a ragged exit wound in the back of his arm.

Madison crashed into Crowe, screaming in pain. Crowe's knees buckled, and he fell to the floor from the impact.

Across the room, Quiz jammed the heel of his hand against a metal button in a panel on the wall. The lights were instantly snuffed out, plunging the server farm into darkness, illuminated only by the revolving red emergency lights from the alarm system.

Ninety-six

"Run!" shouted Madison, stumbling across the room, grabbing Grace by the arm, and propelling her forward toward an open door.

"Quiz, get Ambergris out of here!"

Quiz sprang into action and yanked Dr. Ambergris by the arm toward a narrow corridor, away from Crowe and his 9mm.

Crowe slowly rose to his feet.

Madison turned to face Crowe, planting his feet shoulder-width apart and bending slightly at the knees, lowering his center of gravity.

You're not killing anyone else. I won't allow it.

Madison took a quick glance toward Grace.

"Go! Get out of here!" he yelled.

From just beyond the open doorway, Grace hesitated for a moment. Then she saw the determination and resolve in Madison's eyes. She held his gaze for another moment, nodded once, then turned and ran.

Crowe balled his hands into fists, narrowed his eyes, and charged toward Madison. The flashing security beacon sprayed the room with waves of red light, casting long distorted shadows across the bundles of wires and metal conduits running along the narrow ceiling.

As Madison focused on Crowe's massive form hurtling toward him, he spotted something in his peripheral vision. Leaning against the wall in a shallow recess, just out of reach, was a four-foot length of metal conduit about two inches in diameter.

Madison lunged for the metal pipe, but Crowe was remarkably fast.

Just as Madison's hand closed around the cool metal conduit, Crowe plowed into him at full speed, knocking him back against the wall. Crowe's crushing weight forced the air from Madison's lungs as he smashed against the wall. His head smacked into the concrete with a loud crack as Madison struggled to draw breath. But with iron will, he refused to loosen his grip on the metal pipe.

With all the strength he could muster, Madison slammed his right knee upward into Crowe's groin.

Crowe's knees buckled, but he didn't go down.

Grimacing in pain, he cursed Madison through clenched teeth. Slamming his shoulder into Crowe's chest, he shoved Crowe backward away from the wall.

Caught off guard, Crowe stumbled backward several steps, flailing his arms to regain balance. Like a home-run hitter at bat, Madison cocked his elbow, drew back his arms, and stepped forward toward Crowe as he swung the metal pipe.

Crowe's reflexes were still unbelievably fast.

As the pipe arced toward him, Crowe locked his arms in a tae-kwon-do-style block to protect his face and neck, twisting his arms to catch the blow against the meaty muscle of his forearms.

But as Crowe moved to protect his upper body, Madison changed the arc of his swing, drawing the pipe downward toward Crowe's legs. Unable to move quickly enough to ward off the blow, Crowe howled in pain and anger as the metal conduit slammed into his left knee, pivoting on the balls of his feet to avoid taking a hit directly on his kneecap.

The pipe connected with the muscle and ligament just below and to the side of the kneecap. His leg gave out, buckling beneath his weight, and Crowe started to fall.

Madison's hands and wrists ached from the force of the impact. A sharp pain lanced through the bones of his left wrist. Madison drew back for a second swing, intent on finishing Crowe with a blow to his head as he fell.

But Crowe did not make the same mistake twice. Even as he fell toward the floor, Crowe locked his focus on the pipe as Madison swung again.

Crowe's hands darted out, seizing the end of the conduit and deflecting Madison's swing. Crowe held tightly to the end of the conduit and yanked hard in the direction of Madison's swing, yanking the pipe from his hands.

As Crowe slammed into the floor, taking the brunt of the fall on his left shoulder, the metal conduit flew from his hands and spun across the room, clattering across concrete. Crowe rolled with the impact, avoiding serious injury as he minimized the force of the impact.

I'm outmatched, Madison realized. *Going head to head with this monster is suicide.*

Madison turned and ran.

Ninety-seven

SUBBASEMENT, LEVEL C
MILLENNIUM TOWER
MANHATTAN, NEW YORK

Grace ran down the narrow hallway, taking one turn after another, searching for an exit sign or a window. Almost every door she encountered was locked. Slowing to a jog to catch her breath, she realized that she was utterly lost, with no idea of how to escape from the subbasement of the Millennium Tower.

Fighting rising panic, she closed her mind to the images of explosions and collapsing buildings that tried to worm their way into her conscious thought.

Grace turned another corner and came to a dead stop.
Crap.

The hallway ended abruptly twenty feet ahead. A single door at the end of the hall was the only means of egress.

Grace sprinted up to the door and grasped the doorknob. She could hear the whining hum of some sort of machinery beyond the door. She closed her eyes and turned the knob.

Unlocked!

Grace pulled the door open and stepped inside.

The cavernous room extended well beyond her range of vision in the dim light. A narrow corridor ran down the center of the room between tall rows of industrial machinery that hummed and buzzed. Dull silver ductwork snaked from large air handlers and ran across the ceiling. Air compressors and exhaust fans populated the room with a chorus of metallic noises.

Water condensate on overhead pipes dripped an intermittent rain on the metal grating that covered the floor. Steam hissed from pipes overhead, belching plumes of white fog into the moist, musty air.

Grace advanced down the corridor, through the forest of machinery, pipes, and electrical equipment. Beneath her feet, gaps in the thick metal grate revealed a yawning chasm below.

Ahead and to the right, she saw a phone mounted to a steel column. Tacked above the phone was a yellowed paper listing last names and phone extensions.

She removed the handset and placed it to her ear. There was only silence. She clicked the receiver several times in rapid sequence.

Still no dial tone.

Frustrated, she slammed the handset against the wall.

Goddammit!

Her muscles ached with fatigue, and pain lanced through her head. Her breath came in ragged gasps.

High overhead, a burst of steam jetted upward into the darkness. At the end of the room behind her, the door through which Grace had recently passed swung open with a groan. Faint fluorescent lighting backlit the figure that stepped through the doorway.

Grace froze.

Not big enough to be Crowe.

The figure walked into the room, pulling the door shut behind it.

Definitely a man.

"Christian?" she called out tentatively.

The figure paused.

"No," he replied. "Not Christian."

Ninety-eight

SUBBASEMENT, LEVEL C
MILLENNIUM TOWER
MANHATTAN, NEW YORK

Crowe rose slowly to his feet, careful to avoid placing any weight on his right knee. He tried to raise his right arm. Coupled with the sharp pain radiating down his arm, his right shoulder's refusal to move indicated to Crowe that it was dislocated.

Crowe tested his injured knee.

Remarkably, it held his weight, but spikes of pain lanced through his right leg.

Time for the Queen's cocktail.

He reached into a pocket inside his blazer and withdrew a syringe packaged in plastic. Crowe tore off the plastic wrapper and jabbed the needle into a vein on the underside of his wrist. He depressed the syringe's plunger, draining its contents into his bloodstream.

Crowe recalled the first time he felt the euphoria of the Queen's cocktail, an injectable mixture of painkillers and stimulants used in combat to fight injury and fatigue.

God save the Queen.

Crowe palpated his dislocated shoulder with two fingers. He gingerly rotated the ball-and-socket joint, lining up the bones on either side of his torn rotator cuff. Then he unbuckled his belt, pulled it through the belt loops of his trousers, and folded it in half.

The aroma of leather filled his nose as Crowe stuck the belt in his mouth and clamped his jaw down against the soft leather. He made one final adjustment to his dislocated shoulder and turned to face the wall.

With a grunt, Crowe threw the weight of his body against the wall, driving the bones of his shoulder joint back into place with an audible pop.

Feeling the effects of the Queen's cocktail flowing through his veins, Crowe rotated his injured shoulder.

Much better.

Crowe retrieved his 9mm from where it lay on the concrete floor. Squeezing the grip, he tested the laser sight. A thin beam of red instantly shot across the room.

As the stimulants kicked in and the painkillers flooded his body with synthetic endorphins, Crowe felt euphoric.

Powerful.

Acutely aware of his heightened senses.

He took a moment to deliberate and consider his options.

Observe. Orient. Decide. Act.

Coming quickly to a decision, Crowe sprinted toward an open doorway. As he stalked his prey in the bowels of the Millennium Tower, his thoughts surged in random directions, drifting undercurrents of thoughts and memories colliding in the hyperstimulated synapses of his brain. His mind drifted back in time. He could almost smell the hot desert wind as his mind's eye recalled the Iraqi city where he had lost his humanity.

After Saddam Hussein's military had collapsed under the onslaught of the American and British invasion in the Second Persian Gulf War, Omar Crowe's SAS unit roamed the streets of Basra, rooting out insurgents and remnants of the Iraqi Republican Guard hiding among the civilian population.

One moonless night during the first week of Ramadan, his six-man squad was searching a dilapidated apartment building for Iraqi insurgents when Crowe walked through a thin trip wire hidden in a dark narrow stairwell, detonating a pipe bomb affixed beneath the rickety steps. Three of Crowe's men were cut down instantly in the storm of shrapnel that exploded in the confined space. The remaining two were gunned down by insurgents who rushed into the stairwell after the detonation. Only Crowe, who had himself triggered the explosion that caused the violent deaths of his men, remained uninjured.

Their dying screams filled his ears as Crowe killed the two insurgents, emptying his assault rifle into the bodies of the young Hussein loyalists. One of Crowe's men screamed for help, lying in a twisted heap on the stairs, his body shredded by the violent blast. The dark red blood of his brother-in-arms soaked through Crowe's desert fatigues as he cradled the young man, whose last breath bubbled on his lips.

It seemed to Crowe that a demon had possessed him that day in the silence that followed those horrific moments. With the terrible rage of an avenging angel, he stalked the apartment building, indiscriminately slaying the Iraqi men, women, and children who huddled together in desperate fear in their tiny apartments. When a second SAS unit finally found Crowe, he had run out of ammunition and was frantically beating the mutilated corpse of an elderly man with the butt of his rifle.

The British government quietly discharged Omar Crowe from military service. The incident was never disclosed to the public. Crowe returned to England, drifting from town to town, shunned by his former comrades. The demon inside him remained.

Two weeks later, in a seedy bar in London's East End, a beefy sailor from the British Merchant Marine accidentally bumped into Crowe, spilling his pint across the bar. Crowe snapped, his fiery rage consuming all reason, and savagely beat the man to death with a barstool.

The next morning, Crowe awoke in shackles, charged with homicide. The trial that followed was swift and just.

A jury of his peers and countrymen gave Crowe a life sentence in London's infamous Wormwood Scrubs Prison.

Just when it seemed his life was over, salvation came to Crowe in the form of a bespectacled prison warden with a tattoo of two intertwined serpents on the inside of his wrist. He offered a simple choice: die in prison or serve a new master. For Crowe, the decision was easy. He was spirited out of Wormwood Scrubs Prison in the dead of night. The Order gave Crowe a new identity and a new sense of purpose. He was reborn. Now Crowe served a new master. And so did the demon inside him.

Ninety-nine

SUBBASEMENT, LEVEL C
MILLENNIUM TOWER
MANHATTAN, NEW YORK

Madison froze in the darkened hallway and listened intently. For a moment, all he heard was the faint sound of an alarm from the floor above.

Then there were footsteps.

In his flight to escape from Crowe, Madison had lost his bearings in the maze of corridors and passageways in the subbasement. In the utilitarian hallways and rooms beneath the Millennium Tower, there were no signs to direct him toward an exit, and no windows or other visual cues to orient himself.

Madison's thoughts turned to Grace, alone in the subbasement, trying to make her way out of the building. Guilt weighed heavily on his conscience for leaving Grace by herself to find her way to safety.

He couldn't bear the pain of her loss. Not that kind of pain. Not again.

Justin was a ghost of a child, lying thin and frail under

the starched white sheets of a hospital bed. A tangle of tubes and wires crisscrossed his chest, connecting his dying body with IV bags, monitors, and machines.

The monotonous beep of a heart monitor ticked off the passage of seconds. Christian Madison sat at his bedside, gently holding his son's hand.

Most of time, Justin didn't seem to know what was happening. He stared straight ahead, his eyes glassy and vacant. His breathing was labored. At times, the rise and fall of his chest would stop completely. He would make a small gurgling sound, swallow, and then his breathing would start again.

The sound of footsteps came again, closer this time.

More than one person, thought Madison.

They were close, and coming closer.

Madison tried to spot a place to hide. The only door in his immediate vicinity was locked. The smooth walls of the hallway afforded no protection.

The yellow oval of a flashlight beam flickered around the corner in the hallway ahead.

Too late.

Madison tensed, readying himself for either fight or flight.

The flashlight beam swept around the corner, momentarily blinding Madison. He crouched down, squinting at the figures behind the bright light.

"Christian?" asked the figure holding the flashlight.

Quiz lowered the flashlight, pointing the beam away from Madison.

"Thank God," said Madison. "I don't think I have any fight left in me."

"You look like hell," said Quiz, grinning.

"You should talk," said Madison.

"How's the arm?" asked Quiz.

A makeshift bandage around Madison's arm was soaked with blood. His face was ashen. Dark hair was matted against his forehead.

"I've been better," he said. "But at least the bleeding seems to have stopped."

Madison noticed that Quiz was gripping his left hand, rubbing his right thumb against his left palm. The fingers of his left hand arched backward in an involuntary muscle spasm.

"Quiz, you okay?" asked Madison.

Quiz nodded. His eyes darted back and forth. "I think so. But I don't have my pills."

Madison looked at his watch.

"We have to get out of here," said Madison. "Do you know a way out?"

"Yes," said Quiz. "Well, maybe. I'm not that familiar with this part of the subbasement. But I think I can get us back to the server farm. From there we can make it to street level."

"Let's go," said Madison. "We're running out of time."

One Hundred

SUBBASEMENT, LEVEL C
MILLENNIUM TOWER
MANHATTAN, NEW YORK

Five minutes later, Quiz led Madison and Ambergris to a steel door leading into the Triad Genomics computer core. His security badge triggered the locking mechanism on the door with an audible click.

"We're back at the server farm," said Quiz, looking over his shoulder at Madison. His forehead was covered with tiny beads of sweat.

Quiz opened the door and the trio walked through. Inside the server farm, the temperature was a good fifteen degrees colder, with almost no humidity. Evaporative condensers removed the moisture from the air to protect the sensitive processors and machinery.

Quiz pointed across the room, beyond the rows of tall black servers interconnected by a tangle of colored cables and wires.

"The door we want is there."

Fifty yards away, a nondescript door marked *EXIT* beckoned from the opposite wall. Flashing red security beacons pulsed in the darkness.

"Let's move," said Madison.

Quiz edged toward the center of the room.

Walking closely behind with an unsteady Ambergris in tow, Madison almost plowed into Quiz when he stopped abruptly. Madison lowered his voice to a whisper and scanned the room for any signs of danger.

"What is it?"

Quiz turned around. His face was a mask of fear. Sweat streamed down his forehead.

"I think I'm in trouble . . ."

His speech became garbled and Quiz's eyelids began to flutter. With a loud clack, his jaw snapped shut. The muscles in Quiz's neck bulged as they tightened involuntarily.

"What's the matter with him?" asked Ambergris.

Madison released his hold on Ambergris' arm and took a step toward Quiz.

"He's having a seizure," said Madison. "Sit down if you feel unsteady on your feet, Dr. Ambergris."

Quiz's body convulsed and his back arched uncontrollably. Madison grabbed him in a bear hug, and gently eased Quiz off his feet to the floor.

"What should I do?" asked Ambergris. "How can I help?"

"It should pass," said Madison. "We just have to wait it out and try to make sure he doesn't hurt himself."

As Madison lowered Quiz to the floor, Quiz's head jerked back and forth violently. Madison tried to cradle Quiz's head in his hands to keep it from striking the concrete floor.

Quiz cried out—a loud, terrible wail.

* * *

Crowe silently stalked the hallways around Quiz's office near the Triad Genomics server farm. He reasoned that Quiz, when confronted with a threat, would try and make it back to familiar territory. Dr. Ambergris would be with him.

A faint cry echoed down the hallway.

How very predictable.

Crowe raised his weapon and sprinted in the direction of Quiz's cries.

One Hundred One

SUBBASEMENT, LEVEL C
MILLENNIUM TOWER
MANHATTAN, NEW YORK

Madison struggled to keep Quiz's flailing body from smashing into anything.

"See if you can find something to put under his head. Anything soft," said Madison.

Ambergris surveyed the room for a blanket or a piece of insulation. Anything.

"I don't see anything . . ."

Quiz coughed violently, sending a spray of pinkish red foam across Madison's face. A rivulet of blood trailed from the corner of his mouth.

"Shouldn't you put something in his mouth, like a spoon or something, to keep him from biting off his tongue?" asked Ambergris.

Quiz's legs thrashed wildly.

"No, I don't think that's a good idea. He could break his teeth if we try to cram something into his mouth."

Quiz's right arm shot up and smacked Madison in the face.

"Christian . . . ," said Ambergris.

"Trust me, dammit," said Christian. "We just have to wait it out. It will—"

"No," interrupted Ambergris. "It's not about that."

There was panic in his voice.

"Someone's coming."

One Hundred Two

SUBBASEMENT, LEVEL C
MILLENNIUM TOWER
MANHATTAN, NEW YORK

Quiz rolled onto his side and curled into the fetal position, limbs twitching, as Crowe stormed into the climate-controlled chamber housing the Triad Genomics server.

"What's wrong with him?" asked Crowe, leveling his 9mm at Madison's crouched figure.

"Seizure," said Madison. "He has epilepsy."

"Shame."

Crowe shifted his eyes to Dr. Ambergris and smiled.

A red dot appeared on Ambergris' forehead.

"How's the arm, Doc?"

"Fuck you."

Crowe's smile vanished and his eyes narrowed.

"Run," yelled Madison at Dr. Ambergris.

Ambergris slowly shook his head.

"I won't die running away from the likes of him. I'd rather take it in the face than in the back."

"As you wish," said Crowe.

Crowe stilled his breathing and applied pressure to the trigger.

The fog began to lift from Quiz's mind. His body ached terribly, muscles screaming in protest. The floor was cold and hard against his face.

His eyelids fluttered open. Indistinct shapes swam in his field of vision.

"Christian?" His voice was a raspy whisper.

As his eyes began to focus on a figure across the room, a shot rang out. Then a scream.

Madison watched helplessly as Ambergris stared into Crowe's eyes, facing down his executioner. Quiz stirred on the floor beside him, mumbling his name.

Behind Crowe, the door silently swung open and a darkly clad Asian man edged through the narrow opening.

A long, thin knife glinted in his hand.

Grace followed Arakai through the door into the Triad Genomics computer core. As her mind registered the scene within, Arakai drew his knife.

Before Crowe could react, Arakai leapt into the air onto Crowe's back, driving the knife down into soft flesh at the base of his neck, severing Crowe's carotid artery with a vicious twist of the blade.

Blood spurted from the gaping wound.

Screaming, Crowe pulled the trigger of his 9mm.

Ambergris watched in amazement as Arakai leapt onto Crowe's back, plunging a knife into the side of his neck. Crowe cried out in shock and pain, his knees buckling beneath him. Dark arterial blood jetted from the base of his neck.

Crowe squeezed the trigger and fired.

The shot went wide, slamming into the server next to Ambergris in a shower of sparks. Bullet fragments ricocheted off the ruined metal housing of the server, tearing into his chest and shoulder. Ambergris screamed as he fell to the ground.

Crowe fell hard, the weight of Arakai's body driving him to the floor. He hit the ground chest first, his limp arms making no effort to break the fall.

And then Crowe was still, the crackling buzz of electricity from the ruined server filling the air, a widening pool of blood beneath Crowe's lifeless body staining the concrete floor.

Hidden in a van in the lower level of the parking garage above, a digital timing mechanism ticked away the seconds toward detonation.

One Hundred Three

SUBBASEMENT, LEVEL C
MILLENNIUM TOWER
MANHATTAN, NEW YORK

"Help me with Ambergris," said Madison. His right shirt-sleeve stuck to his arm, soaked with blood.

Grace unbuckled her belt and pulled it off.

"You're not going to get very far unless we stop that bleeding," she said, wrapping the leather belt around his upper arm and pulling it tight.

Madison grunted in pain. His vision blurred, then cleared as the pain subsided.

"You take his other side," he said, putting Ambergris' arm around his shoulders to help support his weight.

Together, Madison and Quiz carried Ambergris toward the corridor leading to the exit. Grace led the way, running just ahead of them, watching the time tick away on her watch.

"Faster!" she yelled, urging them to pick up speed.

Madison's arm screamed in pain as they finally reached the exit to ground level. Grace slammed open the door, and sunlight streamed into the darkened hallway.

Outside in the street, police and emergency vehicles had cordoned off a perimeter around the Millennium Tower. Flashing lights and police barricades blocked the streets and sidewalks. A ring of officers in body armor, helmets, and riot shields guarded the perimeter.

"Help us!" cried Grace. "We need help!"

Several police officers in body armor ran from the police line and sprinted across the pavement.

One of the policemen grabbed Dr. Ambergris in a fireman's carry, hoisting him over a broad shoulder. Another placed an arm around Madison's waist, helping him to stand on trembling legs. Together, the group sprinted toward the perimeter of barricades and flashing lights.

One Hundred Four

SUBBASEMENT, LEVEL C
MILLENNIUM TOWER
MANHATTAN, NEW YORK

Grace glanced back at the Millennium Tower as she ran past the police barricades. She stumbled and began to fall, slipping from the grasp of the policeman. A young woman in an orange vest reached out, grabbed Grace by the arm, and kept her from falling to the ground.

"I've got you," said Jennifer, slipping an arm around Grace's waist. Together, they ran across the pavement toward a line of police cars and emergency vehicles.

In the back of the van parked in the lower level of the parking garage, a timing device ticked away its last remaining second. As the display on the digital timer hit zero, it sent an electric impulse down two thin wires to a detonator.

A tremendous explosion shattered the windows of the first eight floors of the Millennium Tower, blasting out a billowing cloud of smoke.

Police officers and civilians alike dove to the ground, covering their heads and diving behind anything that would provide shelter from the explosion.

A rolling fireball erupted from the Millennium Tower in a swirl of fiery orange and yellow. Glass, concrete, and debris filled the air. Clouds of thick smoke darkened the sky and blotted out the sun.

The shock wave from the explosion ripped through the concrete structural support columns in the parking garage at a rate of three thousand feet per second.

Shards of metal and concrete pounded against the pavement of the street like tiny missiles, ricocheting off its surface. Windows in the surrounding buildings shattered and imploded from the concussive blast. The deafening roar of the shock wave drowned out all sounds.

When the sky finally stopped raining glass and debris on downtown Manhattan, the Millennium Tower had disappeared, collapsing inward on itself and into the massive crater left by the explosion.

One Hundred Five

MILLENNIUM TOWER
MANHATTAN, NEW YORK

Madison lay on his side on the hard cement. Blood ran down the side of his face from a gash in his scalp as he looked up in horror at the Millennium Tower. He watched helplessly as a tremendous explosion rocketed through the mammoth skyscraper, blasting a maelstrom of dark smoke, glass, and concrete into the dawn sky. Above the deafening roar of the blast, the screams of men, women, and children echoed in the air.

One scream rose above the din.

Madison shut his eyes.

Justin was a ghost of a child, lying thin and frail under the starched white sheets of a hospital bed. A tangle of tubes and wires crisscrossed his chest, connecting his dying body with IV bags, monitors, and machines.

The monotonous beep of a heart monitor ticked off the passage of seconds. Christian Madison sat at his bedside, gently holding his son's hand.

Most of the time, Justin didn't seem to know what was happening. He stared straight ahead, his eyes glassy and vacant. His breathing was labored. At times, the rise and fall of his chest would stop completely. He would make a small gurgling sound, swallow, and then his breathing would start again.

Madison was utterly powerless. He worshipped science like a religion, but science refused to perform any miracles for one of its most faithful disciples. He prayed to a God he didn't believe in, bargaining for the life of his dying son.

Madison intellectualized the biological processes taking place within Justin's body.

He pictured Justin's lungs, struggling to draw in enough air.

His cells starving for oxygen.

His heart growing weaker, as it tried to pump more blood through his arteries.

Madison had expected a dramatic end, a domino-like collapse of one system after another.

But that didn't happen.

Justin just slowly faded away. Finally, as the last rays of the evening sun winked out over the horizon, he took one last small breath.

Then he was gone.

"Good-bye, Justin," he whispered softly.

A voice rang out.

"Christian!"

The scream that rose above the cacophony of voices was Grace, frantically calling his name.

"Christian!"

Madison rolled over onto his back as Grace reached his

side, kneeling down and taking his head in her hands. As Madison looked up into her eyes, small fragments of glass fell from his hair and shoulders.

"I'm okay, Grace," he said.

Tears rolled down his face.

She leaned over, kissing Madison fully on the lips.

"We're going to be okay," he said, reaching up to brush a finger across her cheek.

Several feet away, Ambergris sucked in a deep breath and called out.

"Christian . . ."

Two paramedics lifted Dr. Ambergris onto a stretcher. His face was deathly pale and blood streamed from a gash in his forehead.

"I'm sorry, Christian. For everything."

He reached out a shaky hand.

Madison clasped the hand between his own. "I am too. But none of that matters now."

A grave look descended on Ambergris' face.

"If I die, you must decide—"

He coughed violently, and dark blood bubbled against his lips.

"You must decide for yourselves what to do with this knowledge. You must decide whether to reveal the secret of the Genesis Code."

The paramedics hoisted the stretcher off the ground. A third EMT slipped an oxygen mask over Ambergris' face. His voice became a rasping whisper.

"You must decide . . ."

After the ambulance sped away, its flashing lights receding in the distance, Grace turned to Madison.

"We can't keep this a secret," she said finally. "We can't keep the secret of the Genesis Code from the world."

Madison sighed. "I know."

"But how do we spread the word?" asked Madison. "And without endangering our own lives?"

Grace thought for a minute.

"I have an idea," she said.

One Hundred Six

The Sikorsky RAH-66 Comanche perched on the helipad like a giant bird of prey. The helicopter's rotors beat a steady rhythm in the thick air.

"This doesn't exactly look like a transport helicopter," said Grace to their military escort. She smiled at Madison.

"No, ma'am, it isn't. As I said, my orders are to transport you as quickly as possible to the project site and to ensure your protection and safety. The Comanche can do a hundred and sixty knots and sure as hell can take care of itself. Pardon my language, ma'am."

She noticed two 430-gallon auxiliary fuel tanks strapped to the underside of the Comanche.

"Just how far are we going, Colonel?" asked Grace.

He smiled. "You know I can't tell you that, ma'am."

Within minutes, the Comanche was airborne. The ground rushed by a thousand feet below. Grace sat back in her seat and looked at Madison.

She looked down at the thick file in her lap. On the cover was stenciled:

THIS FILE IS CLASSIFIED TOP SECRET
Examination by unauthorized persons is a criminal
offense punishable by fines and imprisonment
up to 50 years and $200,000.

It was titled: "THE GENESIS PROJECT."

"I feel like Alice right after she went down the rabbit hole," said Grace.

After Madison had been treated for his injuries at Mount Sinai Medical Center, Grace and Madison had gone directly to the FBI. After learning of Dr. Ambergris' discovery of the ancient warning hidden in the human genome and its dire predictions of global cataclysm, the U.S. government launched a massive program to decipher the rest of the Genesis Code. Grace and Madison were recruited to serve on the Genesis Project team, housed in a secret military installation in a remote corner of Nevada.

"So what will Quiz do now that the government has finished debriefing him?" asked Grace.

Madison chuckled. "They used the carrot-and-stick approach with Quiz. Set him up with his own consulting firm, complete with lucrative government contracts. If he cooperates, he'll be set for the rest of his life. But if he breathes a word of what he knows about the Genesis Code, he spends the next fifty years in a military prison."

Grace looked out the window. "I'm going to miss him."

"Me too."

They passed the next few minutes in silence.

Grace reached over and took Madison's hand. "So why did you run away from me after Justin died?"

Her eyes searched his face.

After a moment, he spoke.

"I think maybe it hurt too much to care about someone. Or maybe I didn't believe I deserved to feel happy again. I don't know."

Grace smiled. "Or maybe you were just being an ass," she said, as tears spilled down her cheeks.

"Okay, I guess I deserved that," said Madison, squeezing her hand. The lines of his face softened.

"But I'm here now," he said.

Grace leaned in and kissed him gently. Her lips were soft and warm on his mouth. After several long seconds, she pulled away.

"How's the arm?" asked Grace.

Madison moved his right arm up and down, pivoting his shoulder joint along a vertical axis.

"Still pretty sore," he replied. "My shoulder too. But the doc says I'll heal over time."

Grace chewed on her lower lip.

"I still can't believe that they're gone," she said softly. "Giovanni. Ambergris. And Bowman and Vasquez."

"I know. I try not to think about it. I don't do very well with death and loss."

Grace smiled and took his hand.

"You're going to be okay," she said. "We both are."

Flavia Veloso sat in her cubicle at WXNY, staring at the headline above the fold on the front page of *The New York Times*.

FBI SAYS AL-QAEDA BEHIND MILLENNIUM
TOWER BOMBING

She didn't believe it. Not for a minute.

Rumors were circulating about a government cover-up. In the days following the bombing, sources from Triad Genomics told her about the murder of Dr. Ambergris just days before the attack. There was talk of a groundbreaking scientific discovery, and the government's suppression of that discovery to keep it from becoming public knowledge.

But she had no proof. No hard evidence.

A runner from the mailroom interrupted her thoughts.

"FedEx for you, Ms. Veloso."

She took the FedEx box. It was addressed to Flavia Veloso, WXNY. No return address.

Strange.

She opened the box. Inside was a thick manuscript. Four hundred white pages filled with black type.

Madison and Grace had decided that the story of the Genesis Code must be told to the world. But perhaps there was some logic to the Order's concerns that most of humanity simply wasn't ready to face the dire warnings it contained. So they decided to preserve and present the story of the Genesis Code in the same manner that it had been preserved throughout mankind's past—hidden within our myths and stories.

Fictionalized in the pages of the manuscript sent to Veloso, Grace and Madison told the story of the Genesis Code to those with the insight and wisdom to discern the kernels of truth hidden within paragraphs of fiction.

Flavia turned to page one and began reading.

She laid the cover page aside on her desk. On it was written the title of the manuscript:

THE GENESIS CODE